I0607560

Northern Horizons

REPENTANCE AND ABSOLUTION

AE LISTER

Repentance and Absolution
ISBN # 978-1-80250-997-7
©Copyright AE Lister 2022
Cover Art by Erin Dameron-Hill ©Copyright November 2022
Interior text design by Claire Siemaszkiewicz
Pride Publishing

Published in 2022 by Pride Publishing, United Kingdom.

Pride Publishing is an imprint of Totally Entwined Group Limited.

REPENTANCE
AND
ABSOLUTION

Dedication

To secrets well kept.

Chapter One

Shadows
But go and learn what this means:
'I desire mercy, not sacrifice.'
For I have not come to call the righteous, but sinners. ~
Matthew, 9:13

Oscar was gone, and I couldn't find him.

The brush surrounding the new homestead — if that's what you could even call it — grew dense and completely impenetrable in some spots. A fella could easily get lost, especially a city fella who couldn't tell an oak from a birch and fell o'er his own outsized feet on occasion. There were wolves in these parts that could kill a man Oscar's size in an instant — not to mention the bears, coyotes and panthers.

I'd told him time and again not to go wandering around without me, to stay near the ramshackle rooms we were fixing up and not to go looking for whatever he thought he wanted to see.

The kid was trouble. Had been since I'd first laid eyes on him, back in Dawson City, and there wasn't any way of taming him, much as I'd tried. I supposed, when it came down to it, I didn't want to tame him any more than I'd wanted to smother the fire that kept us both warm at night and reared up inside me when he looked at me the way he did. He'd nigh burned me with a primal passion that I was still trying to control — or at least understand. It still didn't make no sense how the two of us came together like we did. But there was no turning back now.

"Oscar!" I shouted into the trees, trying to see my way and take heed of any movement ahead of me. I'd searched all around the sorry excuse for a house that he'd inherited from his dead uncle, and he was nowhere to be found. So now, I headed into the brush toward the creek. I'd already checked the well and he wasn't there, neither fallen into it nor trying to get water up for a drink. I didn't know where he was, and I was beginning to panic.

"Oscar! D'you hear me? Get back here right now or I'm gonna tan your pretty hide so bad you won't be going anywhere for a week!"

As I stepped past a big boulder, something caught my eye. T'was the peacock-blue frayed edge of a shawl, and I stopped in my tracks when I saw a familiar person standing there, looking off into the distance.

"Cal? Is that you?" I said.

But it couldn't be Cal. Cal was back in Telegraph Creek, whispering scandalous things into the ears of men who paid for her time and attention. The person wearing the shawl turned with a languorous ease and smiled at me. T'was Cal sure enough, even though it couldn't possibly be.

"Jimmy! My, I'd almost forgotten how handsome you were."

I blushed, taking off my hat and giving her a puzzled look. "What're you doing here? How did you get here?"

Cal simply smiled, the dimple in her cheek on the opposite side to Oscar's. "Has that naughty boy wandered off again?"

She'd rouged and painted her face till there was no sign of the handsome boy underneath, the boy who was a girl for all intents and purposes, except for the tackle between her legs.

"Yes, he has," I said. "And I'm gonna haul him o'er my knee when I find him."

Cal laughed and pursed her lips. "Oh, I don't think he minds that, do you?"

"He'll mind it this time," I promised. "And he'll mind me."

No matter what games we liked to play involving my hand on his behind, giving him a pretend walloping for being a brat, I'd give it to him this time — like I had once before when he'd wandered off and scared me half to death.

"You know which way he went?" I asked Cal, since I had nothing else to go by.

"There," Cal said, pointing through the brush. "I heard a gunshot by the river."

My blood went cold. *Fuck.* God only knew what he'd wandered into, and for a goddamn second, I almost fell to my knees.

In a moment I'd moved past Cal and I was running, tearing through the brush toward the river, terrified of what I'd find. The crack of a rifle pierced the silence, and it echoed for long minutes as my breaths ripped through my chest.

When I found him, if he hadn't been shot or eaten by wolves, I was gonna kill him.

Just as I reached the edge of the brush, where it opened up onto the river, another shot echoed through the trees and I opened my eyes, gasping huge gulps of air and blinking at the darkness.

"Hey, hey, shhhh, it's okay. It's a nightmare. You're dreamin'."

Oscar's shadow loomed above me in the darkness of the room that was barely a room — just a space with four walls and a fireplace, the fire banked now but the coals glowing red.

I grabbed him and pulled him down to me, hugging him so fierce that he squirmed and protested.

"Stop. You're hurtin' me. I can't breathe."

I loosened my hold a little so he wouldn't try to get away, but t'was hard not to keep him in a death grip after that god-awful dream.

"What the hell's wrong with you?" he said, clutching my shoulders.

"I couldn't find you," I whispered, my heart beating a drum in my chest. "I couldn't find you." I was breathless, even though I'd not left my bed.

"I was right here — right here in this bed beside you, all night long."

I nodded against him, keeping him close to prove to myself he was here and he was all right — and so was I. His hair smelled of wood smoke and sweat, and I reckoned we could both use a wash.

"You need a bath," I murmured, kissing him under his ear where it smelled of his own special musk that I loved.

He snorted. "So do you. I reckon we oughta change into fresh underwear, too, and wash these ones."

I slid a hand under the blankets, popping the buttons of the flap of his union suit so's I could skate my palm o'er the swell of his ass, making him squirm in a delicious way, his small, stiff cock pressing against me.

"Well, dammit, it sure is you, Oscar. No one else has a nubby so small and sweet what wants to pretend to be big enough to cause any mischief," I said, teasing him the way he liked to be teased, so that he felt dainty and delicate and half the man I was. It had seemed strange at first and like he should be offended by that kind of talk. But he loved it, and that was a fact. And I didn't question it at all no more.

Sure enough, he groaned and pressed his fingertips into my shoulders, rutting against me like a dog.

"Goddammit. What were you dreamin' about? You were sayin' my name then you said *Cal*. Was it *scandalous?*"

"No. T'was terrifyin'. You were lost, and I couldn't find you."

He pressed against me, his nubby rubbing against my thigh through the fabric of his union suit. We'd bought the sets of red flannel underwear when the weather turned right cold at the start of November. Guess we'd had enough of freezing our asses off on our journey and we wanted to be warm, even if it meant looking ridiculous. "Well, you did, didn't you? You found me good, since I was right here all along."

"That's a fact. Thank the Lord," I murmured, turning his face to mine and finding his lips in the darkness. He opened to me in that sweet way he had of assuring me there weren't nothing I couldn't do that he wouldn't want, as far as any intimacy with his body went. We'd nigh explored every damned inch of each other by now, and I never could get enough of him. I wasn't sure I ever would.

I pulled away from his mouth and nuzzled into his neck, just to sniff that scent of him I was so fond of. "I'm just so relieved you're here and t'was all a dream."

He relaxed into me and offered his long neck for my kisses and for me to run my nose along. The bit of stubble there did something to ignite me, and I lapped my tongue o'er his Adam's apple, then bit it gently.

"Oh. Jimmy. Hell," Oscar breathed. "It ain't even dawn yet, and you wanna keep me awake?" He yawned.

"I'm sorry. Never mind. Just cuddle under these here covers with me. I need to know I got you."

Oscar stifled another broad yawn. "You got me, all right, in every sense of that word. You prob'ly won't want me after a few more months. I'm already a nuisance most of the time, ain't I?"

I didn't know if he was playing up being a brat or if he truly thought he was a nuisance.

"No, you're just— My ma used to call it restlessness, when I couldn't sit still. Said I'd grow out of it, and I guess I did."

"Yeah? What if I never grow out of it, huh? What if I'll always be like this?" Oscar said, snuggling into me, wiggling his ass, even though he'd just told me he wanted to sleep.

"Keep still. I'm tryin' to go back to sleep, and you ain't helpin'."

"What if I'm always this restless?" he asked again in a whisper. "Will you still love me?"

I laughed. He was all that and more, this twenty-one-year-old man-child.

"I reckon I will. Can't seem to help it," I grumbled, as if me loving Oscar was an inconvenience rather than the miracle of a lifetime that had been wasted with broken men.

"Good," he said, laying his head down on the feather pillow. "I reckon I'll still love you, too."

* * * *

In the morning, we woke to bright sunshine streaming in the new glass windows. We needed curtains. Next trip into town we had a list of things to buy. The big wad of cash I'd looted from Spook and Whitlaw—the outlaws who had stolen and almost raped and killed Oscar—still had some bulk to it. I reckoned that the money was rightfully ours, what with all the heartbreak and fear they'd put us through. Although, in the end, it had shown me plain as day how I felt about him—that I'd go through hell and back just to keep this man safe and by my side. I'd shot both of them outlaws dead without a thought, even though I'd sworn off killing when I'd left the gang. Figured I was doing the world a favor in that case.

Oscar and I—with help from Carson Moore, Timothy Jensen and Timothy's son, Frank—had managed to shore up one small room of the broken-down homestead that Oscar had inherited from his late uncle. T'was a decent-sized space with a fireplace and a cookstove to keep us warm and fed, but with the big bed on the other wall and a chair and a table in it, the room felt small and close.

That suited the two of us, though, for now, and made it cozy and easy to heat, although we were eager for spring to come so's we could finish the job and get at least a couple of more rooms added on to this one. T'was a huge job, for sure, but we had a will and the means, and I reckoned we could get some kind of decent home built for the two of us in time.

For now, I was content to wake up under the wool blankets and quilts we'd bought, snuggled beside Oscar, who sighed softly and blinked like an angel, even though the thoughts in his pretty head were more devilish, surely.

"Mornin', Jimmy."

"Oscar. How'd you sleep?"

He rolled onto his side and watched me. "Well, 'cept for you makin' so much noise and hollerin' my name, pretty well I guess."

I'd forgotten about my nightmare. Now it came back to me with all its ball-shriveling fear and sense of loss. I frowned.

"Don't remind me. I never want to have it again."

"I'm sorry. Maybe you won't."

I shrugged. The truth was, I'd been having a lot of bad dreams. Most of them were flashbacks to long-gone days, when I'd watched Whitlaw and Spook do some horrible, bloodthirsty things. And I'd done some myself. Seemed all that was coming back to me in my dreams, and I couldn't hardly get rid of it. I woke from those nightmares feeling hopeless and riddled with guilt, full of disgust at the way I'd lived my life. But this last one, when I was out of my wits trying to find Oscar, brought back all the terror of losing him to Spook and Whitlaw near the beginning of our journey and how lost I'd felt when I didn't know where he was or how I would find him before they killed him — or did something worse.

I gazed at Oscar, wondering how I'd ever deserved this handsome, heartbreaking lamb of a man and feeling like any moment God was gonna take him away from me. I didn't deserve Oscar. I felt that deep down in my bones, and I guess t'was coming out in my dreams. But for whatever reason, he loved me, he wanted me and he'd stayed with me all this time. Now we were setting up a home together, the way we'd do if Oscar was a lady and I wanted to marry her, make her happy and protect her.

I truly didn't see a difference. The fact that he had a cock instead of a cunt seemed entirely inconsequential. I'd bedded whores more masculine than Oscar. He had the sensitivities, delicacy of feeling and ability to nurture that a woman might. He'd taken care of his horse, Sprite, and he'd nursed the kitten we'd got when we'd first arrived in Port Essington. He'd coddled her like she was his baby, and now she was a big mouser with a fierce disposition that still had the tendency to curl up in his lap for loving when she needed it.

Of course, we couldn't let on in town what we were to each other, and that was a shame. But t'was a price I'd pay to keep Oscar close. I reckoned I didn't have to tell anyone what they didn't need to know. What me and Oscar did in our home was a private thing, and t'was gonna stay that way.

Oscar yawned and gazed back at me out of his sweet brown eyes.

"You look like you're havin' your deep thoughts again, Jimmy."

He kneeled up and took my face in his hands.

"You know it don't do to brood about stuff. You just wind up workin' yourself into a mess of feelings you ain't got no control o'er."

15

I nodded and sighed, because he was right.

"I guess t'was different when we were on the road. I was too busy getting us safely from one place t'other, I didn't have time to dwell on things from my past—or worry beyond our survival."

"The past is the past," Oscar said. "I told you that once, and I'll tell you that again. You ain't the same man. You told me a bit of what happened back then, and it truly is horrible. But you was misled and mistreated, and you ain't responsible for the things those men made you do. You gotta believe me."

I nodded in order to placate him, but I did feel responsible. The truth was, I could have left the gang earlier than I had. I could have distanced myself from those men when I'd realized what they were capable of—and I hadn't. I'd run with them for years, helping them with their thieving and killing and all-around terrorizing, because I was too lily-livered to leave. True enough that I'd hung in the background, but that wasn't an excuse.

But Oscar was right. There were things to be done and we'd better get at them, rather than brood under the blankets on this chilly, late-November morning.

"Let's get them horses fed and watered," I said, as a lump under the blankets at my feet started moving and making muffled mewls.

Oscar reached a hand underneath and pulled Sprite out into the day. The gray and white cat with enormous ears, named for the horse we'd lost to wolves just outside of town, blinked and stretched on the top of the blankets. She let Oscar pet her for two seconds, then jumped onto the floor to search for mice.

"I swear, those ears get bigger every day," I said. "She part rabbit?"

Oscar laughed. "Maybe. Anyhow, I think they're cute."

He hopped out of the bed and grabbed the poker from where it leaned against the iron stove, opening the hatch and stirring the embers that had mostly faded.

"We'd best get this stove goin'," he said, "before it gets too cold in here."

"Sure," I said, grabbing my pants and pulling them on. "Don't forget to do up your access hatch," I said, reaching out to cup his bare bottom in my hand.

"Fuck. That's your fault," he said, reaching behind him to button up the fabric flap.

I grinned. "It mostly always is. Pretty convenient to have that bit of cloth be moveable, I'd say."

Oscar laughed and gave me the wide, impish grin that I loved.

"That's a fact."

He winked as I pulled on my trousers and shirt, then sat to do up my boots, while Oscar threw a couple of logs in the stove and stoked it so that they caught and crackled.

We'd spent close to a week chopping wood that now stood in a huge pile against the outside wall of our makeshift house, helping to keep the cold out and in a convenient spot to grab when we needed it. Oscar had learned real quick how to use an axe, and his muscles had bulked up, although he'd always be on the lean side.

He was strong and he was healthy, and that was all that mattered.

Back when I'd found him—an aimless, wisp of a stray in Dawson City—he'd been skin and bones, and filled with a desperation so raw that it hurt to look at. I'd fed him and taken him back to my room to get him cleaned up so's he'd have half a chance. But what had happened the next morning I don't think either of us had expected.

Oscar had been full of gratitude for the kindness I'd shown him, and I'd been horny for something I couldn't hardly imagine until he'd put his lips around me and got me off that first morning, to my shock and his satisfaction. Those were the only skills he thought he had at the time, and I guess he'd wanted to show them off and thank me for what I'd done.

I'd been blindsided by his bold actions and the confusing feelings he'd aroused in me, but I should have known there wasn't any going back from that moment—that he'd claimed me then and there, and t'wasn't no use to fight it. As if something had possessed me in that room, I'd hauled his naked ass o'er my lap and spanked him like he was a misbehaving child, when he was the farthest thing from that. But we'd both got off and my world had tipped upside down and backward.

And now we were here, in Port Essington, building a home and making a life together. Back when I'd left the gang and taken up a good, honest career hauling supplies, I never would have expected anything near to this, and now I couldn't rightly imagine anything else.

Chapter Two

A Trip into Town

"We gonna chop up some more trees today?" Oscar asked as he finished getting dressed. He took up his hat from its spot on the nail by the door and popped it onto his head, ready to go.

I turned from the window to see him standing there, looking fetching in the clothes we'd bought in Whitehorse. They'd traveled well, and I'd had them cleaned and mended when we got to Port Essington—mine, too—so that they'd last a while.

I looked him up and down and smiled a long, slow smile.

"Oscar Yates, you are a vision."

T'was true. He had filled out in the time since we'd first become acquainted, and the months of staying put and eating well had done him good. He'd always be a bit on the small and skinny side, but I didn't mind that one bit. His skin was clear and glowing from the hard work he continued to put in on our little house and keeping the wood stove stocked with firewood. He'd proved he could be counted on and that we were in this together. T'was the chores inside the house he wasn't so fond of, but that didn't bother me much.

He grinned and tipped his hat. "Yes, sir, I know it. So, you gonna put me to work or you gonna stand there starin' at me all mornin'?"

"Hmm." I scratched my chin where the stubble had grown in o'er the days since I'd last taken a razor to it, as if I was considering what to do, when I'd already made up my mind. "I reckon we should ride into town and get you a horse."

The look that came o'er his face just then held about five different emotions — sadness and regret at the loss of his beloved Sprite, joy and excitement at the thought of getting his very own horse and curiosity as to why I'd decided today was the day.

"You for real?" he asked in hushed tones, taking off his hat and slapping it against his thigh. "A *horse*? For *me*?"

He blinked rapidly, as though trying not to cry, and my heart burst for this young man who was full of emotion and had a pure, pure soul. T'was true that Oscar liked to get up to filthy business with me between the sheets and lots of other places, but he was the sweetest, most affectionate person I'd ever met. He loved with his whole heart, Oscar did. Sometimes t'was almost too much, but I'd take it.

"Reckon we won't get a better day than this. The sun's shining, and there don't look to be much wind right now. We best go and get it done. We'll get some foodstuffs while we're in town then we'll have what we need until Christmas."

"Jimmy, I—" He choked on his words as his forehead creased and his lip quivered.

"C'mere," I said, opening my arms and beckoning him to me.

He was against me in a moment, and I held him while he succumbed to his tears. Then he sniffled and pulled back, wiping at his eyes in an angry way. "I'm sorry."

"What for? For bein' sad about Sprite? He was a good horse, and I miss him."

Oscar shook his head. "Nah. For blubberin' like a baby. Will I ever be a real man, Jimmy?"

I almost laughed then, and I gave him a look like I thought he'd plumb lost his mind.

"Oscar Yates, you are more of a man than those goddamn outlaws I ran with. You got balls the size of yams with the things you say and do, the way you make me feel. I never met anyone braver 'an you."

He smiled and laughed, his eyes twinkling with his leftover tears. "Yeah, I s'pose that's true. I got some guts on me a lot of the time. But why do I tend to cry so often? I ain't never cried so much in my life before, and we ain't even in danger or nothin'. Why are my moods so up and down?"

I'd noticed that, and t'was different than when we'd been on the road. But we'd been so busy surviving then, trying to get where we were going and there had been a lot of distractions.

I shrugged. "I don't know. You lost your horse, though, and you found out your uncle, who we'd traveled that long journey to find, was long dead. That's a lot to take in, Oscar. I reckon you're still grievin'."

He gazed at me out of puzzled eyes.

"And maybe you're still dealin' with what happened with Spook. You ain't had much time to sort all that out 'till now."

He frowned and looked angry all of a sudden. "Nothin' even happened."

I gave him a serious look, because that wasn't true at all. Sure, he hadn't been raped or maimed or killed, but it had been a close call. There hadn't been any space for him to process it, and by the time we'd got to Telegraph Creek, we were both so relieved to be in a safe place that we'd put it behind us. But now that we were staying in one place for so long, those memories were bound to return. I knew Oscar'd been having his share of bad dreams. When two people shared a bed, t'was easy to know when the other person was unsettled.

He looked away, frowning at the floor. "Nothin' happened."

"You know that ain't true. Spook threatened you. He was going to—"

Oscar's gaze came up and blazed fierce into mine. "I know what he were gonna do. You don't have to tell me. But he didn't, because you shot his head off."

I didn't say anything.

He started blinking again and looked up to the roof, then back at me. "I don't want to cry again. Can we talk about somethin' else?"

"Sure," I said.

Oscar looked around him, saw the sourdough wrapped in a towel on the wood slab that was our kitchen counter. "Should we bring some bread and cheese for our lunch?"

All of a sudden I wanted to treat this boy to a grand day out. He'd get a new horse, and we could enjoy the fine weather.

I smiled. "Nope. We're gonna have lunch at Annie's."

Oscar parted his lips, and he looked as if he was going to float on up into the air. "Annie's? You jokin'?"

"No, I ain't jokin'. I wanna see your eyes go all glassy when you taste those flapjacks she makes."

Annie's was a little restaurant on Main Street run by a widow named Annie Price, who made the best flapjacks and sausage this side of the Yukon border. She had a devoted clientele who filled her place every weekend and most weekdays during the busy summer months and made it profitable enough for her to stay open during the off season.

Oscar couldn't help but laugh. "My eyes go glassy?"

I nodded. "They do. I know how much you like 'em."

"I do. I surely do," he said, looking like he wanted to get going right away, now that he knew what awaited him.

"Well, let's go and get Dixie fed so we can saddle her up. You wanna ride behind me or take Poke?"

Poke was our brave mule, who'd carried Oscar strapped to his back for a couple of miles after he'd got knocked out near Telegraph Creek. He was a solid and reliable animal but not much fun to ride.

"I'll go behind you."

I gave him a stern look. "You gotta make sure you're not holding on to me too tight now, when we get into town. Remember? We're only supposed to be buddies."

"I'll remember. I'll sit up straight and act like I'm not too happy to be on the same horse as you, e'en though I love it."

After Oscar's horse, Sprite, had been killed and we'd rode into Port Essington doubled up on Dixie, he'd been torn up with grief and plumb exhausted, so he'd about draped himself onto me. I reckoned we'd looked enough like worn-out travelers for it to come across fairly normal. But now that we were living here and trying to keep our private lives private, it wouldn't do.

T'was a shame we had to hide who we truly were in order to live together so near a town without any trouble. But t'was the price of what we had and what we wanted to keep, and we'd pay it so's we could keep this thing that was so dear to us.

"You love it, do you? Really?"

"Gawd, of course I do. All snugged up and grabbin' onto you? Makes me feel like a goddamn princess in a fairy tale," Oscar said, and I laughed.

"I reckon a princess would use better language," I said.

"Maybe...maybe not."

* * * *

Carson and Tim had helped us fix up the barn, too, and repair the wood fence around the paddock and small corral. The stable was a basic structure with three stalls, and, like our little kitchen-house, t'was warm, dry and weather-proof. Luck had been with us, and the integrity of the groundwater and well on the property had been intact. We'd installed a new pitcher pump and trough in the yard outside the barn to water the horses, and we'd put in a pump at the sink in the house, too—a luxury, as was the stove. Neither of us fancied lugging buckets of water back and forth. We'd done that enough on our journey.

Oscar helped me to feed and water Dixie and Poke. We brushed them down while they ate, then I tacked up Dixie, and we were ready to ride out. I pulled Oscar up behind me and he snugged in close and wrapped his long arms around my waist.

"Mmm, you smell so good," he said, snuffing at my neck where t'wasn't covered by the collar of my jacket.

I laughed, resting my gloved hand atop his. "I ain't had a proper wash for days, Oscar. I think you're deluded."

"Maybe we should get baths while we're in town. Make it a proper holiday."

I gave him an astonished side-eye. "Je-sus. I offer you a meal and to buy you a new horse, and now you want a bath? My goodness."

He laughed, knowing I was teasing. T'was a good idea, in fact, to get cleaned up proper. There wasn't a way to have a bath at our place, although we had access to cold water and tried to keep our bits clean using a basin and a cloth every night before bed.

Oscar's hot breath puffed across my ear. "I want you to do something for me when we get back from town, and you prob'ly want me clean for it."

My cock twitched under the thick cloth of my trousers, and I inhaled a sudden breath. "That a fact?"

"Mmm-hmm. Though I reckon you'd still do it if I was dirty, wouldn't you, Jimmy?"

I could hardly speak now that my wanting had gone from zero to a hundred with one soft suggestion. I cleared my throat. "Prob'ly. I'm sure I have before."

Oscar laughed again and pressed himself against me so's I could feel his own excitement. So much for a clandestine ride. At least it would be a few miles 'till we were anywhere near other folks.

"Oh, you have—and I liked it."

"I reckon you did. I reckon you like most of the stuff I do to you, e'en if it involves treatin' you rough."

"'Specially if it involves that." His gloved fingers slid o'er my trousers to press against my stand, and I made a vulnerable sound.

I pulled Dixie up and craned my head around. "Oscar, you need to fuckin' behave or we'll have to turn around right now so's I can bed you—and you won't get your new horse. You want that?"

He had to think about it for a minute, his gaze burning hot coals as he stared at me. Then he sighed.

"Fine."

He took his hand from o'er my privates and clasped me at the waist as he sat up straight, so that he wasn't leaning on me.

"Good boy."

"Aw, fuck, now you gone and said that? I'm all hard and achin' now."

"Good. So'm I. You might as well be, since you're the cause of it."

"All right. I'll stop teasin' you. 'Cept it's so much fun."

"Yeah, I know. But I swear, if you do one more thing to provoke me, I'm gonna turn this horse around and take you home."

T'wasn't much of a threat, because it would only be to take him inside the stables and fuck him o'er the feeding trough, then we could be on our way again. But if we wanted to get his horse, have a nice lunch and treat ourselves to full baths, we had to get going.

"All right, all right. Sheesh. Grouchy."

I laughed at him and urged Dixie forward, determined to enjoy the nice weather and a trip to town.

* * * *

It took about a half hour to get to town on horseback. It would probably take twice that in a wagon, but we'd be able to haul more. I'd thought about using some of our money to buy one, but they cost dear, and we didn't plan to come into town much o'er the winter — only to get supplies when we needed them. I was hoping that would be about once a month, and we could always load up the mule to bring them things back.

Which was more reason to buy another animal. If we were gonna make do without a wagon, we needed to each have a horse. Plus, I figured a friendly new pet would distract Oscar from his sadness o'er losing Sprite and the trauma of almost being the victim of a violent rape and murder. T'was worth a shot, since we needed one anyway.

I'd heard about a gentleman wanting to sell a Morgan horse that was only about five years old and sound. I'd had Carson put a word in that I wanted to look the mare o'er with an intent to purchase. I was hoping she hadn't been sold and that we could have a look at her.

The town itself was mostly empty at this time of year. Most folks went to parts south where they could find work, since the Port Essington fisheries closed down when the Skeena River froze up every year. But there were a few people out and about on this pleasant day.

We stopped at Jensen's and hitched Dixie up, then went in to speak to Carson. He was behind the bar as usual and cleaning some of the spigots with a cloth so they'd keep their shine.

"Hello!" I said, before the door had shut behind us. We'd gotten to know him and Tim Jensen pretty well while they helped us fix up the kitchen part of our house.

He looked up and smiled.

"Jimmy! Oscar. Nice to see you."

"How're things with you?" I said, taking off my hat. I glanced at Oscar to make sure he remembered to remove his. Sometimes he forgot the basics of decency, and I had to remind him.

"Oh, you know. Nothing changes around here. Well, not much," he said. "Can I get you something?"

"No, thank you. Do you know if that horse has sold yet? The one we spoke about last week?"

"Oh, the Morgan? I don't think so. You want to go see her?"

"Yeah. Oscar needs a horse of his own, and I reckon she might be all right for him."

Oscar rubbed at the brim of the hat in his hand and shifted his feet. I imagined he was worried she was already sold and he'd have to wait for another suitable animal — which, of course, would be tragic now that I'd got him all worked up to get one today.

"Sure. I can take you. I don't start at the bar for another hour." Carson grabbed his coat and hat. "It's just down the road."

We walked along the planked sidewalk, the heels of our boots ringing against the wood. The smell of the sea drifted in from the Skeena and for once wasn't hidden under the stench of fish being gutted and processed. The wind was colder here, coming off the partially frozen river, and I pulled up the collar of my coat. I hoped Oscar was warm enough. He was so focused on looking at this horse that he probably didn't feel it.

"How are you, Oscar?" Carson asked. "The room we shored up keeping tight?"

"Yes, sir," Oscar said. "I reckon we did a good job with it, thanks to you and Mr. Jensen."

"It was my pleasure to help out. As I've said before and probably will say again, it's good to see the place getting fixed up, even if it'll take a while."

"I never had the learnin' to do any construction, so I'm eager to see how it's done. And I think Jimmy feels the same."

"I do," I said. "I know how to do a lot of things, but I've never built a house or anything close to one before. I'm very happy to get some help."

"I figure when the spring comes, we can get to work on the rest of the place. You got big plans for it?"

I shrugged. "I reckon we don't need much space."

"You'll probably want to put in a second bedroom…and maybe a sitting room?"

"Oh sure. Another bedroom would be good," I said. "Although we're managin' for now."

Carson chuckled. "You two probably kept close quarters while you traveled, so this isn't much different," Carson said. "I'm sure you can put up with each other till the spring."

Oscar huffed. "Well, now, I dunno. Jimmy here has an awful loud snore."

Carson laughed again, and my cheeks flushed with embarrassment. But t'was a good deflection, so I joined in.

"You think you're all that quiet? Sounds like a chainsaw half the time. It's a wonder I get any sleep."

Oscar threw me a devilish look that Carson didn't see. It only lasted a second, but it showed he was getting a kick out of our deception.

"Well, then, we'll have to get you sorted out," Carson said. "And you'll just have to put up with each other until then."

"I guess so," Oscar said with a sigh.

"Here we are," Carson said, leading us into the yard of a small house with a blue door. He stepped up to the porch and knocked.

After a moment, the door opened to an old woman in a wool shawl. She seemed to recognize Carson but gazed with good-natured curiosity at me and Oscar.

"Oh, hello, Mr. Moore. You here about the horse?"

Carson took off his hat and nodded. "Yes, ma'am. I've brought some friends who're needing one. They'd like to have a look at her, if that's okay?"

The woman nodded, smiling. "Of course. Peter's around back in the stable. You g'on around, and he'll sort you out."

"Thank you so much, Mrs. Morris."

The woman closed the door, and Carson led us around the side of the house to a small, square paddock in the back. There was a plump gray horse standing near the fence with one hoof lifted.

"That her?" Oscar whispered to me.

I shrugged. "I ain't got a clue. Though it don't look young, so maybe not." I gestured. "Also, it's a stallion."

"Oh…yeah."

"Peter?" Carson said, walking toward the covered end of the paddock. "You there?"

An old man with a wrinkled face and kind eyes came out of the shade and moved toward us, wiping his hands on his rough trousers.

"Carson Moore, how d'you do?"

"I'm just fine, Peter. These are the men I was talking about, wanted a look at that mare you're selling. Did you find a buyer yet?"

Peter looked us o'er carefully before he shook his head. "Nope. She's here. Hold on. I'll bring her on out."

We waited near the fence while Mr. Morris went into the stable. Soon he came out leading a medium-sized horse. She was bigger than I'd anticipated but smaller than Dixie, who was on the large side.

Oscar gasped.

The delicate mare was black all over but for a swipe of white all down her nose, as if a paintbrush had got her by mistake.

Peter led her into the paddock and had her walk around for us. She seemed sound. She was certainly a pretty thing.

"If you don't mind my asking, sir, why're you sellin'?" I asked.

Carson gestured to me. "Peter, this is Jimmy Downing and his friend Oscar Yates. They just came to Port Essington about a month or so ago. They're fixing up Mr. Yates' old place."

Peter raised his eyebrows as the mare regarded us with clear, curious eyes.

"That a fact?"

"Oscar here is Mr. Yates' nephew."

"Well, now, it's good to meet you, then," Peter said, giving Oscar and me a kind look.

"Likewise," I said, and Oscar said, "Hi."

Peter looked the mare o'er, then turned back to us. "Well, I reckon this horse ain't much use to me. I got old Sam there, and I need cash more than I need a second horse. I got this horse for my granddaughter, in fact, but"—his voice cracked—"she ain't here no more."

I didn't know if he meant she'd passed away or that her family had left Port Essington for someplace else. It wouldn't be polite to ask, so I got down to business.

"How much you want for her?"

"Well, now..." Peter examined the horse again, petting her arched neck and scratching under her chin. The mare sniffed him and nuzzled against his shirt. "I paid a hundred for her last year. I reckon I'd need close to that. She's a fine horse."

I couldn't argue that, but a full hundred seemed steep and more than I wanted to pay.

Oscar clutched at my sleeve. "Jimmy, she's so pretty!" he said, then he let go of me and stepped back, in case he was being too intimate.

"Do you mind if we come in and meet her? I'm getting her for Oscar here, because he don't have a horse at all right now. I need to see if they'd get along before we talk serious about cost."

"Surely. Come on in," he said, gesturing to the gate.

Oscar had unlatched the gate and was in the paddock before I could blink, walking up to that horse with an eager smile and an outstretched hand.

"Hello, girl," he said, his voice smooth and soft.

Watching him made my heart hurt, as I recalled the way he'd bonded with Sprite once we'd got rid of the wagon.

The mare regarded him warily for a moment, then reached her muzzle out to sniff his hand. She nickered and tossed her forelock, as if she were saying hello.

His smile broadened. He glanced at me, then returned his gaze to the fetching mare.

"You sure are a beauty," he said. "And I reckon you know it."

Chapter Three

Onyx

Carson and I laughed and Peter smiled, because it did look as though the mare was preening with all of us looking at her.

"You wanna lead her around, son? That way Jimmy can see that she's sound and comports herself well."

"Yes, sir," Oscar said, excitement in his voice as he reached out for the mare's lead.

We watched as Oscar led the coal-black mare around the edges of the paddock. The old gray stallion simply stood and watched them, giving a snort of contention every now and then, but otherwise paid no interest.

"Sam don't care about her one way or the other," Peter said, laughing. "I reckon he'll be glad to get the stables back to himself, if you decide to buy her."

I nodded, watching Oscar and the horse. The mare seemed content to follow him around the ring as if they were already fast friends. He glanced at me, his eyes shining with delight. I had to remind myself to watch the way the mare walked. I didn't want to waste our money on an unsound horse, no matter how nice she was or how much Oscar might want her.

She moved well—exceptionally well, in fact—but I wasn't gonna say that to Peter. I scratched my chin, frowning.

"She flighty?" I asked.

Peter chuckled. "Well, she's spunky and full of energy, but I'm sure Oscar can manage her. She's pretty well-behaved."

"He just learned to ride. He ain't got much experience," I said, as Oscar's smile dimmed, and he threw me a glare.

"I can manage her, Jimmy. She's a pussycat."

Sure enough, she was still following him around the paddock like an obedient puppy. I didn't know if I wanted to spend so much, but I'd perhaps made a mistake bringing Oscar here. Peter could likely tell how much Oscar wanted this horse. I reckon t'was obvious to all of us—which put me in a tricky position.

"She's all right," I said. "A bit young for an inexperienced rider like Oscar."

I lifted the latch and went in through the gate, approaching Oscar and the mare. She regarded me warily, then lifted her head and blew a snort my way.

Oscar laughed. "I agree, pretty girl. You tell 'im."

I rolled my eyes and extended a hand to the mare. "Lookit. You gotta get along with me, too, if you wanna come home with us. Not just him."

The mare considered that, then stepped toward me and nibbled at my shirt as if she might find a treat in my pocket. She did seem friendly and good-natured. I figured we wouldn't find a better horse in this town, but I had to keep those feelings to myself.

I turned back to Peter. "You say you're wantin' a hundred for her?"

Peter leaned against the fence. "She's a Morgan horse. A good one. They ain't cheap."

"I know it," I said, frowning. I looked at the horse, and at Oscar. "I wasn't plannin' to spend more than seventy, to be fair. We gotta lot of work to do on the property still. That's gonna cost a pretty penny."

Peter grunted. "She can pull a plow or a wagon, e'en though she's on the small side. That's the breed, though. They're sturdy and tough little horses."

"Yes, sir, that's true." I walked beside the mare, taking off my glove and running my hand along her flank, although I could already see she was a fine horse. I didn't truly care that she was so young. In fact, that just made her a better option. She had lots of good years left.

Oscar was being quiet, stroking the mare's broad forehead and whispering his secrets in her ear.

"Hmm," I said, as though I were having a hard time deciding. "Would you take seventy-five?"

Peter frowned. "I don't know if I can go that low," he said. "The wife would be upset with me if I let her go for less than ninety."

I nodded, squinting at the horse and looking at Oscar. Acting like I didn't have a wad of cash in my satchel back home that could have paid for three horses. Fact was, we did need to save that money for living until we could find ourselves a means of a regular income. But I'd already got him down ten dollars. Maybe he'd come down more.

"Yes, sir, I understand. I just don't know if I can go as high as ninety."

Oscar glanced at me and seemed to understand what I was trying to do. As much as it must have killed him, he stepped back from the mare and stayed quiet.

But Peter wasn't stupid. "Seems like young Oscar's already got a bond with her."

Oscar gave Peter a measured glance. "She's a fine horse, sir. But now that I think about it, I was hopin' for a bay with white socks."

I had to work hard to school my features. I knew there was nothing Oscar wanted more than this midnight black horse right now, only he was playing the game and I was thankful for it.

"That a fact," Peter said, sounding a little put out.

I turned to Carson, hoping he'd play along. He knew I wasn't trying to scam a crazy deal, only to bargain in a gentlemanly way. I reckon Peter would have thought less of me if I'd simply handed o'er a hundred, anyway. No doubt he was hoping for eighty or so and had started high.

"Didn't you say there was someone with a bay for sale, Carson? I can't remember."

Carson grinned. "Yeah, I thought I heard of one — fella lives down by the harbor. We can go see it this afternoon if you want."

"Now hold on," Peter said. "Could you give me eighty-five?"

I scrunched up my face as if that was still just a bit too much. I thought for a long moment.

"Would you take eighty?" I said. "I can't go higher than that."

Peter took off his hat and swiped it against his thigh, and for a second, I thought he was getting mad. But then he laughed, and his eyes twinkled.

"You drive a hard bargain, Mr. Downing," he said. "Eighty, then. You give me another five, and I'll throw in all her tack."

I grinned, more than happy with that deal.

"Done."

I walked o'er to Peter and counted the money out, handing the bills to him—and Oscar had himself a horse.

* * * *

We told Peter we'd pick her up on our way out of town later in the day.

"You thought of a name, yet?" I asked Oscar as we walked along the sidewalk toward Annie's. Carson had gone back to Jensen's.

The sun was high, and I checked the time on my pocket watch—twelve-twenty.

"Yes, sir, I have. Her name's Onyx."

I'd never heard that word before. "Onyx? What the hell is that? Is that a different language?"

Oscar gave me a look. "Hell, Jimmy. You mean there's somethin' I know about that you don't?"

"Very funny. Just seems like a strange name for a horse, that's all."

"'Onyx' is a mineral. It ain't gold, but it's awful pretty. Back in Dawson, I learned the names of all kinds of rocks from them miners who were obsessed with finding gold. The best bits of onyx are solid black and smooth, just like my horse."

"Well, she ain't so smooth with her winter coat comin' in. But she sure does look solid and healthy."

Oscar's eyes sparked. "Thank you for buyin' her for me. I don't know what I'd have done if we'd had to leave her behind. I think I fell in love with her when she first came close, to be honest."

"Just like I did you."

He shot me a secret glance. "Exactly."

I cleared my throat and kept my distance, like we were just two men walking through town together. The intimidating landscape of Port Essington rose up around us, dwarfing the town itself in the shadow of mountains and thick banks of forests.

I thought back to that day in Dawson City when I'd encountered a bedraggled and starving street rat. "Although, if memory serves, you weren't as friendly."

Oscar laughed. "No, that's true. Not sure why you put up with me. I was so surly."

I nodded. "You had every right to be. The world had treated you pretty bad, I reckon. I'm just glad I found you."

"When I think what my life might have been like if you hadn't—" Oscar said, shaking his head and quickening his step, as if he wanted to leave those thoughts behind him.

I kept up with him and pointed down the street. "You ready to get some lunch?"

Oscar lifted his head and beamed, his gaze fixing on the sign of a petite white house that said 'Annie's Kitchen' in bold yellow letters on the side.

"Yes, sir. I'm starved."

"Then let's go in."

As we stepped up onto the porch, the door opened, its metal bell jingling as two women came out, laughing about something. I grabbed Oscar's elbow to get him to move aside.

"Oh, excuse us," one of the ladies said, while her companion smiled and said, "Thank you."

"Ma'am," I replied.

We stepped into the cozy interior where there were about six tables set up, ranging in size from six-place settings to two, all covered in white linen. I gestured toward a table for two in the corner, and we sat down.

T'was homey and smelled of good food and coffee. Only a couple of the other tables were taken. It didn't take long for a young man about Oscar's age, wearing a short white apron o'er his trousers, to come on o'er. In the back of my mind, I wondered if someday Oscar might get a place at Annie's or at Jensen's, serving food and drink. He was pretty enough to please the public, if only I could teach him the good manners he'd need.

"Good day, gentlemen. Can I offer you a menu?"

"Oh my gosh, yes," Oscar said. "I'm so hungry."

The man laughed. "That's what I like to hear. My ma likes to feed hungry people. That's why she set up this place, of course."

"Look, Jimmy. I can get those flapjacks again," Oscar said, pressing his finger on the menu.

"We always have them," the young man said, "I'm Henry. You new in town? I don't think I've seen you, though it sounds like you've been here before."

"I'm Oscar Yates, and this here's Jimmy Downing. We came all the way from Dawson City."

Henry seemed astonished. "Up in the Yukon? That's a mighty long way."

I nodded. "We're fixin' up the Yates' old homestead, just outta town. It's gonna be a job, that's for sure."

Henry laughed. "I heard it was gone to ruin. You gentlemen sure are bold to take on such a task. But welcome to Port Essington, Oscar, Jimmy. Let me get you something to drink, and I'll put your order in. You want the flapjacks, too?" he asked me.

"No, I think I'll have the pork and beans. Them flapjacks taste good, but I feel I need something a more solid to sustain me."

"Fair enough. You want some bacon with your flapjacks, Oscar?"

"Oh, yes, please. Thank you."

We settled in, observing the other guests and enjoying the smells coming from the kitchen. So far, the people in Port Essington had been welcoming. T'was a different atmosphere to Dawson City, that was certain—and even to Whitehorse, which was a big city. Port Essington was more of a village, in a pleasant, lucrative spot. The salmon canneries kept folks employed during the milder seasons, and those that worked there went south for other employment during the winter.

Carson and Tim said the railway was coming, and they didn't know what the town would do when that happened. The railroad was slated to go on the land across the Skeena from Port Essington, and the implications of that would remain to be seen. Tim and Carson were doubtful the town would survive it in the long run. But it would take some time for the railway to be built out here then to get running properly, so the town would be all right for now. And maybe they were wrong.

Folks who stayed for the colder months hunkered down and led slower lives, making the most of the warmer weather so they could take it easy through winter. There was still hunting and trapping, and many of the local indigenous people stayed and made use of Port Essington's conveniences. Port Essington didn't have a slum, because the only people who came were industrious, hard-working types who weren't afraid of the perseverance it took to even get to the place. If you made it, there was opportunity enough to make a go of it. If Oscar and I had to make a home somewhere, this seemed like a promising spot.

Henry brought a plate piled high with fluffy flapjacks and crispy bacon for Oscar and another with a side of juicy pork with baked beans in a little bowl for me. He had already put a basket of fresh-cut bread in the center of the table, and he filled our cups with coffee and milk.

"Can I get you anything else?"

"No, I reckon this'll do. Thank you kindly," I said. I gazed at the food laid out and noticed that Oscar's eyes had gone all hazy. "There you go, looking at them flapjacks like you been starved for weeks."

He picked up the little jar of syrup that Henry had brought and poured a copious amount o'er the pile. "I feel as though I have been." He looked at me with a puzzled frown. "We got the ingredients to make these at home?"

"I can make sure we do. You want me to make them for you sometime?"

He nodded vigorously. "Oh yes," he said, slicing his flapjacks and lifting a forkful to his lips. I watched as he chewed and slurped, my mouth curving with amusement.

"They may not be as good as Miss Annie's, though."

"I don't even care. I reckon they'd be pretty okay."

We ate quietly, since we were hungry and the food tasted delicious. T'was fine to sit in town at a fine establishment and enjoy a meal together.

Oscar gazed at me as he slowed down and took a break from shoving food into his mouth. "I reckon I want to learn to rope the way you do, Jimmy. Can you teach me that?"

I snorted, finishing up my beans. "What you wanna learn that for? We ain't got any cattle or sheep."

"Not *now*. Seems like a skill I'd like to know." He gazed at me, and I knew what he was thinking. My trousers felt tight all of a sudden.

"Oscar," I said, giving him a look.

"Jimmy, there ain't no reason I shouldn't learn it."

"Sure. I guess," I said, wiping my mouth. "But first you'd better get used to—what did you say your horse's name was gonna be?"

Oscar spoke around a mouthful of flapjack. "Onyx."

"Right. You'd better get used to Onyx and let her get used to you, and don't try any tricks or nothin'." I gave him a glare. "I mean, be sensible."

Oscar grinned, as if there was nothing for me to worry about. "Ain't I always?"

I raised my eyebrows. "Well—"

He pointed at me with his fork. "Don't answer that."

I laughed, content with my belly full, knowing Oscar was happy and fed, and that we seemed at the beginning of a promising adventure. Fixing up Oscar's late uncle's place was an overwhelming undertaking, but today it felt manageable and like we were fated to it.

When Henry brought our bill, I asked about the best place in town to get a bath.

"The Front Street Hotel offers a hot bath for a dollar. And they have a fancy bath for one-fifty, if you want fresher soap and softer towels." He smiled. "I recommend that one. Nothing feels better than a fluffy towel once you've cleaned up."

"I reckon we can indulge ourselves. We're havin' a special day in town. Oscar just got a new horse, and we've put in a lot of work on the homestead."

I left money on the table to cover our meal and a tip for Henry.

Walking next to me on our way to the hotel, Oscar looked so untroubled that it made my heart sing. I liked to see him that way. Doubtless, that came from my memories of finding him starving on the streets of Dawson City. He'd been trying to make money in questionable ways, and I'd taken pity on him and given him a meal he could hardly enjoy because his stomach was so shrunk in on itself. Then I'd brought him up to my hotel room, and he'd washed all the stink and dirt off. I remembered how quiet he'd been, sitting there in the cooling water, and how long it had taken me to realize he was crying.

My initial interest in Oscar had been honorable and charitable. At least, I liked to think so. That had changed upon waking up the next morning with his mouth on my cock, which had shocked and confused me but had also pleased me in a way I'd never contemplated.

There had been no turning back from that moment, and Oscar and I had become more and more intimate as time had gone on and fate had thrown us together.

An imposing structure at the north end of the street facing the harbor, The Front Street Hotel served a diverse clientele. This was where Oscar and I had stayed on our arrival at Port Essington. The rooms were affordable and decent, clean, and the hotel offered upgrades for the more particular traveler, such as the luxury bath with fine soap and soft towel that Henry had explained. We paid for two of those, and Oscar made a point not to remark or look at me with regret when we had to go into separate rooms.

T'was pleasant to be alone for a hot bath and simply let my mind wander as I washed my hair and body and soaked for a spell. The soap I was given smelled of lemon and sandalwood and lathered up real good. I held it between my palms like t'was a cherished keepsake, and, honest to God, I wanted to wrap it up and take it home. But I resisted that impulse in the interests of not alienating the people who worked there.

When I'd finished and rinsed the suds off, I stepped out onto the mat and wrapped myself in the towel I'd been provided. T'was plush, and the proprietor had said t'was made from the finest cotton. I'd only ever paid for the most rudimentary of services in the past. This was a new experience, and I vowed then and there we would spend the money on such luxury every now and then. And one of the must-haves for the new house would be a space where we could keep a copper tub, so we could bathe in the comfort of our own home. Now that would be living the high life!

We'd brought our fresh union suits and clean clothes to put on after the bath. There was no point spending a fortune to bathe then putting on your soiled clothes again.

Renewed and refreshed, I was ready to take on the world when I stepped into the parlor of the hotel. Oscar sat there waiting for me with an indulgent look on his face. He raised his eyes.

"What?" I asked.

He spoke with a lackadaisical air while drifting his gaze o'er my body. "What the hell were you doin' in that bath, Jimmy?"

I glanced at the gentleman behind the desk in the next room, but he was busy with some paperwork and not paying attention.

I turned back to Oscar, giving him a stern look. We needed to be cautious.

"I was enjoyin' it. Did you even wash yourself properly? Or did you just dip yourself in and climb out without usin' the soap we paid so much money for?"

Oscar stood up and ran his fingers through his damp hair. "As you can see for yourself, I've washed my hair. The rest you'll just have to take my word on."

Until we get home, I thought as I forced my face to stay straight.

Oscar lifted his chin as if I were an annoying friend to question him on his cleanliness. Kid could act when he wanted to.

"Fine. Anyhow, I'm ready now. We should go to the store and get those things on our list."

"Then we can go and get my horse?" Oscar gushed, reverting to his regular demeanor.

I sighed, nodding. "Then we can go and get your horse."

* * * *

We found everything we needed at the general store. In a moment of impulse, I asked the shopkeeper if they happened to have any lemon soap?

"As a matter of fact, we do. The Front Street Hotel has a standing order for this one," he said, holding up a yellow bar with bits of solid lemon rind in it, exactly like the one I'd used. It cost dear for a bar of soap, but I figured we deserved a bit of luxury, especially making do with such primitive living arrangements. If a simple bar of soap could make our evenings more pleasant, then I reckoned t'was worth the price.

"That's it. I'll take one of those, please."

"Of course. I'll wrap it up in some paper for you."

"Thank you."

By the time we got back to Peter Morris' place, the afternoon was beginning to wane. We had a couple of hours of daylight left if we were lucky. Best to get on home and get the horses settled before dark.

"I gave her a grooming and tacked her up. She's ready to go."

"Thank you," I said. "Oscar's eager to ride her."

Peter looked at Oscar. "Now, you need to show her who's boss. She's a nice horse but she's young, and she'll take advantage if she can."

"Yes, sir."

"I'm very glad to have sold her to such nice fellas as you and Jimmy. I know you won't mistreat her, and this way, I can see her from time to time, whenever you come into town."

"That's so. Thank you kindly," I said.

For a second, Oscar looked a little green around the gills. It had been a long while since he'd ridden on his own. His very last solo ride had ended with tragic results, and I reckoned he was fielding some unpleasant memories.

"Could I try her out in the paddock first?" Oscar said to both me and Mr. Morris.

"Of course, you can, son," Peter said, giving Oscar a kind look. "That's a good idea. Give you both a chance to get your bearings."

Peter led Onyx out of the barn and into the middle of the paddock, where Oscar went to meet her. The saddle she had on was sturdy but fancy, with elaborate stitching around the edges and pressed designs in the leather.

Peter apologized. "I got this stuff for my granddaughter, so it's a bit on the feminine side. I hope you don't mind."

Oscar was busy petting his horse and talking gently to her, but he glanced at the saddle and smiled. "At least it ain't a sidesaddle. That would have been a little hard to explain."

Peter laughed. "True. Times are changin', you see, and I didn't see any reason my granddaughter couldn't ride a horse like her pa does." He sighed with a sadness he couldn't conceal. "They decided to go out east a few months ago. Ain't even heard from them or nothin'. Missus and I are hopin' for a telegraph soon, else we'll have to believe they perished. It's a tricky business, this overland travel, especially when you have a family. I just hope they're all right."

Oscar's forehead creased. "I surely hope so, too, Mr. Morris. And the saddle suits me fine. I like it."

Peter nodded, blinking quickly. "You need a hand up?"

Oscar came around Onyx's left side and grabbed the pommel of her pretty saddle. "Nope, I got it."

He fit his boot into the stirrup and swung up in a graceful movement, as I recalled teaching him the basics of riding on our journey. Being a city boy, he hadn't had any riding experience, which hadn't been an issue until we'd abandoned the wagon after encountering a member of my old gang and I'd decided it would slow us down. I'd had to lead Oscar on Sprite for the first day or two, until he'd found his seat and was ready to try to handle the horse himself. But, by the time we'd ridden across the Yukon to Whitehorse, then to Telegraph Creek and most of the way to Port Essington, he'd become an excellent horseman, although the downing of Sprite by a pack of wolves had ruined his confidence. At least Oscar had survived. I didn't even want to think about the alternative. It had been bad to lose that horse, but it would've been a million times worse if I'd lost Oscar. I don't know if I'd have been able to go on, especially being in Port Essington on my own, when the only reason I'd come here was for him.

Peter moved out of the way and Oscar shifted in the saddle, getting comfortable. Onyx's ears flicked back and forth and she shied to one side, but Oscar clucked to her and urged her forward with an instinct that came back to him.

Onyx began to walk, and Oscar turned her to go by the fence. When they passed close to me, he threw me a grin as his eyes sparkled.

"She moves like a dream, Jimmy. She's perfect."

Chapter Four

A Lustful Interlude

"You remember how to ride," I said, grinning and crossing my arms on the fence of the corral. "That's good."

"I reckon you're a good teacher," he said o'er his shoulder as he turned Onyx to walk the other way. The horse responded to his signals, her ears flicking back and forth as he clucked to her and gave her encouragement.

I blushed at Oscar's praise, remembering those early days of fumbling about and finding our way together. I had taught Oscar to ride a horse, but Oscar had taught me things I'd never imagined. Best not to think of those things right now, though, lest I were to embarrass myself in front of Mr. Morris and reveal the truth of our relationship.

Oscar took Onyx around the edge of the pen several times, all the while with that childlike smile on his face as he coaxed her into a trot then a canter. I soaked it in while trying not to look like I was staring. He gushed with pleasure and confidence, sitting so comfortably in the fine saddle that I knew we'd made the right decision to buy the black mare. The two of them together made my heart sing because they made such a pretty picture.

"He named her yet?" Peter asked me. "I wanted to let my granddaughter name the horse, so I've just been callin' her 'girl'."

I nodded. "Yeah, he named her Onyx."

Peter frowned. "Onyx. That's a peculiar name. Is it just made up or does it mean something?"

I shrugged. "Oscar says it's a type of mineral. He spent most of his recent life in Dawson City. Knows all about minin' and rocks and such. Onyx is a black rock, he said."

"Hmm. S'pose that makes sense then, e'en though it sounds queer."

"Sure enough," I agreed.

Oscar pulled Onyx to a stop and slid down, then gave her a kiss on her smooth black nose. "You're a good girl, and you're mine. And we're gonna have so much fun, Onyx. I promise."

"All right, all right. You don't have to sweet talk her. I reckon she'll like you well enough if you're the one to put feed in her trough," I said, laughing at the way he was treating her — as though she were his pet and not a needed form of transportation. Oscar had always seen horses for more than what they were, but I didn't hold it against him. T'was a part of his nature, the way he showed affection to all living things. He had a huge heart that didn't seem to have been tainted by all the hardships he'd endured, which was a goddamned miracle if you thought about it.

But he frowned. "I know I don't have to. I want to, because she's my pretty girl and I already love her."

He stuck his tongue out at me.

My goodness. I suddenly had a very strong urge to get home and give him a turn o'er my knee for that cheek. My face heated as I put on my hat and turned back to Mr. Morris.

"Thank you, sir. It's an honor to do business with you," I said as Peter opened the gate so Oscar could lead Onyx to where I'd hitched Dixie.

"Likewise. It's nice to meet new folks. I hope you do well here. My wife and I have lived in Port Essington for most of our lives, and we can't think of a better spot."

* * * *

I had Oscar ride ahead of me on the journey home, so's I could keep an eye on him and make sure Onyx was behaving herself.

They did make a handsome pair, truth be told, and seemed to be made for each other. She was just the right size for him, and he was already smitten. I could see that much. They seemed to be communicating the whole trip home, with Oscar murmuring sweet words and Onyx's dainty black ears angling toward him. I recalled he'd done the same with his horse, Sprite, and, as a result, they'd formed quite the bond. He had a way with animals. I reckon there weren't too many beasts that could resist him, me included.

T'was satisfying to watch him as we rode. I enjoyed the sight of his lithe but solid body rocking in Onyx's saddle as he guided her with ease o'er the grass and between the trees. I felt free enough to be able to keep my gaze on him, since there weren't any other folks around this far out of town.

By the time we got to the homestead, I'm afraid I was in an indecent state.

But Oscar seemed oblivious. He pulled Onyx up and slid to the ground, going right away to her head to thank her for such a nice ride. Then he turned to me and didn't notice the strange way I was moving.

"Jimmy, she's such a nice horse! I love her so much!"

"I'm glad you like her. I think we got our money's worth, and that's a fact."

"You were drivin' a hard bargain, though. He asked for a hundred and you got him down to eighty-five with free tack."

"I know it," I said, basking in his approval.

"T'was impressive to watch you."

Warmth flooded my belly and even more went into my groin. I couldn't help making a small adjustment to my trousers and Oscar finally noticed my predicament.

"Jimmy, you ain't swoll' in your trousers right now?"

I shrugged. "Maybe."

He stared at me, then at the front of my trousers, then at his horse, then back at me, with a tortured look on his face. "But...I got to get Onyx settled and groomed right now. I can't just—"

He seemed so conflicted that I had to laugh, even though there was nothing funny about the way I wanted to grab him and pull him to the house—or into the stable.

"Seems I've got some competition for your affections. I reckon I'll just have to wait, won't I?"

His face softened and he smiled. "I reckon you will. But as soon as my horse is sorted out and comfortable in her stall, well, then I'll attend to you."

"Fair enough," I said, leading Dixie into the barn and trying to think of things that would make my dick stop its stand.

We spent the next half hour looking after the horses and checking on Poke, giving Dixie a bit more feed and all of them some hay. Peter had advised us not to give Onyx a full meal until tomorrow as she'd probably be out of sorts at the change of scenery, and a horse's digestion could be delicate. But Oscar ran to the house to get Onyx a carrot to make sure she didn't starve. Tomorrow, she could have the grain mix, same as Dixie and the mule. We'd picked up another bag of it in town that I'd strapped behind my saddle. I put it with the rest of the feed.

We decided to let them all out into the paddock to let them figure things out together, but we did stay to watch in case anyone put up a fuss or acted less than friendly. T'was amusing to watch Dixie and Poke as they observed the coal-black mare who waltzed right up to the trough and took a long drink as if she didn't care one bit that she was in a different spot to where she'd woke up. Dixie watched Onyx for a moment, then glanced our way as if to say *Who the hell is this now?* but soon ambled o'er and nudged Onyx out of the way so she could have a drink. Onyx whinnied and tossed her head, but she moved aside and let Dixie by, so that was good. Dixie was the leader here, and Onyx had better figure that out.

Poke didn't seem to care one way or the other and waited until the horses had drunk their fill before heading o'er there. I reckoned he wouldn't be much of a problem. He'd always been easygoing and had stood the myth of the ornery, witless mule on its head more than once. He was a sweetheart and braver than some horses. We'd been lucky to get him.

"She seems all right," Oscar said, his brow wrinkled as he waited for one of them to make trouble, but it didn't look like that was gonna happen.

"She's fine. Looks like they all get along all right," I said, leaning on the rail of the fence and trying not to make my close observation of Oscar's stance too obvious. But after so long being with him in town where I couldn't touch him then watching him ride his horse all the way home, I was raring to go.

Oscar nodded and gazed at me from under the brim of his hat. "You reckon we can leave 'em?"

I cleared my throat as my cock jumped at the thought of getting Oscar into the house. But I kept myself calm and inclined my chin with what I hoped was a look of sage wisdom.

"I reckon so. We can check on them in…a little bit." Hopefully after I'd had my way with Oscar the way I wanted — *needed* — to. But I wasn't worried. We'd hear it if one of them got nasty, but I didn't expect it.

We walked back to the house. I added some wood to the stove and poked it around until it caught. Then I pumped some well-water into a basin in the sink, and we took turns washing our hands with the fine lemon soap, not saying a word. But there was a buzzing electricity in the air and a knowledge that words had been said and references made to something that needed to happen.

I risked a glance at Oscar. "You're awful sweet with that horse. She don't stand a chance. I reckon you stole her heart already, like you do with everyone."

Oscar grinned and winked. "I never expected that a hasty 'thank-you' suck in the hotel room in Dawson would steal your heart, Jimmy Downing. Reckon I just got lucky with that one."

I blushed, remembering that morning. "I reckon you did."

"I was lucky you didn't wring my neck, you bein' an ex-outlaw and all. I didn't really think about what I was doin' — no doubt I was still addled from bein' so hungry and so many days without sleep. You'd said you didn't want that so many times — but I guess I sensed that, secretly, you did want it...or might." He frowned and cocked his head. "You know, if you had told me to stop, I would have. You know that, right, Jimmy?"

"I know it. T'was a shock, for certain. But there wasn't a point that I didn't want what was happenin', e'en though it seemed daring and took me a bit by surprise."

He raised his eyebrows. "A bit?"

I blushed. "I might have...thought about somethin' like that on occasion," I mumbled. "Didn't much admit it to myself until after things had progressed between us. But I reckon I'd had some...*questionable* desires, to be certain." I glanced at him shyly. "You got good instincts, Oscar Yates," I admitted.

"Why, thank you," he grinned, drying his hands with the linen towel. "Weren't nothin' but a grateful gesture. Now, what happened afterwards...? Well, that was somethin' truly special."

"You mean when I hauled you o'er my lap and spanked you till we both spilled?" My voice was a little shaky. That entire experience was engraved on my memory like a film reel. What had happened in that room with Oscar had been a revelation and a shock, not to mention the dirtiest thing I'd ever fucking done with anyone, although I'd done my share of whoring.

I'd gotten more out of a clandestine gamahuche and delivering a spontaneous spanking to Oscar than I did going full bore with a woman. It had been nothing I'd ever been expecting, but when it had happened, it had felt so right.

I reckon I'd gone and lost my mind a little, and that was why I'd not been able to leave Oscar behind when I'd left for Whitehorse. We'd only been separated once since then, and that was when Oscar had been taken by Spook and Whitlaw, and I didn't want to remember that.

I took the towel and dried my hands, my fingers trembling with anticipation.

"You still hard for me, Jimmy?" Oscar's soft voice came from behind me.

When I turned around, he was standing by the bed, gazing at me out of dark, hooded eyes. He'd taken off his coat when we'd come inside, and now he hooked his thumbs underneath his gray braces and flicked them off his shoulders.

"Why? What have you got in mind?" I said, my mouth going dry.

He smiled slow. "Oh, I don't know. But why don't you come here and undress me?"

I swallowed, my throat feeling thick. "Okay."

I walked o'er and put my quivering fingers to the buttons of his shirt, making quick work of pulling the tails from his trousers and the sleeves off his arms. His union suit was clean, but it presented a barrier to his flesh that I needed to dispense with.

Instead of going for the flap of his trousers, I undid the tiny buttons of his underwear until I could peel the red flannel back from his shoulders and unwrap him like the gift he was. He helped me get his arms out of the tangle of cloth then stood before me, naked to the waist, his hair still tousled from the wind.

"Like what you see?" he asked.

"S'pose I do."

He laughed then, because t'was obvious I was spellbound.

"Hmm, you look like you want to eat me, Mr. Wolf," Oscar purred in seductive tones.

I smiled, pleased to be compared to such an animal. Even though the wolves had got Sprite, I admired their fearlessness and their savage beauty. I supposed they had to survive.

"I do, sweet lamb. I wanna eat you all up."

"Fuck," he cursed. A shiver took him as he lifted his chin. "Take off my trousers now. I wanna be naked for you."

"I want that, too," I said. I pulled down his trousers and the union suit, smelling the lemon of the soap we'd used at the hotel and back here and the scent of Oscar's own musk and maleness, without the overlay of dirt and sweat we'd both had going on for a few weeks. T'was a heady moment, and I closed my eyes and inhaled as I knelt before him. I opened them when Oscar put a gentle hand on my shoulder and stepped out of his clothes and underthings until he was standing there with nothing but a cheeky grin.

"Boy, you are so lovely," I said, eyeing him up and down and all o'er. "Whatever made you fall for a crusty, old, wasted fella like me?"

"Psssh. You ain't wasted. And you ain't old, neither. Just old enough." He shrugged, his gaze dropping to my feet and climbing up my body while my cock grew progressively thicker. "Old enough to be my daddy, though."

The breath whooshed out of me, and I surged forward, grabbing him and tackling him to the bed. "Barely. I ain't your daddy. And it's a good thing, considering what I'm about to do to you."

His mouth opened on a gasp as he met my gaze. "What are you gonna do to me, Jimmy? You gonna fuck me?"

I made a sound—a desperate, vulnerable sound deep in my throat—as I grabbed at my trousers, pulling the buttons apart on them and on my underwear as my gasps got louder and Oscar squirmed beneath me, spreading his legs as I took my cock out.

"Goddammit. Where's the grease?" I muttered.

Oscar moaned and reached to the little table beside the bed, grabbing the jar of saddle grease that we were using for slide when we fucked or did other things.

"Here. Open it and I'll help you," Oscar panted.

The crackle and pop of the wood in the iron stove accompanied our harsh breaths as I dipped my fingers into the tin then pressed them between his legs. He leaned back on his elbows, watching me with his eyes wide and his lips parted. There were so many things we liked to do together, but I hadn't been inside him for a while. Seemed we could hardly contain ourselves.

"Remember the first time you mounted me?" he said as I breached his hole with my fingers, spreading the slippery cream inside and around him.

I groaned. "Yes. Yes."

"You liked it so much."

"I did. I loved it."

I pushed my two fingers into him, into that silky soft, hot place, spreading him as he quivered and gasped, closed his eyes, then opened them again. They were burning coals now.

"You gonna mount me now? Make me yours again?"

"Yes. God, yes. Every day. I'm gonna fuck you every day, Oscar Yates—here in our bed, so's you'll know you're mine."

"Jimmy!" he panted as I pressed my cock at his hole, ready for his body to swallow me up and obliterate me.

The muscle yielded and I sank in as Oscar keened, his head thrown back as I bottomed out in one slick move. Then I had to stay still or I'd finish too soon and he'd curse me for ruinin' our fun. It had happened once or twice, and he was touchy about it—only because there wasn't a thing he liked more than having my cock up inside him like this, and he wanted to enjoy it.

He was all heat and softness, panting breaths and little mewls of pleasure. I held my breath, closed my eyes and tried to get ahold of myself.

"Hell, Oscar. I could stay like this all winter. You're so fucking *warm*."

He gave a breathless laugh. "I reckon we'd freeze to death once the fire went out."

I opened my eyes and laughed, too. "Christ. Imagine if they found us like this?"

He looked shocked but laughed and pushed at my shoulders. "I reckon you'd better start to move, then, so you can tumble me proper and make me spurt. Come on, now."

His words got me moving right quick. I found a rhythm that he liked and didn't make me get close right away, although t'was always a battle. I'd never known what I was missing before I did this to him, but there wasn't any going back from it.

"Oh, God. Jimmy, God. You got such a big dick. I'm so lucky you're so big and manly. I love your cock so much..." Oscar liked to talk dirty, and I liked to listen to him. T'was one of the things that had taken me by surprise at first but that I soon found I craved. In a society that liked to emphasize polite manners and decorum, t'was a refreshing thing to give it all up and act like randy animals.

"I'm glad I gotta big dick, too, so's I can do this properly."

"Oh God. Oh God. I'm close," he said, his hand going to his nubby. That was what we called his penis, even though t'wasn't all *that* small—just a little smaller than average, I reckoned, having seen my share of flaccid and hard cocks when I camped out with the gang for so long. When Oscar's cock was the way t'was right now—red and raging and stiff, it looked pretty damned impressive. But he liked it when we made a fuss of how it compared to mine—something about feeling small and less than a man. It made Oscar happy and allowed him to feel soft and delicate and looked after. It had seemed strange at first, but now t'was just a part of who he was and who we were together. And I liked it, too, because I surely enjoyed bein' the big man when it came to him. I liked to treat him nice, take care of him and bed him the way he deserved.

I grabbed his ankle and lifted his leg up, spreading him nice and wide as I pounded him. I batted his hand away from his cock and took o'er, my fingers still greasy, stroking his nubby fast and hard and pounding into him the way he liked.

Oscar enjoyed things rough, whether I was fucking him or spanking his behind, and I had no problem with that.

After a moment, his body arched up from the bed and his nubby spurted o'er my fingers, as Oscar cried out louder than any girl I'd ever had and cursed me for giving him so much pleasure.

I lasted maybe two more thrusts then my whole body stiffened as I pressed deep and exploded with bliss, spilling inside his sweet heat.

"Oscar, Oscar. Fuck. I love you. I love you so much."

We lay there, connected in such an intimate way as our desperate, frantic breaths evened out. My head lay on his chest, and he stroked my hair gently as the wood in the stove crackled. The small room felt cozy and warm now, and there was a slick of sweat on us both.

Oscar laughed. "Now we need to bathe again."

I clicked my tongue. "We should have bought a little tub to stand in when we were in town. Even a small bath would be something. We could heat the water on the stove."

"Next time," Oscar said, "when we have Poke to carry it back."

His fingers in my hair felt so sweet and soft as my dick shrank and finally popped out when I shifted.

"Oh," Oscar groaned. "Je-sus."

"What?"

His eyes had a faraway look as he smiled with smug satisfaction. "I feel you leakin' out of me."

I caught my breath. "Oscar, that's so…filthy."

His gaze on mine sparked fire again. "I love it. God, Jimmy. I'd have your babies if I could."

I gaped at him, startled at first. But the way he'd said it, with complete and utter honesty, expressing the way he felt about me, went straight to my heart.

"You would? Truly?"

"Truly," he said, tracing his finger o'er my cheek. "Maybe if we try hard enough, it might happen."

I rolled my eyes. "Well now, I ain't no medical doctor, but I have to say I got my doubts about that."

Oscar shrugged. "Well, there ain't no harm in you *tryin'* to knock me up. We can pretend, can't we?"

I grinned, once again taken aback by Oscar's sense of himself and willingness to be whoever he wanted.

"I reckon so. You want me to get you with child?"

"Oh fuck. Yeah, I do. I want you to fill me so full of your seed that a miracle happens."

"What would we say to the townsfolk then?"

Oscar sobered. His lips set in a firm line. "We'd tell 'em I was havin' your baby, and I was nothin' but a strange-lookin' woman, I s'pose. Think they'd believe that?"

I shook my head. "Doubt it. But you never know."

I kissed him all o'er his handsome face, staying close and warm and not wanting to get up and do any chores. I'd stay like this as long as I could.

Chapter Five

Secrets

As the dark days of winter approached, the weather became colder and the nights longer. Since there wasn't much to do to keep up the homestead except chop firewood, clean dishes and clothes, cook and look after the horses, Oscar and I spent time exploring our new home. Oscar and Onyx needed to get to know one another, and t'was enjoyable to ride out for an hour or so for the heck of it. T'was pleasant to be out in nature, and the scenery here at the base of the forests and mountains of the Lower Skeena was majestic and awe-inspiring — when we could see it, that was. Most of the land around our homestead was dense pine forest, and we had to be careful to notice landmarks and use the compass to make sure we knew where we were at all times. After several meanders, though, we got used to the surrounding landscape, and we knew where the easiest routes were.

When I'd teased Oscar about Onyx being competition for my affections, I'd been half joking, although it soon became apparent that I wasn't all that wide off the mark. Oscar spent a good deal of his time in the stables, talking to his horse, telling her all his secrets, even when he wasn't riding — so much so that I did begin to feel a might neglected.

T'was silly to feel that way, of course. Oscar spent lots of time with me, and there were many things he got from me that he couldn't get from his horse. I knew t'was so, in theory. As a result, I pushed those feelings down and went about my business, trying to find ways to occupy myself when he wasn't around or finding an excuse to be in the stables when he went there. But I reckoned that most of the time he went to talk to Onyx, part of t'was a need to get away and be on his own, which did hurt me, even though I tried not to take it personal.

Oscar and I were different in a lot of ways. I'd spent most of my life in the company of others, even when those people had been men with questionable morals. Truth was, I liked being around other folks, and there had been times I'd found my job hauling cargo for Mr. Henley a might on the lonely side. Perhaps that was why it had been so easy to help Oscar — because I'd been desperate for some kind of companion. What I hadn't guessed was *what* kind of companion Oscar would want to be with me. As luck would have it, that had turned out to suit me just fine in the end.

But Oscar had spent much of his life on his own, even in a crowded, cramped city, and he liked to be free of other folks sometimes so's he could think his own thoughts without getting distracted. And I understood it, I did. But it still sometimes smarted when he took off to the barn to be with his horse. Only I felt silly feeling jealous of an animal. So I buried those emotions until they got so thick and unruly inside me that I guess they just busted out.

"Where you goin'?" I said, as Oscar pulled on his coat and reached for the door handle.

"I need to go check on Onyx. She seemed a bit sad this mornin'."

I stared at him. "*Sad*? How can she be sad? You pamper her so much, I reckon she's gonna start thinkin' she's a goddamn fairy princess."

Oscar pursed his lips. "Anyhow, I need to check in on her."

"Fine." My tone held more annoyance than I'd planned.

Oscar's hand stayed where t'was, motionless on the handle of the door, as he gave me a strange look.

"What the hell's wrong with you? You mad 'cause I wanna look after my horse?"

I put down the plate I'd been drying. "She ain't goin' nowhere. She's fed and watered and out in the paddock, and she's got Poke and Dixie to keep her company."

Oscar examined me for a long moment, not saying anything. I felt embarrassed about my rude words, but I hadn't been able to help myself. Seemed he spent more time in the barn with his horse than he did with me, and it hurt.

"Jimmy."

"What?"

He licked his lips and frowned. "Are you jealous?"

I laughed but it came out sounding wrong. "Jealous of a goddamn horse?"

He shrugged. "You're actin' like you're mad at me 'cause I ain't at your beck and call all the time no more."

"I thought…" I put the dish on the shelf and picked up another. "I thought you liked bein' at my beck and call."

Oscar rubbed a hand o'er his temple. "I do, Jimmy. Goddammit, I do. But Onyx is —" He scuffed the toe of his boot on the planked floor. "She's mine, and she's pretty and warm and soft and she listens. Jimmy, she listens t'all my problems, and I —"

My head jerked up. "You got problems? What kind of problems?"

"Oh, I don't know. But I can talk to her about anythin'."

I put the wet plate down on the counter and laid the towel on top. Then I ran my fingers through my hair and gazed at Oscar. "What? You can't talk to me?" My voice came out all quiet, like I was scared to hear the answer to that question.

Oscar took off his coat and hung it back on the hook. "'Course I can. It's just…different…when I'm talking to Onyx, out in the barn."

"Uh-huh," I said, turning back to the sink and the dishes I'd been wiping clean. But I only curled my fingers around the edge of the wood counter and stared out of the window at the trees.

"She don't care what I'm sayin'. I don't gotta think about what she might suppose from what I'm tellin' her."

"Like what?" I asked, staring straight ahead. "What can you tell that horse that you can't tell me?"

He was quiet for a spell. I picked up a dish and the dish cloth, and I was just about to ask him again when he started talking.

"Stuff like — like, if Spook had carried through with his plans for me…and somehow didn't shoot me after…that I were gonna go to the river and take care of things myself."

The dish in my hand slipped out of my fingers and thunked into the tin bowl, making a ringing sound that went straight through me. I stood there a moment, trying to collect myself and think about what I wanted to say to that—and how I wanted to say it.

I took a deep, steadying breath. I didn't turn around.

"Are you sayin'…? Are you sayin'…you wouldn't have come back to me?"

"Jimmy, I—"

I meant to give a sort of a hollow laugh, but it came out more of a gasp.

"I wouldn't have known what happened. You would have disappeared, and I'd never have known Spook got you or where you were. I'd have thought you'd just decided you were done with me."

Oscar made a sound of frustration behind me, and I flinched.

"See? This is why I tell them private things to my horse, because she don't judge me or make demands like you do."

I did turn around then, because I was so surprised by what he was saying.

"*Demands*? What kind of demands you think I make on you, boy, except for the ones you want me to make? I thought you liked when I was demandin'?"

"I'm not talkin' about that! I'm not talking about what I like when we play our games. I'm talkin' about… Hell, I don't even know." Oscar threw his hands in the air and sat down hard on the mattress of our bed. I gazed at him for a long while, and I realized he may just have had a point.

"I'm sorry. I'm sorry I reacted that way to you tellin' me what you did, and I reckon I can't blame you for them thoughts. But why do you think I'd judge you?"

"You said I was selfish for not thinkin' of you, when all I could think about was Spook and what he was prob'ly gonna do to me!" Oscar brushed at his face with his hand. "How the *hell* was I s'posed to know you were gonna come and shoot 'im? I thought you were still asleep at the camp, or you'd only supposed I'd fucked off and wouldn't even come lookin'?"

I blinked several times, putting myself in his place for maybe the first time since that incident. We were quiet for a long time, neither of us wanting to address what was happening.

"Why're we fighting?" I said, after several minutes, when I couldn't stand the silence any longer.

"I don't know. I don't rightly know," Oscar said. "'Cept you don't want me to go the barn and tell all my secrets to Onyx, and I don't know why."

"'Cause I want you to tell all your secrets to me," I said. "I thought you loved me." I'd never expected in all my life to sound so needy as I did in that moment. But as soon as I said it, I realized how selfish t'was.

"'Course I love you. But that don't mean I gotta tell you everything I think in my silly, stupid head, do it?"

The absurdity of this discussion came to me in an instant, like a spark of illumination.

"No. No, I suppose it don't." I gave a little laugh, and t'was genuine this time. "What the hell do I know, anyway? I ain't never been in love with nobody before. I don't know how any of this works." I held up my hands, the dishtowel in one of them.

Oscar nodded, and the corners of his sweet mouth started to twitch.

"I'm just as confused as you."

"C'mere," I said, tossing the cloth to the counter and opening my arms, hoping he'd forgive me.

He hesitated a second then he ambled o'er and let me pull him to my chest. His sinewy arms went around my waist, and he clutched onto me like he was afraid he was going to float away, and I was the only thing anchoring him.

"Jimmy, I—"

"Shh. Just be still," I said, holding him like the precious thing he was.

We stood together like that for a spell. Then I started to speak.

"Now, I wanna say somethin'. I want you to know that I don't blame you for anything goin' through your head while Spook and Whitlaw had you. You hear me? None of it. That was a terrifying situation, and you had to deal with it however you could. I got no right to judge you on that or put my selfish needs ahead of you tryin' to sort it all out. I'm sorry. I truly am."

"Me, too, Jimmy."

"You ain't doin' wrong by me goin' out to talk to that horse. I reckon it's a good thing you do that."

"I love her so much. I think she likes me, too. Maybe she's startin' to love me."

I laughed and kissed the top of his head. "How could she not?" I tipped his chin so's he'd look me in the eye. You make people love you just by doin' what you do. The kindness you shown me, and now the way you are with that horse? 'Course she's gonna love you. She prob'ly loved you in that corral at Mr. Morris's, like I loved you when I saw you scramblin' for cash in Dawson City. I didn't know it at the time, but you were mine from that very moment, e'en though I didn't understand exactly how. Reckon you sorted me out right quick."

Oscar laughed, the sound of it making my heart sing. "Yeah, I reckon I did. But that weren't exactly *love*."

"G'on. I know that. But I think I started to fall for you e'en before you showed me your skills at gamahouching."

Oscar's face screwed up. "At *what*?"

"Ain't you heard that word? It's what you did that morning…with your mouth."

"Oh, I *know* what I did that morning with my mouth. Never knew t'was called that!"

"Well, you do, now." I stepped back and took hold of his arms, giving him a quizzical look. "You ever get any schooling?"

"Not much. I reckon I wouldn't have learned *that* word, even if I had gone to school."

"No, I reckon that's true."

He cocked his head. "How do you know so many big words? Did those outlaws teach you?"

I rolled my eyes. "I suppose they did teach me the bad ones, but my ma was a teacher. She made sure I was educated. She wanted me to have a good life. Didn't quite work out, though—till now, at least."

Oscar nodded then smiled in a shy way, as if he was tryin' not to feel proud. "You gotta good life right now?"

"Best life I've had so far, and that's the honest truth. And it's all because of you."

Now his smile was big again, and he nodded, satisfied. "E'en though you're still outside the law?"

"Well now," I said, letting go of him and folding my arms o'er my chest. "I've decided to make my own decisions when it comes to that. Those laws that stop cruelty and evil? Yeah, I'll obey those ones, now that I'm outta that fearful spot with the gang. But the laws and rules that get in the way of the good things, like love and pleasure that don't seem to be harmin' anyone? There shouldn't be laws against those things, in my opinion." I scratched at my chin. "Anyway, there ain't no law can stop me from loving you, Oscar Yates."

We gazed at each other for a long moment, caught up in where the conversation had led us. But he'd been wanting to go and see his horse before I'd waylaid him with my baseless insecurities.

"Now, go and look after that horse. I got things to do."

Oscar smiled. "Maybe we can saddle up Dixie and Onyx and take a ride later? Just for fun?"

I thought about it. "Sure. I don't see why not. Prob'ly a good idea to keep up our explorin'. The more familiar we are with the lay of the land, the better, I reckon."

"I think so, too," Oscar said. "And riding out with you reminds me of our travelin' days, when I was so grateful you didn't leave me behind."

I cleared my throat, remembering the decision I'd made to bring him with me and where that had led. "You don't have to worry about bein' left behind no more."

* * * *

Later, when the sun was high and the wind had died down, we put Poke in his stall, saddled up the horses and headed out. A large proportion of the trees surrounding our small homestead—pine, spruce, hemlock—kept their foliage through the colder months, but the loss of leaves from their deciduous neighbors made the forests seem sparer and the sightlines clearer. T'was easier to find your way, except in spots where the evergreens grew thick and plentiful.

The landscape was starkly beautiful and full of wildlife. I'd already hunted rabbits and foxes, coyotes and badgers. We had our fill of meat available to shore up our store-bought goods, at least for now. Eventually, some of them would go into hibernation and the pickings might be scarcer, but I doubted the land here was anywhere near picked clean of game, like some of the more populated areas.

Spokshute Mountain loomed in the distance. Named by the local people, it stood guard between the British Columbia mainland and the town, with our homestead and probably a few more nestled at its feet. One day, maybe in the summer, Oscar and I wanted to climb it. Maybe not all the way to the top, but we'd give it a try.

The horses seemed excited to be out, and Oscar and I picked up on that feeling of adventure. But I was also filled with an overriding sense of peace and calm. We'd made a risky journey to get here, and we'd never expected that things would work out the way they had. The shock of finding out that Oscar's uncle had perished had been tempered by the fact that his broken-down homestead had been ours for the taking. I'd convinced Oscar that we could make it what we wanted, and now we were living that dream, cozy and warm in our tiny kitchen, with big plans to build a whole house come spring.

The day was a nice one. The cold wasn't too biting, although the clouds portended snow and I expected it would start to fall soon. We hadn't had a but a few flurries so far, but I reckoned we were overdue for a dumping.

I was used to snow and, to tell the truth, I liked it. When the world was blanketed in white, the stillness settled me and made me feel like a bear in a den — safe and protected. I don't know what t'was exactly, but I liked the feeling.

My thoughts returned on their own to all the times I'd ridden out doing reconnaissance for the outlaw gang, back when I was nothing but a stooge for those men. Recon had seemed like a benign sort of thing, compared to what the others liked to do, so I fastened onto it as something they could count on me for. I could ride well, and I could keep quiet. And I had a way of explaining the landscape that would make it easy for the others to find what they needed.

Of course, I had enabled them in so many ways, and perhaps I was in a large way responsible for all the things they had done. But I figured someone else would have done the recon if I hadn't, and they'd have found folks to rob and murder just the same. Only I had to live with the fact that it had been me.

"Jimmy, what are you thinkin' about?" Oscar said, as he pulled Onyx up beside Dixie. "You're frownin' like you need to use the outhouse."

I forced my features to relax and gave him a look. "Nah, I used it this morning. Stank it up real good."

He narrowed his eyes at me. "I reckon that's true. Still, whatever you're thinkin' don't sit too well with you. I can tell."

I raised my eyebrows. "Oh, you can, can you? What am I thinkin' right now?" I said, running my gaze along his body and back up again, then licking my lips and giving him the most sultry look I could manage. I figured distraction was better than telling him about all that darkness I wanted to forget.

His eyes widened and he swallowed, his cheeks flushing and a smile forming.

"Hmm. I don't know if I can say it out loud. 'Tis so very scandalous."

"Never stopped you before," I grunted. "Never mind. Let's just keep goin'. This was a good idea."

Oscar nodded, keeping pace beside me and Dixie through the clearing. "Good. I'm having fun, too."

"I think Onyx is enjoying herself. Her eyes are so bright, and she's swishing her tail. What sort of secrets are you tellin' her when you whisper and her ears go back?"

He winked. "Oh, you know. All the dirty things we do, you and me."

"That poor animal."

He laughed. "She don't care. I reckon animals ain't as particular as people, and they're better for it, truly."

"Yeah, you might be right. Although I've known some people could have cared a bit more about some things."

"Sure. Only I think the code most people are using could stand a fix or two."

"I agree with you there."

We continued on for a spell. When we hit the tree line again, we needed to go single file to find a way through, but we'd had to do that plenty of times on our journey to Port Essington, so t'wasn't any different. I ended up behind Oscar as we circled around and started to head back in the direction of our homestead. We'd ridden in a rough circle to explore as much area as we could.

I smelled woodsmoke before we came to a small clearing. For a second I thought I'd misjudged the distance and we were already back at our place, but that couldn't be.

Oscar pulled Onyx to a stop.

"Hey, look."

I peered around him. An impressive, planked farmhouse loomed at the far edge of the clearing, smoke drifting from its chimney. A moderately sized barn sat between us and the house, beside a large paddock. Two horses — a bay and a chestnut — grazed inside a sturdy wood fence.

"Guess we got some neighbors," I said, uneasiness creeping in. On the one hand, t'was good to have folks close enough to ride to in an emergency. But, on another hand, it seemed like an invasion of our space and privacy. What with the secret nature of our relationship, it suited us to be isolated and alone. I wasn't sure how I felt to know there were people so close.

As we watched, a man came out of the front door of the farmhouse and headed to the barn. We had come out of the thick trees, and I figured we were visible, so there was no point trying to hide. The man stopped and stared in our direction. He remained motionless, as if he'd seen a dangerous animal, when t'was only me and Oscar on horses, plain as day.

I raised my arm to indicate that we were friendly, but the man didn't move and kept staring for a long moment. Then he turned right quick and hastened back to the house, slipping inside and shutting the door. I reckon he probably latched it, too.

"Why's he so scared of us?" Oscar said.

"I don't know."

Dixie was getting restless. She didn't understand why we'd stopped. I reckoned we could do one of two things. We could go forward and introduce ourselves or we could avoid the place and head home.

"What should we do?" Oscar asked.

"Well, now, this ain't the town or a city. This here's wild country, and God knows who you'll find out here. Folks have a different way of doing things. I don't fancy coming at the wrong end of a rifle, do you?"

"No, sir," Oscar replied.

"Then let's go home." I turned Dixie around. "We can ask Carson or Tim about them, maybe. See what's what before we put ourselves in harm's way."

"Good idea."

"Let's loop around and go back the way we came. We got time, and I'm not ready to be done ridin' yet."

By the time we made it back, the sun was on the decline. Once the horses and mule were tended and fed, we walked to our small house in the fairy light of a charming sunset.

"You suppose we'll get some snow soon?" Oscar said.

"Yeah. I reckon we're long overdue."

Chapter Six

Regrets

The snow did come.

It arrived the following day in plump white flakes that drifted down from a gunmetal sky. More came the next day and another inch or two a few days later, until there was enough that stayed on the ground to make a scene out of one of them fancy greeting cards. By that time, t'was December, and I realized we were gonna have our very first Christmas together, all nestled into our cozy little half-house in the thick forest around Port Essington.

T'was amusing to watch the animals in the paddock after the first fall of fluffy white hit the ground. They pranced about and whickered at the snow, as if asking it why it had taken so long to come. They snuffled their muzzles into it and snorted, then shook their heads as if the snow had played a trick on them.

"So, what do you want for Christmas, little boy?" I said one afternoon as my thoughts became tender and sentimental.

Oscar's head snapped up from where he sat at the small table on a wood stool, going o'er some letters and easy words I'd written out for him. It had taken me some time to discover Oscar didn't know how to read or write. He had a bigger vocabulary than he realized, and the fact that he hadn't had much schooling didn't hit me until I'd asked him. I'd bought him a slate and a slate pencil in town, and he was letting me teach him the alphabet and some basic words. Sometimes he'd get frustrated and tell me t'was no use, that he was too old to learn it, but I stopped that kind of talk right quick. I'd tanned his hide for it enough times that he only did it now to incite me—and in a deliberate and teasing way. He was really trying to learn, and I was proud of him for it.

"Excuse me? What do I want for *Christmas*?"

I couldn't tell if the look of shocked indignation he threw me was because I'd called him a little boy or because I'd mentioned Christmas. I stared back at him in silence for a moment, then raised my eyes, uncrossed my legs and half sat up from where I'd been lying on the bed, reading a weekly I'd picked up in town.

"What? You tellin' me you didn't have Christmas in Dawson City?"

He huffed and turned back to his slate. "Not much of one. Not me, anyways. Maybe other people."

He lifted his gaze to me and screwed up his forehead. "You tellin' me you had Christmas with them outlaws?"

I blinked. Then I smiled and straight up laughed, picturing it.

"Of course not. But I did with my family for a long time…before everything went bad."

He kept looking at me, probably deciding if he wanted to ask me about that.

Instead, he turned back to his slate. "Just a lot of Godly nonsense, I figure. What did Jesus e'er do for me?" He sounded like an old man who'd had enough of the world, and I couldn't blame him. Oscar had lived a long life in his twenty-one years.

"Now hold on a minute," I said, not willing to give up my dreams of making a cozy celebration just between the two of us, with some of the traditions from my childhood. "Just because religious people thought of it don't mean it has no value."

He snorted.

I sat up. "Come on now. What do you got against feasting and merriment?"

He looked up again. "Feasting, Jimmy? What the hell are we gonna feast on?"

T'was true, our diet was a little sparse. We wanted this money to last, so we were making do with basic foods that we could get easy and cheap. But that was even more reason to splurge on a special dinner that we might remember for a long time.

"It's our first Christmas together in our new home, for all it's just a kitchen with a bed. I reckon I can shoot a duck or a goose or somethin'."

"A goose?"

"Sure."

"Ain't all the birds flown south?"

"Not all of 'em. There's gotta be a few around, down by the river."

"Well, if you were to shoot one, I reckon I'd eat it," Oscar said with a lazy resignation.

"Oh, I know you would eat it. I seen you go hog wild on just about anythin' I bring home."

"Stop talkin' about it. You're makin' me hungry."

I laughed. "Tell you what. You spell out the word 'eat' on that slate, and I'll get you something we can roast up on Christmas Day."

"Fine." Oscar focused on his slate and wiped it clean with a rag, then used his slate pencil to scratch out some letters. He held it up toward me.

On his slate were the letters E T.

I nodded. "That's a good try."

His face fell. "You mean, that ain't right?"

"Nope. There's an A where the second E is."

He frowned at the letters and grunted with indignation. "What? Where the fuck does the A go? I thought A made a 'ah' sound. There ain't no 'ah' sound in the word 'eat', Jimmy."

I couldn't help laughing. "I know it. English is a...peculiar language. It ain't easy to learn, and you're doin' just fine."

Oscar stood up and brought his slate o'er. "Here. You spell it."

He got onto the bed beside me and passed me the slate. I took it from him, wiped the second E away and put an A there instead.

Oscar blinked. "Of all the fuckin', stupid, damn, shitty—! What the fuck? *Why*?"

He was so damn angry about it that I couldn't help finding it more amusing than anything.

"C'mere," I said, throwing the slate and pencil onto the bed and wrapping my arm around Oscar, bringing him on top of me so's I could kiss and cuddle him. He was still mad, though, so he squirmed and complained, which made me even more determined to kiss him.

"You're a good learner, and you'll manage."

"I don't know, Jimmy. It don't make a lot of sense."

I growled in his ear and closed my teeth gently on the lobe. "Neither do you sometimes, but I would never give up on you."

"Hmph. I reckon I make more sense than this here language."

"Maybe. You're startin' to be more responsible, that's true."

He gave up and stretched out against me, wrapping his hand around my neck and finding my mouth with his. He kissed me sweet and gentle, like his anger at the English language was fading and his interest in other things might be rising.

"Jimmy—" he said as I started to undress him, "I been meaning to ask you…"

"Ask me what, beautiful boy?"

He giggled, lay back and let me unwrap him like a pretty package. I loved the way Oscar seemed so slim and delicate but had the strength and heart of a lion.

"Well…you know how we like to take the horses out together for a ride. And how much fun it is."

"Sure." I parted his shirt and his long underwear so's I could kiss him along the light trail leading down his belly. He twined his fingers in my hair.

His words came out breathy and like a sigh. "I want to take Onyx out for a ride on my own."

I stopped kissing him, my head all of a sudden filled with fear and trepidation. But I recognized real quick that t'was leftover alarm from what had happened with Spook and Whitlaw and all the other dangers we'd faced on our journey. So, I tamped my panic down…or tried to. I wanted to be reasonable.

"Why? Don't you think it's safer to go ridin' together?"

"Sure, but I like to be on my own sometimes, Jimmy. And me and Onyx, we're like, best friends, except for you n' me, Jimmy. You're my very best friend, and my sweetheart, and everythin', a course. But I want to take Onyx out for a ride by myself."

"But...you know there are dangerous animals around." My belly clenched at the thought of Oscar being out in the woods on his own, even though I knew t'wasn't reasonable. He was a grown man, even though we played at something else. I looked up in time to see him roll his eyes.

"We ain't seen none. We're near enough to the town that I reckon they stay away."

T'was true, we hadn't encountered any large animals yet, but I knew they were out there.

"Ain't you heard the wolves howlin'?"

He nodded. "Not the last few nights. And they were so far away, Jimmy."

I sighed. I was so fearful of letting him out of my sight.

"Hey," he said, tilting my chin up to meet his gaze, "I can take care of myself, y'know."

"Can you?"

He frowned. "Well, I aim to."

I found one of his nipples with my mouth, knowing that would distract him. Sure enough, it did, and he didn't say no more about it. And I finished undressing him and fucked him hard enough that he forgot about everything else.

But I knew I hadn't had the last word on this.

* * * *

The next day, when we got back from feeding and watering the horses, and I could tell that Oscar was waiting for the right opportunity to bring up riding out on his own again, I sighed and pulled open the bottom drawer of the dresser we shared. He watched as I pushed the clothes aside and picked up something wrapped in a white cloth.

"Here. If you're gonna go out ridin' by yourself, I reckon you're gonna need this."

I placed the cloth-wrapped item in his hand. He stared down at it while I fetched a cardboard box from the same place.

"What is it?"

I nodded at him to see for himself. He unwrapped it and stared at it, then swallowed hard.

"It's a revolver," he stated in a reverent voice, then lifted his gaze to mine. "When did you get this?"

"The last time we were in town. You remember, you went off with Carson for a bit and left me at the store."

"Oh."

"It ain't got any bullets in it right now." I held up the little box. "I reckon you'll need some teaching before I let you use it on your own and loaded."

He touched it with the same reverence, then lifted the gun carefully from its wrapping, gazing at it from different angles. "It's real pretty."

I scoffed. "That thing can kill a man. It *ain't* pretty."

"Well, it sure is *shiny*. And it feels good in my hand."

Oscar had tossed the rag aside and now stroked that revolver like t'was a precious stone.

A chill passed through me as I remembered watching my baby brother, Robert, with his first gun. A part of me recoiled from teaching Oscar how to handle a weapon, but a bigger part of me wanted him to be able to protect himself. I'd bought it for him, but I hadn't been able to bring myself to put it in his hand until now.

"That's neither here nor there," I said. "It's to keep yourself safe. I don't—" I took a deep breath. "I don't like the idea of you out there on your own with Onyx, e'en though she's a good, sensible horse. But if I have to put up with it, I'm gonna need you to learn to shoot."

"Okay."

I went o'er the safety aspects to begin with. T'was to be kept in the drawer, unloaded, unless he was going out riding. He needed to be respectful and careful with it, because he didn't want to shoot himself or his beloved horse, or *me*, by accident. And he was only, *only*, to use it in self-defense, or to practice his aim with tin cans on a stump, and only when I knew he was doing so. No shooting for fun or trying to bring down an animal, no matter how good he thought he was, or how pleased he imagined I'd be. I told him I'd be prouder of him for following my instructions. He seemed to acknowledge that.

We spent some time each day outside, using a can on a log as a target. Oscar took to it pretty well and hooted with satisfaction every time the bullet made contact. Soon, he was hardly missing his target. Still, that was while standing, with an object in his sights that didn't move. It would take more time and practice, but his aim wasn't bad. I hoped he could at least scare off an animal and make it home alive. I still wasn't comfortable with the idea, but Oscar was a grown man, and I couldn't keep him at home like a child, as much as I might wanted to.

The first time he went out on his own was rough. I'd convinced him to stay close to the homestead and not to go near the neighbor's place just yet. We hadn't been back to town since we'd encountered him, so I hadn't been able to query Carson. I reckoned t'was better to steer clear for now.

For the first bit that he was gone I couldn't sit still, and my mind was filled with horrifying images. I figured distraction was the only way I'd get through it.

There was cleaning to be done, so I got to it. Truth be told, Oscar tended to be slovenly. I couldn't blame him, considering the time he'd spent on the streets and without proper guidance. I'd told him in no uncertain terms that he needed to take his boots off inside the door where we had a mat and not track mud and grit and snow inside our small place, but sometimes he forgot. I tried not to get mad, and if I asked him to help clean, he was willing. T'was a small bone of contention between us, and I reckon every couple had to deal with problems like that. T'was frustrating, but if you loved someone, you put up with it and just tried to manage, and you focused on all their other, good qualities — of which, Oscar had plenty.

Since that first ride, from which he'd returned home so content and proud of himself that I couldn't begrudge him wanting some freedom, he'd rode out a handful of times. He made sure to be back within an hour or so, and I simply tried to distract myself from fretting while he was gone.

But one day, about a week after he'd started on these occasional forays, he rode out on Onyx around three in the afternoon. I'd asked him not to be long because it looked like it might snow, and the sun went down sooner in the evenings these days. He assured me he would be quick, and I trusted him on his word.

Almost as soon as he'd ridden out with his revolver in its holster on his saddle, it did start to snow. T'was not unusual this time of year, and I'd expected it, so I didn't worry much at first. I went out and got Dixie and Poke into the barn where t'was dry and gave them their evening feed and some fresh hay.

Carson Moore and Tim Jensen had insisted on stocking the barn with enough hay to get us through our first winter, and I couldn't have been more grateful. I'd protested that t'was too much, since they were helping us with everything else, but they'd insisted t'was their duty to do it, after what had happened to Oscar's uncle. I reckon they'd always feel responsible for that outcome, even though t'wasn't their fault.

I stood between the barn and the house for a few minutes, watching in the direction Oscar had left, hoping to see him coming home, but with no luck. T'was getting awful cold, so I went back inside.

O'er the next hour, the snow got real thick really quick, and the time ticked by and Oscar didn't return.

I felt restless, anxious and like maybe I should saddle Dixie and go out looking for him. But then, I thought that was being silly and that he'd roll in any minute, looking pleased as punch to have been out in such a pretty snowfall. I was glad he had his revolver, but it wouldn't be much help to him if he couldn't find his way home. The more time went by, the more anxious I became, and my thoughts began to spiral. I stood staring out of the window at the falling snow as vivid images assaulted me.

Thick flakes of snow fell, making it hard to see, but the desperate man that Spook had robbed and tormented turned and somehow toppled the skinny outlaw in a frantic attempt to escape. Spook's gun slipped from his drunken grip and the man lunged for it, grabbing it and aiming it at him with crazed eyes.

"Shoot him!"

"Goddammit, shoot the fucker, Jimmy!"

Spook and Whitlaw shouted at the same time, because I'd aimed my gun the moment the man had moved, mostly to protect myself. But I pulled the trigger, because t'was either that or become a victim. He jerked and fell back in an instant, gurgling and twitching on the ground like a squashed insect. That was the first time I'd ever shot a man.

I had been in a state of shock for days after, and neither Spook nor Whitlaw could figure out what was wrong, since to them two, cold-blooded killing came natural. I got to thinking that maybe I should have simply lunged in front of Spook, so the desperate man would kill me, and I'd have found a way out from the sticky spot I'd been in. But I had wanted to live too much for that, and I was glad I'd lived, because I'd escaped them and found Oscar and...

Maybe this snowstorm was God's way of punishing me for all that. I blinked hard and stepped to the door to get my coat and boots. Maybe Oscar was lost or he was already dead, but I had to find him. I had to know for sure. Maybe God had taken Oscar from me to punish me for what I'd done.

Before I even got close to where my coat hung, I fell to my knees and placed my trembling hands together in a prayer—something I'd never, ever done before. And I started talking to God in my head. Because I knew that if I didn't make amends with him, right this minute, he was going to take from me the only thing that mattered.

I know I ain't been a good man. I know I done terrible things for the wrong people, and I'm sorry for that, I truly am. I wish I could go back, change everything and never leave with Spook and Whitlaw after Ma died and...and Pa...did what he did. But I let them convince me I could do manly things and make a strange kind of life with them. I regret it every day. I do, Lord.

And Oscar? Well, he loves me and...he forgives me, and I know that don't matter, but I hope you can forgive me, too. I blinked up at the wood roof of our little home, my eyes stinging and blurring. *I know you understand what we are together, and I know... I know you don't think it's wrong. I know that in my heart, because what Oscar and I have is so...pure and, and...it's the most holy thing I've ever felt, Lord. I know you understand that. And I'm beggin' you...I'm beggin' you...please, please, please don't take him away from me.*

I shuddered a desperate breath and rose from the floor, shoving my stocking feet into my boots and pulling my coat off the hook, feeling the absence of Oscar's things like a knife in my gut. I grabbed my rifle from its hook, where it stayed loaded and ready to use in an emergency, with Oscar forbidden to touch it unless he absolutely needed to. And I went out to the barn.

The snow was still falling, and by now, the daylight had faded and I knew Oscar would be in trouble. How he'd find his way in the dark and the snow — well, I didn't want to think on it. I reckoned Dixie sensed my fear and the state I was in, because she was quiet and subdued as I saddled her. Or maybe she didn't want to go out in the storm.

I got her ready as quick as I could and led her out of the barn, knowing there was a good chance I'd get lost in this damn storm before I ever found him...but needing to try.

Chapter Seven

A Buffalo Coat and an Act of Kindness

As I led Dixie out of the barn and into the storm, the sound of my name reverberated in my ears o'er the howl of the wind. I glanced up from under the brim of my hat, peered into the swirling flakes of snow and almost fainted with relief when I saw a bobbing light ahead beside the shape of a horse and rider — except there were two of them.

I watched as the glow of a lantern got closer, the heavy grip on my chest loosening. One blur was a horse and a man I didn't recognize, holding a lantern that illuminated them both, but the other became Onyx and Oscar.

"Oscar!" I yelled out, but he didn't hear me.

The other man, wearing what looked like a buffalo fur coat with a high collar and thick leather gloves and holding a lantern, moved forward as Onyx and Oscar followed.

"Jimmy! Ho, Jimmy, what a fucking storm!" Oscar yelled from his seat on Onyx's back as they came into the yard. Relief washed through me as I let go of Dixie and ran to them, grabbing one of Onyx's reins and following it to Oscar's knee.

"Oscar! Christ almighty, I thought you was lost!"

Oscar's familiar laugh came through the howling wind. "I *was* lost! I found our neighbors, though. And Clarence helped me to get back."

"Thank God!" I said, reaching my arms up to circle them around Oscar's waist, not caring who saw me. Oscar lifted his other foot from its stirrup and slid down from Onyx's back, so's he could hug me close and laugh in my ear.

"It's all right, Jimmy. I'm all right."

I wanted to kiss him, but I figured we'd already been much too affectionate in the presence of a stranger. I increased the force of my embrace for a brief second, then forced myself to let go, stepping back and clearing my throat. At least the snow in my face disguised my tears.

"Go inside and warm up," I told Oscar. "I'll look after Onyx."

"Jimmy, I can help you," Oscar protested.

I turned sharply. "You won't be much good to either of us if you lose a finger to frostbite. Now get inside."

Oscar opened his mouth to keep arguing but the other man's — Clarence's — voice pierced the wind. "Listen to him, boy. Get inside."

Clarence shifted in his saddle, and the tone of command coming from him brooked no argument.

Oscar gazed back and forth between Clarence and me, then realized he was outnumbered.

"All right. Fine." He made his way to the house. We watched until the door closed behind him then gave each other a glance.

"Let's get these horses into the stables," I said.

Clarence dismounted and we got the horses out of the wind. Clarence hung his lantern on a hook and hitched his bay to another and helped me get the tack off Dixie and Onyx. I gave Onyx's damp coat a quick brushing to help her dry off while Clarence stood and stroked the neck of his bay mount, giving him access to the water trough that I'd filled for Dixie in preparation for riding out.

"Thank you for bringing Oscar home. He ain't got much experience bein' out and about in the wilderness, and I didn't know there was a storm coming or that it would get this bad." I held out my gloved hand. "I'm Jimmy. Jimmy Downing."

Clarence didn't smile back. He assessed me with a cold glance. Then nodded again.

"Clarence Trelawney."

I couldn't get a read on him. He'd been very kind to bring Oscar back to me, but he wasn't acting all that friendly.

"Well, I thank you for bringin' him home. I was goin' outta my mind with worrying."

Clarence regarded me calmly. The bulky fur coat and his sizeable hat notwithstanding, he wasn't that tall — a little bigger than Oscar — and what I could see of his face, most of which was hidden by his wool scarf and the collar of his coat, was fresh and young-looking. T'wasn't the grizzled, old timer face with a thick beard I'd been expecting.

"I reckon."

I cleared my throat, feeling uneasy. "You want to come to the house before you head back? I'm gonna make some hot coffee for Oscar, and you're welcome to have some."

"No, I need to get back, or my wife'll worry."

"Fair enough," I said.

I put Onyx into her stall with some hay and water, then followed as Clarence led the bay out into the snow and wind. He mounted his horse and gestured toward the house.

"You get that boy warm, now."

"I will. Thank you."

Clarence brushed the brim of his hat with his glove and turned his horse, leaving in a flash of lantern light as the dark and the cold enveloped me.

I walked toward the glow of the windows of our little half-house, thanking the stars above for Clarence and the fact that Oscar was at home, safe.

When I got inside, Oscar looked up from his spot on a stool near the stove. He was holding his hands out and staring at them in the lamplight.

"You okay?" I said.

"Yeah." He lifted his hands, spreading all his fingers out. "I think I get to keep them all."

"Thank God," I said, ripping my coat off and stepping out of my boots so I could go o'er to him. "Let me see."

I took his wrists in my hands and examined his fingers. They were still a bit red, but there weren't any gray patches that would indicate frostbite.

"Okay. How are your toes?"

"My toes?"

I pulled up a stool and sat down, gesturing to his stockinged feet. "Give me your foot."

Oscar gripped the edges of his stool and lifted his right foot so's I could take it and rest it in my lap. Carefully peeling the wool sock off of it, I held my breath, praying that his feet were okay. Again, there was redness, and when I laid my palm against the pad of it, t'was cold.

"'Tis burnin'," Oscar said, with a wince. "Your hands are so warm."

"It's gonna hurt as the blood starts movin'. Give me the other one. Go on."

Oscar did as he was told, and I rubbed both his feet with my hands, checking each of his toes, while he sat there watching me and giving me the softest little smile.

"Jimmy, I'm fine. I'm gettin' warmer now."

"Good. I don't think you've got any frostbite. Does it hurt?"

"Some. I guess that's a good thing. Means the blood's flowin', right?"

"That's it. Better'n the alternative."

He looked away, at the walls of our little house, then back to me. "You know this ain't the first time I been caught out in the cold." His voice was quiet.

I stilled my hands and stared at his foot, thinking about the times he must have been out in harsh weather in Dawson, when he didn't have a home to go to.

"Sure. I guess," I said, tracing a finger along his arch and over the sole of his thin foot, his precious skin rosy with returning circulation, then resumed my actions, rubbing and chafing him to help it along.

"Anyway, I'm fine. I'm feeling warmer now."

I kept up my foot massaging, though, because t'was a way of staying connected when I'd feared he was lost to me. Oscar was silent, but then he asked, in a soft voice, if I was mad he'd gone to the neighbor's place when I'd told him to avoid it.

"No, I'm not mad at you for goin' to their place, not in that situation. T'was the exact right thing to do, and

I'm glad you had the sense to disobey me. But why on earth didn't you just stay there?"

He gaped at me. "What? And not come back here? You'd a gone outta your mind!"

Well, he was right about that.

I ran a hand o'er my face and through my hair. "All right. All right. That's true enough."

"What did you think of Clarence?"

I thought about it. "Well, t'was awful kind of him to bring you home, and that's a fact. I'll always be grateful to him for that. But he didn't say much. Didn't seem overly friendly."

"Well, he needed to get home. We left Irene, and I could tell she was worried about Clarence going out in that storm."

"Irene. That's his wife?"

"Yep. She's awful nice. She gave me a cup of tea and her seat by the fire to warm up before we left."

"Thank God." I looked at the boots he'd left by the front door. "We need to get you a new pair of boots, I reckon. Those're old and beat up."

"How much you reckon one of those fur coats would cost? Like the one Clarence has?"

I let go of Oscar's feet and stood up, going to the counter and finding a can of beans and the can opener.

"Don't know. Probably pretty dear," I said.

"Oh."

"Anyway, you ain't gonna need a coat like that. Because you ain't goin' out riding if there's any chance of a storm from now on."

"Oh, I see. You're fixin' to keep me here in this tiny house with you, so's you can protect me from the elements and keep me all toasty and tumbled."

I'd been expecting an angry protest but Oscar didn't sound mad. When I gazed o'er at him, he was sitting there watching me with a benign curiosity and a plain affection that made me tingle from my toes to the top of my head.

"I reckon I will."

He smiled then and leaned forward with his elbows on his knees.

"Well, okay. As long as I'm allowed to go out when the weather's fine."

"You are."

He looked at his feet that were still bare and pale against the floorboards.

"Maybe you need to warm me up from the inside out, Jimmy."

I stared at him, my cock thickening at the look he was giving me.

"Maybe that would be best."

Oscar stood and came o'er to where I was standing at the counter with the can of beans in my hand. He took it from me and set it down. Then he led me to the bed and climbed up onto it.

"All right," he whispered. "Now you show me just how glad you are to have me back and set me aflame so's I can get warm again."

I crawled atop him and kissed him hard and desperate, then I showed him just how hot I could make him.

* * * *

The following week, on a sunny, mild day without a cloud in the sky, we decided to go into town for supplies to get us through most of the winter. Since we planned to stock up, we brought along Poke and some packs and rope to load him up. The storm had been a wake-up call, that we needed to make sure we had the essentials to get through the winter without needing to make too many trips into town.

We'd bought Poke in Whitehorse, instead of replacing the wagon we'd had to abandon. We'd wondered about his temperament, although the fella who'd sold him to us had assured us he was generally good-natured, and that had proven true.

He plodded along behind us at the end of his lead rope as we rode into town on that bright day in mid-December. T'was cold, sure enough, but with our long underwear on and our warm coats and hats, we didn't fare too badly.

Tim Jensen let us stable the horses and the mule behind his saloon. So far, we had only found kindness in this town. I hoped our luck would continue.

The place was even quieter than it had been a month ago. Carson said a lot of folks went south to Vancouver or Victoria once the Skeena closed, due to the ice. The climate was milder there and they could find work that wasn't available in Port Essington o'er the winter months. Still, there were enough folks remaining that Jensen's Saloon could stay afloat, and enough through-travel that the hotels stayed busy.

Carson said that in the height of summer Port Essington was a sight to behold, with a bustling economy and a profitable trade. The dance halls and concert venues filled up with revelers, and there was even a small red-light district. I didn't reckon any place would ever live up to Miss June's resthouse in Telegraph Creek, so I had no interest in goin' near it. Anyway, I had a warm body and an even warmer heart beside me whenever I needed it, and I was mighty thankful.

Salmon was the most prevalent commodity in this town on the Skeena estuary. I recalled the strong odor of the fish canneries when we'd come into town back at the end of October. I reckoned the smell would be even more putrid in the heat of summer. I wasn't bothered by the numbers in town decreasing o'er the winter. Oscar and I were trying to keep a low profile. We didn't need the whole town wondering and gossiping about us, at least until we'd found our footing.

Oscar needed a pair of boots, so we went to the cobbler's first. My boots were standing up well, and I figured I could probably get another couple of years out of them.

It had occurred to me that the way Oscar and I were when we were together seemed a tad on the strange side, considering we were supposed to be friends and not lovers. I liked to look after Oscar, and Oscar liked to be looked after, so at home, that worked out pretty well. But in town, if we were pretending to be buddies, we needed to act differently to that.

"What, you mean you ain't gonna look after me like you do at home?"

"Not when we're among other folks, no, I ain't. You gotta act like you're offended if I fall into the habit of bein' the gentleman instead of the companion. Okay? Because sometimes I ain't aware I'm doin' it."

"You think you treat me like a…lady? When we're out and about?" Oscar gaped at me, demonstrating that he could act *very* offended.

"Not on purpose. No. I guess, just because of how I found you, and how we are together, sometimes I treat you kind of fatherly, and I don't know how that'll be taken, since we ain't supposed to be father and son." T'was hard to explain, and I was embarrassed. "Never mind. Forget it."

"Oh, I ain't never gonna forget it, Jimmy. I will let you know in no uncertain terms if I believe you're tarnishin' my masculinity. I reckon I deserve more respect than to be coddled like a child."

I stared at him, surprised at such vehemence and certain he was being sincere, until he broke into a toothful grin and I realized he was teasing me. Oscar didn't care a whit about preconceived or socially acceptable notions of masculinity. He was his own man and would do as he pleased — which was one of the things I loved about him, truly.

I, on the other hand, had a fragile-enough ego and didn't like to think I was feminine, although Oscar teased me sometimes about the way I liked to keep the house clean and make the meals. T'was all in good fun. But I wanted to make sure we presented a believable picture of camaraderie in town, since our very survival depended on being accepted as friends who lived together for convenience.

It soon became clear that t'was a state of things we'd have to try harder to break.

"What kind of boots should I get, Jimmy? I ain't got a clue," Oscar said, looking at the footwear on offer at the cobbler's.

I gave him a narrow-eyed look.

"What?" he said. Then realized how that had sounded.

"Oh. I mean, I's just askin' for your opinion, you know. I s'pose these ones would do."

He picked up a pair of boots that I considered completely non-functional, and I had to bite my tongue.

I gestured to a pair of leather stovepipe boots with a thick sole and high, supple sides.

"Well, I would have thought these might be good for riding and walking. Of course, it's your choice. You're the one...payin' for 'em."

I'd given him five dollars to spend on a new pair of boots and an extra dollar for anything else he wanted. I figured he'd load up on sweets at the general store with that dollar—or a part of it.

"That's a fact," Oscar said, putting the fancy boots down and picking up the other ones, giving me an amused glance, like we shared a private joke. "I s'pose you're right. Although, 'tis a shame. I reckon I'd look nicer for the *girls* in t'other ones."

Out of the corner of my eye, I noticed the shopkeeper stifle a smile as he shook his head, doing some figuring up with a pencil at the cash.

"The girls don't care about boots, Oscar. They want a man can walk a few miles without gettin' his feet wet."

"Is that so?" he said, with a twinkle in his eye.

I shrugged, pretending to examine another pair of leather footwear sitting on a wooden box. "I reckon."

Oscar sighed, looking at the boots in his hand. "You're prob'ly right. These ones are very fine, and that's a fact. I think they'd look good on me, too."

"Who cares how they look? You oughta be more practical, Oscar," I scoffed, as if I did think he was annoying.

"Can I get those in your size, sir?" The clerk had made his way o'er and now stood in front of Oscar.

"Yeah, sure. 'Cept I don't know what size my feet are..."

He started to turn toward me but stopped himself and simply shrugged.

"That's quite all right. Have a seat— I have a measuring instrument."

The shop clerk measured Oscar's feet and declared him a size ten. I was a twelve, so I figured that must be about right. I focused on some leather cording on a hook that was available for saddles or... *Hmm*. I touched it with my fingers. T'was soft and pliable and might be perfect for—well, for what I had in mind. I wondered how much it cost. My mind went places it shouldn't while I was in a public place, and I had to adjust myself with a subtle movement.

"What do you think?"

Oscar's voice startled me. I turned as he lifted a booted foot up onto one of the display boxes and flourished his hand.

I was about to say they looked real good, but then my gaze slid to the shopkeeper, who watched us with a smile.

"What're you asking me for?"

Oscar caught on. "True. You don't know a thing about style."

I laughed because he was right.

"Get 'em if you like 'em. I reckon they'll do. And you don't need my permission," I huffed.

"Nope, I surely don't," Oscar said, stomping around and checking them out, making sure they were gonna be all right. "The fit's good."

I bit my tongue for about the fourth time since we'd come in here. Next time we tried this, I'd have Oscar go into the store on his own. We'd avoid any of this nonsense.

He paid for his new boots, and the shopkeeper asked if Oscar wanted him to dispose of the old ones. I could practically hear the gears turning in his head as he must have resisted asking me. He glanced at me while the clerk wasn't looking and I shook my head.

"No, thank you. I'll keep 'em for chores."

"Of course. I'll give you a bit of moleskin in case you get blisters from the new ones. Although these boots are so fine and fit you so well, they may not need much breaking in."

"Thank you." Oscar turned to me. "You ready, Jimmy?"

I lifted the roll of cord off its hook and held it out for the shop keeper to see. "How much you want for this?"

Oscar looked at the cord in my hand, then met my gaze. Something in his eyes told me he knew what I was gonna use it for. His nostrils flared and he lifted his chin, but I reckon the shopkeeper didn't notice.

"That's five yards of fine-tooled leather cord. I can't let that go for less than a dollar fifty."

I gazed at the cord in my hand, wondering if I should spend that much. Then I looked at Oscar and said. "I'll take it."

"Wonderful. It's very strong. Perfect for wrapping around a post or a fence for support."

"Yeah, that's what I need it for," I lied.

"It'll shrink when it gets wet, so it'll hold real tight."

I nodded, licking my lips and trying not to think about my intentions as I gave my money o'er.

"Do you need a bag?"

"No, sir. I'll just put it in my pocket. Thank you." I grabbed Oscar's old boots from the bench and tucked them under my arm before I wondered if it might look strange. We left the store and started walking down the street, Oscar's new boots making a fine sound on the wooden sidewalk.

He glanced at me. I could feel how hot my cheeks were. There weren't many people about.

"What'd you buy that cord for, Jimmy?" Oscar asked, with narrowed eyes.

"I reckon you know," I whispered, barely loud enough for him to hear.

When I met his gaze, his eyes burned fire, and I wished we could go straight home. But we had a substantial grocery order to fill.

"Never mind," I said. "I reckon you'll find out, soon enough."

Oscar huffed out a breath. "It won't be, though," he muttered. "Jesus." And scuffed the toe of his boot on the planks.

"Don't ruin your new boots, now. I may not be stylish, but I reckon they'll stay nicer if you don't purposely wreck 'em."

I smiled at Oscar, and he blushed and shook his head.

"Stop treatin' me like I don't know anything, Jimmy. I'm a grown man."

"I know you are," I said.

On our way to the general store, Oscar grabbed the arm of my coat and pulled me up.

"Jimmy! Is that Clarence? In the buffalo coat?"

I followed his gaze. It did seem like Clarence. He was wearing that furry buffalo fur coat he'd had on when he'd brought Oscar through the storm. And he was with a stunning woman who wore a similar coat with a wide hood o'er her thick wool dress and clutched a paper-wrapped parcel under her arm.

Chapter Eight

Neighbors

When Clarence noticed us, he froze and looked away, leaving me feeling rebuffed. Perhaps he didn't want to get to know us. Folks in small towns could be strange.

But the woman standing with him glanced o'er and saw me and Oscar. She pulled on Clarence's elbow and pointed at us, saying something to him.

Clarence shrugged and said something back.

In a moment, the woman had moved around Clarence and was making her way to us. She smiled and her face lit up like the sun—like Oscar's did when he was happy.

"Hello, Oscar. It's so nice to see you again!" The woman shifted her parcel to her other arm and held out her gloved hand to Oscar, as if she were a man. "You've recovered from your snowy adventure, I see!"

Oscar seemed taken aback, but quickly recovered, and shook her hand. "I—yes. Nice to see you, too, ma'am."

"Oh, call me Irene." She turned to me. "You must be Jimmy. I'm very pleased to meet you."

"Likewise," I said, shaking her hand.

She glanced at her husband, who was busy looking at some wares in front of the hardware store. "Don't mind Clarence. He's a bit of a curmudgeon if he doesn't know you well. Anyway, I guess we're neighbors. What are you doing in town today?" she asked Oscar.

"Well, I needed new boots, so—" Oscar glanced at me for assistance. He seemed taken aback by Irene's interest.

I jumped in to explain.

"We're heading to the general store to bring in supplies for the winter months. I reckon we'll get enough to make it to February. Then we'll have to come back to town, I guess."

"Do you have a wagon to bring all that stuff home, Jimmy?" Irene asked.

I shook my head. "No, ma'am, but we've got a real good mule. Figure if we load him up well, we'll manage."

"Clarence and I have a wagon that converts to a sled in the winter, so if you ever need anything, let us know. We come into town regularly, even during the colder months. I run a mail-order sewing business, so I need to get to the post office every couple of weeks." Irene showed us the large parcel. "Also, it can get pretty lonely out where we are."

"I reckon."

She glanced at Clarence, who had made his way o'er. "Don't mind my husband. He's a big old grump half the time. Likes to keep to himself. But not me. I like people."

Clarence rolled his eyes but otherwise remained silent.

"That a fact?" I said, with some irony since it was pretty obvious.

"It is," Irene replied, inclining her head in a self-assured way and giving me a cheeky smile. "Maybe...maybe since you gentlemen don't live too far from us, you can visit us on occasion?"

Clarence frowned, as if he wasn't sure that was such a good idea. But that didn't seem to bother Irene.

Oscar smiled with genuine excitement and glanced at me. I shrugged.

"Could we?" he said, forgetting that he wasn't supposed to defer to me when we were in town. Old habits died hard, I supposed.

"Sure," I said.

It might be nice to go visiting. We might as well take advantage of our proximity. I wasn't worried about Clarence. I figured he was one of those folks who preferred to keep to themselves and ended up married to someone who was a shade more sociable.

I liked Irene. She seemed genuine, affable and full of energy.

"Wonderful!" she said. "I have a piano and like to play. Oh, Clarence, won't it be fun to have Oscar and Jimmy over?"

Clarence attempted a smile but didn't seem convinced.

"Oscar can sing," I said, because Oscar had a beautiful singing voice but I didn't get to hear it so often—only when I asked him to sing me something to get me to sleep.

Irene turned to Oscar. "Oh! You can sing while I play! It'll be just like a town social!"

"Well, I ain't so good as Jimmy says—"

I scoffed. "You are, too. You got a voice like an angel."

Then I realized that sounded like it meant too much to me. This pretending to be buddies was harder than I'd figured.

"I mean, you can hold the notes and all that," I said, trying to downplay my appreciation of Oscar's skill.

Irene smiled, like she'd decided then and there that Oscar was her special project. She took his arm and leaned in close. "I can tell we're gonna be great friends, Oscar."

Oscar blushed and let himself be coddled and petted. T'was nothing more than a friendly gesture, and Irene was married, so I figured Oscar didn't have to worry about giving her the wrong idea.

"Irene, we need to get to the dressmaker's," Clarence mumbled, side-eying me as if he were afraid I was gonna kidnap his wife.

Irene took it as a cue to keep talking.

"I'm buying some material for a new dress for myself, and I have some commissions to work on. I like to have a few projects over the winter. I'm making some shirts for Clarence, too." Her eyes widened, and she put her hand on Oscar's arm. "If you need any shirts or trousers, I can sew them. I've got a whole book of patterns for men's and women's clothing. You'd only need to buy the fabric, and I'll do it for you…"

"Irene," Clarence said, taking Irene's elbow, "come on."

Irene let Clarence guide her forward, but she glanced back and waved. "Have a good day. I hope to see you again soon!"

We stood there like we'd just been lifted by a small whirlwind and set down in a different spot and watched them walk away down the street.

Oscar turned to me. "Jimmy, I like Irene. And Clarence? Well, he's all right. I reckon he didn't have to bring me home the other night, but he did — and made sure I'd be all right."

"Yeah, and I'll always be grateful for that." I laughed, shaking my head. "I guess it's true what they say, that opposites attract."

Oscar grinned. "Yep. Like me and you. I'm small and your big. I'm friendly like Irene, and you're miserable like Clarence."

"Now hold on a minute," I protested.

"Maybe not miserable. But you're more standoffish than me."

"Only because I'm more sensible."

Oscar gave me a look. "Well, there you go. You and Clarence can be 'sensible' together, and me and Irene will have fun. Sounds perfect."

I rolled my eyes.

We walked to the general store and spent a good forty-five minutes gathering together the things we'd need — staples like coffee and tea, wheat flour and sugar, rice and beans, canned goods, beef jerky, salt pork and fish, potatoes and root vegetables. We even got a couple of wheels of old cheddar cheese that we hoped to be able to protect from mold, since we both liked it and it would be a healthy addition to our diet o'er the winter, when fresh milk wasn't available. Maybe next winter we could get a dairy cow and some chickens, so's we could have milk and eggs all year long. There was a small root cellar under the floor of our little kitchen-house that had been there already and only needed cleaning out so we could use it. T'was accessed by a hatch in the kitchen floor. Thank goodness there was only the two of us. We would have needed a wagon if we'd been storing food for an entire family.

I hoped to supplement our diet with fresh meat that I'd bring in when possible. There seemed to be plenty of game about. I had found a recipe booklet for basics like breads and pies and such. I didn't know how successful I'd be, but I wanted to try my hand at them. Didn't seem like it'd be too hard, if I had instructions. The new stove worked real well, and we might as well take advantage, plus we'd have lots of time to kill o'er the next few months. I might as well learn something new, keep us both fed well and not succumb to boredom and brooding. I made sure to get some canned fruit so we wouldn't die of scurvy, and powdered soups that we only needed to add to boiled water. I wasn't sure how they'd taste, but t'was worth a try.

By the time we'd finished our shopping, it all came to a pretty penny, but since I expected it to last us until spring, I didn't mind. It felt good to get so much at once, since it meant that we could hole up at the homestead. I reckon it would be nice to spend a bit of time with Clarence and Irene, as long as Clarence warmed up to us. But I had no desire to come into town on the regular, especially since it seemed hard for us to pretend to be friends rather than sweethearts. We could practice with Clarence and Irene on our visits there, and maybe when we started coming to town in the spring, it'd prove easier.

Once I'd paid for our supplies and asked the owner to hold them until we brought our mule by in an hour or so, I went to look at the hats while Oscar sidled up to the counter with the little drawstring bag I'd given him. I watched out of the corner of my eye, wondering what he'd get and certain it would be candy or chocolate. I'd seen his eyes about bug out when he saw the display case with all the sweets—fudge, peppermints, imported chocolates and the regular stuff like penny candy, twists and licorice. He hadn't had anything but a few peppermints since that time I'd brought him some back from the store in Dawson City. I recalled the image of him, sitting on the bed in my big shirt, his legs crossed as he sucked on a licorice like he was afraid to eat it too fast.

Gawd, I should have known even then that there wasn't any getting away from him or this thing between us.

Oscar tipped his hat to the lady behind the counter.

"Hello. Would you like to buy something?" she asked.

"Why, yes I would," Oscar said, and I imagined him throwing the full force of his smile her way. "I'm lookin' at all these sweets, and I'm havin' some trouble making up my mind."

"Is that so?" she said, with a lilt to her voice that expressed more than a casual or a business interest in my handsome lover.

"'Tis so. Why, you have more candy in this display window than I've ever seen before."

The young lady giggled, and I had to bite my lip to keep from smiling.

Yes, ma'am, I know just what you're up against.

T'was all I could do not to turn and watch them. Instead, I listened, and picked up a top hat to examine it.

"Our chocolate is brought in by steamer, but this is the last of it until spring when the river opens up again. It's good Belgian chocolate, the finest in the world."

"Well, well," Oscar said, not giving anything away.

"And the licorice is made local, so it's very fresh."

"Why, that looks good, too." Oscar sighed. "I can't make up my mind."

"Well, now, let me see. How much do you want to spend?"

"I got about twenty-five cents, Miss."

"I see. Well, would you like me to put together a collection of things for you to try?"

"That would be wonderful! Yes, thank you so much."

She giggled again. "You got any favorites? Do you like chocolate, or do you prefer hard candy?"

"I do like my candy hard," Oscar said, and I just about choked on a gasp.

I pretended to succumb to a coughing fit as they continued talking. I missed a bit of their exchange, but when I could hear again, Oscar said, "I wonder if you might throw in a few gumballs. I like them, too."

"Of course, I can. Here... I'll give you an extra for free, since you're so nice."

"Why, thank you, kindly."

"My name's Lucy. Are you new to Port Essington? I haven't seen you before."

"Good to meet you. Thank you for helping me with the sweets."

"I—well, of course. You're welcome," she said, sounding a bit put off.

In a moment, I felt a bump against my arm.

"Oh, excuse me, sir, I must have tripped," Oscar said, gazing up at me with good humor. "Oh, it's you!"

I rolled my eyes. "Of course, it's me. I said I'd wait for you."

Oscar's eye glinted as he held up a medium-sized paper bag. "Look what I got!"

"Is that full of sweets? You spent all your —" My voice was raising and I remembered I wasn't supposed to be treating him like my kid. So I moderated my tone and volume. "You spent all your money on that stuff?"

"Maybe there's something else in this bag, Jimmy. Did you ever think of that?" He grinned. "Anyway, it's my money, and I can spend it how I want."

T'was *our* money, but t'was true that I'd given him some to spend how he wanted.

"Fine. Don't come to me when your teeth fall out."

"I won't." He smirked. "Anyway, are we done here? I'd like to go to Jensen's for a drink, if you don't mind."

I nodded. "I reckon we can do that. The weather's still fine, but we can't stay too long. We got to pack up Poke and get home."

"Sure, I know. But it would be nice to see Carson and Tim, if they're there."

"True. I'd like to get their outlook on Clarence and Irene. They seem all right, but it's a good idea to mention them and see what Carson says."

When we walked into Jensen's, Carson was at the bar. He smiled and waved to us.

"Hey! How's that horse working out, Oscar? Afternoon, Jimmy."

"Afternoon," I said, finding a seat on a high stool.

"She's a dream. Thank you for finding her for us," Oscar said, sitting on the stool next to mine.

"I'm glad she's worked out for you. What'll you have?"

"I'll have a pint of whatever's on tap," Oscar said.

"Same here," I echoed. A beer would quench my thirst nicely.

As Carson disappeared to fill a pitcher from the cold barrel, I turned to Oscar. "We don't have time for more than one."

"All right, though I'm feeling a bit peckish."

"Where'd you put that bag of candy?"

"It's here in my pocket. I ain't hungry for any of that, though. I need something more substantial."

"Well, I don't know. When Carson comes back, ask him what he's got."

"Fine."

We had Carson bring us some bread and cheese with our beers, just to take the edge off. We'd had a hearty breakfast before we'd left, and we'd have supper when we got back — probably a can of beans warmed up with some of the fresh bread we'd bought.

"Carson," I said, while we sipped our beers and enjoyed our snack. "You know anything about Clarence and Irene Trelawney? They live near to our place."

Carson nodded, "Yeah, I know them. They're good folks. Been out there about, let me see, must be six or so years, now."

"Clarence brought Oscar back during a storm the other night."

"I was all right," Oscar scoffed.

"You was lost in that storm," I said, a little more harshly than I'd intended, and I dialed it back a bit. "Anyway, they seem all right. Irene's friendly but Clarence is a bit standoffish. Still, I'm grateful he helped Oscar."

"Yeah, Clarence is like that. Don't take it personal."

"Okay, I won't. Thank you."

"I'm glad you met them. Maybe you can visit each other over the winter. Might be a little less lonely for everyone."

"I reckon. We don't plan to come to town too much, at least until March. We might not see you for a while."

"Did you get some supplies in?"

"That's why we're here. We got a load waiting for us o'er at the general store."

"Did you want to borrow my wagon to get it home?"

"That's very kind. But we brought our mule, and we've got smaller packs for our horses. We'll be fine."

We chatted a bit longer and said hi to Tim Jensen, who made an appearance. T'was good to already have a couple of friends in town.

Afterward, we rode o'er to the store with Poke. It took us a little while to get everything sorted on the mule and behind our saddles, but we managed to find a place for everything.

"Maybe we should buy a wagon or a sled, Jimmy."

I side-eyed him. "Why?"

"T'would be easier than doin' this."

"'Cept we only have to do this once or twice a year, I reckon. Once the weather's better, we can ride in every couple of weeks for supplies. We might not even need the mule."

"True."

"Wagons...they're costly. I'm trying to make sure this money lasts us, at least 'till summer, when we'll have to find some jobs in town, I suppose—and save enough of our wages to get us through the next winter."

"Yeah."

"We want to get the house fixed up, don't we? We still gotta pay for that."

"How much we got left? Enough?"

"I hope so."

* * * *

About a week before Christmas, when Oscar and I were enjoying a relaxing afternoon, movement out of the window caught my eye. T'was a woman on a horse, sitting astride, like a man, with her skirts hiked up under her buffalo coat.

"Oscar, look," I said, standing up. "'Tis Irene Trelawney."

Oscar stood from the table and came o'er to look. His eyes lit up like t'was Christmas Day already.

T'was a good thing we hadn't been in the middle of a clinch or we might not have seen her coming. As t'was, Oscar had been practicing his letters while I'd been examining my recipe booklet. I'd tried a few of them, to some success, and I wanted to make something special for Oscar on Christmas Day. I planned to go hunting, to see if I could catch us a goose, a duck or even a rabbit—something fresh that I could turn into a hearty stew or roast in the oven. T'would be our first Christmas together, and I wanted to make it special. I already had a surprise planned. I'd had Carson help me get a special gift for Oscar that wouldn't bring on suspicion but would seem like a thoughtful trinket between friends.

Oscar moved quick to the door and flung it open, calling out to Irene with excitement, as the cat shot out like a bullet into the snow, wondering what the fuss was about.

"Oscar! Don't let the cold in. Tell her to come inside."

"Helloooo!" he hailed. "Come on in! You can hitch your horse to the fence, there, where it'll be out of the wind—or do you want to put it in the barn?"

I didn't hear Irene's reply, but Oscar closed the door and rubbed his arms, as I took in his appearance and stood to pull up my braces.

"Oscar, you ain't decent."

I stifled a laugh as Oscar looked down at himself in a panic.

He wasn't quite *indecent*, but his braces hung down, his shirt had come untucked and he was barefoot.

"Aw, shit," he said, pulling his braces up and tucking his shirt in, then buttoning it closer to the top, like I'd done.

"Here," I said, tossing him a pair of rolled up socks. I didn't know if they were his or mine, but it didn't rightly matter.

He sat on the edge of the bed, pulling them on and grinning. "Good thing we were payin' attention." He blanched. "Jimmy, what if we'd been—?"

I narrowed my eyes at him. "I reckon she'd have knocked, and we'd have had to scramble. T'would have been a fright and a panic, but she'd have had to wait. We'd have come up with some excuse for not answering right away, I s'pose."

"I s'pose."

There came a knock at the door just then. Oscar finished with his socks and jumped up, hastening to pull it open. He flourished a hand and bowed, grinning wide.

"Come in, fair traveler. Won't you rest yourself a bit?"

Irene stepped inside our little kitchen-house and shoved her hood back, smiling and rosy-cheeked. Wet snow caked around the tiny buttons of her heeled boots, and on the hem of her skirt.

"Don't mind if I do! Hello, Oscar, Jimmy." She gazed about her with interest. "Well, this is a cozy little space, isn't it?"

Chapter Nine

A Bit of Leather Cord

"It's all we could fix up this late in the season. This and the stables— It's all we got for now. But come spring, we're meaning to add on," I said.

Irene shrugged as if she didn't care one bit.

"This is a good, solid little house. I reckon you'll be comfortable. It doesn't take much time or wood to keep a small space heated…and clean. Seems like Clarence is always bringing wood in for our place, and I'm always sweeping and mopping." She laughed.

"You and Clarence have a nice place, that's certain."

Irene nodded. "'Tis nice, but it's a lot to keep clean. Never mind. What I'm here about is that Clarence and I wanted to invite you over for Christmas Eve."

Oscar and I blinked at Irene in surprise.

"That's only four days away. I hope you haven't planned anything?" she said, when we didn't answer right away.

"No, we haven't," I said. "That's mighty kind of you. Are you sure Clarence is okay with it?" I couldn't help asking, since he'd seen less than friendly the couple of times we'd seen him.

Irene rolled her eyes. "Clarence is an old grouch, but he likes to keep me happy, so he's agreed to have you over."

"I see," I said, grinning at the way she seemed to find Clarence's stoic coldness amusing.

"Jimmy, can we?" Oscar said, then cleared his throat and scratched at his chin, widening his stance. "I mean, that sounds just fine. I think we should go."

He glanced at Irene to see if she'd noticed his initial deference. But she didn't seem to have marked it. She turned to me and raised her eyebrows.

"What do you say, Jimmy? We've got three bags of sweet potatoes in the cellar and I'm gonna make a pie. Maybe a cake, too. It's Christmas, after all."

Well, I couldn't resist that smile, to be honest. I inclined my chin. "That would be nice."

Irene clapped her gloved hands together. "Wonderful! Why don't you ride over in the morning on the twenty-fourth, as soon as you're done your chores? We'll spend the day telling stories, playing games and eating good food. Does that sound nice?"

Oscar's eyes had glazed o'er at Irene's words, and I almost started drooling myself.

"That sounds... I mean." I glanced at Oscar. "We'd like that very much."

"Oh, I'm so very glad," Irene said.

"Now, ma'am, I was planning to go hunting for something good to cook Oscar for Christmas Day. Did you want me to see if I could get a goose or a turkey or something, for Christmas Eve?"

"Well, Clarence will probably go out. Maybe the two of you could go hunting together? I'll let him know, and mayhap he'll be willing."

I had my doubts, but I simply smiled and nodded.

"Now, I have to get back. But I do hope to see you on Christmas Eve! Hopefully, the weather won't be so bad that you can't make it the two miles to our place. But if it is, we'll understand. If that happens, just come Christmas Day instead."

I nodded. "Will do. Thank you very much."

"Yes, thank you. I can't wait. Truly," Oscar said. The hushed tones in his voice told me he was excited now to have a proper Christmas, something he'd missed out on his whole entire life.

When Irene had left, we watched her from the window as she untied her brown mare from the fence, hitched up her skirts, swung up into the saddle then headed out through the forest. I wrapped my arms around him from behind and nuzzled his warm neck.

"We're blessed to have neighbors like the Trelawneys," I said.

"I know it," he said, covering my hand with his own. "Jimmy?"

"Yeah?" I licked a line up to his ear and took his lobe in my teeth with great care, making sure he felt my warm breath on the wet spot.

He shivered.

"You want to try out them leather cords you bought?"

His words caused my dick to go full hard in about three or four seconds. I reckon he felt that because he wriggled his ass against my groin.

"I reckon I do, now."

"What are you gonna do with them, Jimmy?" he asked, placing his hands o'er mine.

"Hmm, I don't know," I said, sliding my fingers down his side and across the front of his trousers as his breath quickened. I pressed the palm of my hand against his stiffness as I held him close. "If this little nubby of yours wasn't so small, maybe I'd wrap it up in one of them cords till t'was bulging out the sides and ready to blow."

Oscar inhaled a shaky breath and gave a little whimper.

"Then I'd tease you and fuck you until you went plumb crazy with it."

"Fuck," Oscar said. "*Gawd.*"

"And I figure I'd tease you and fuck you so good, you'd come with only those tight cords around your thick little nubby."

Oscar made a choking sound. He cursed again. I grinned against his cheek.

"Oh, Jimmy, you gotta do that. You *gotta* do that," he said, breathless.

I laughed. I'd only been trying to inflame him with wanting. I didn't even know where I'd got the idea of it.

"You really want me to tie up your dick?"

He turned in my grasp and leaned into me, his eyes alight with interest. "Yes. Yes, I do."

"Hmm," I said. "Your nubby might be too small for that. I'd have to get you pretty firm before I started, then wrap it up like a parcel and see how much it fights."

"Oh my *gawd.* You're gonna kill me," he panted.

"What would be the fun in that?" I stroked o'er the curve of his ass under his trousers with my other hand

and pressed my hardness against him. "I need you to do something for me, now."

"Yes, sir?"

I grinned. I loved the way he gave in to me.

"I need you to take down your suspenders then take off your trousers and your shirt. You can leave them long underwear on, for now."

Oscar didn't say anything, but he did as he'd been told, glancing out of the window as if he feared Mrs. Trelawney might come back.

"Don't worry. She's gone. But I reckon we oughta get some curtains hung up since they live near enough to pay an unexpected visit."

He exhaled a laugh that ended with an indrawn breath as I narrowed my eyes at him.

"You think what I'm about to do to you is gonna be amusin'?" I said, in a stern tone that I knew would thrill him. Sure enough, he parted his lips and creased his forehead with seeming delicious tension as he shut his eyes.

"No, sir."

When he opened his eyes and gazed at me, he was on fire with it, and we hadn't even started. It had been a long time since I'd taken him in hand this way, and we both craved it, like a tasty treat that we saved up for a special day. Only there wasn't anything particular about the day, except for the fact we had some leather cords to play with.

"Get on the bed, Oscar...on your back."

He did it without thinking—like the good boy he always was for me, at least when he knew I was gonna take a firm hand with him.

"Now, I want you to reach them hands up o'er your head and keep 'em there. Think you can do that for me?"

"Yes, sir," he breathed, moving them into place, relaxing and twitching his fingers as he settled into position. I might have to bind them later, but I wanted him to do it willingly for now.

"Good boy. You are such a good boy, Oscar Yates. The best boy I ever knew," I purred, giving him the praise he wanted—needed—that made him so hot for me that he'd do anything I asked of him…or just about. "Do you trust me?"

He sighed, his limbs twitching with impatience as he fought to stay still. "Of course, I trust you. I trust you so much."

I knew he did. T'was a miracle and a blessing, his trust in me, and I cherished it. I might not rightly deserve it, but I adored it.

"Okay then. You say your special word if you want me to stop at any point. You remember what it is?"

His sweet lips formed the briefest smile. "Church," he said.

I resisted a smile of my own. "And why did we decide on that?"

He swallowed thickly. "Because this is holy, and what we do together is good and right." His voice was hushed and reverent.

I nodded. "Exactly…no matter what anyone might say. You know it and I know it. And we need to remember it."

"I taught you that, Jimmy."

"You did. And I ain't never gonna forget it. I'm gonna unbutton your underwear now, and I don't want you to move."

Oscar groaned. "Yes, sir."

I pushed my suspenders down and pulled my shirttails out of my trousers, then unbuttoned the shirt and threw it aside. I undid the buttons at the top of my underwear, then climbed onto the bed and loomed o'er Oscar. His gaze held mine as I unfastened his red union suit one button at a time. I went slow and easy, in order to tease him and make him wait, because I knew he loved that.

"Oh, Jimmy," Oscar breathed, trying to stay still as I undressed him. By the time I'd got down to his hips, his little nubby was shoving up hard and insistent under the fabric. I grinned and made a show of wrestling with the buttons so that every move would inflame him further. He made soft sounds of distress as my fingers fumbled against his stand. "Oh God..."

"Shush, now," I said, spreading the sides of his union suit away from his body as a shuddering breath escaped me. He was so lovely. A decent spread of fine hairs on his chest became a sparse trail down his belly until it met with a thicker forest around the base of his arching cock. His deep, quick breaths made his belly dip and fill and his nubby sway. T'was wet at the tip, and it moved on its own when I gave Oscar a hungry, predatory look.

Oscar watched me as I examined him, no doubt seeing how I responded to his partial nakedness and his surrender. We were quite the pair, the two of us, and seemed to fit together—the answer to a peculiar riddle, like two puzzle pieces that joined up when they didn't seem to go together at all. T'was how it had been from the start with him, and once I'd stopped trying to resist it and fretting about it, we'd settled into some kind of acceptance. And now we seemed to have a spiritual appreciation of it. Even though the things we did to each other, or with each other, might seem base and depraved to some, to us they were aspects of our deep connection. And I was about to worship him with bits of leather cord the way a priest might splash his holy water onto the innocent.

Oscar was far from innocent, that was true, and the same with me in different, but equally sordid, ways. But he was God's creature just the same, and I loved every bit of him and didn't see nothing evil in anything he felt for me, wanted to do with me or anything I felt for him. What we had was a blessing and a miracle, and I revered it.

I stroked his little cock — *his nubby* — with my fingers as I grabbed the pieces of cut cord from where I'd put them and threw them onto his belly.

"See that? That's what I'm gonna use to wrap up your nubby with."

Oscar made a sound and squirmed, his cock jerking as if nodding *yes, please.*

"But first, I'm gonna tie your ankles to the bed here, so you're trapped. I'll leave your hands free for now. But if you can't keep 'em up there, I'm gonna have to bind them. Understand?"

Oscar nodded frantically. "Yes, sir. *Yes*, sir."

"Now." I narrowed my eyes at him. "You wanna be naked for this? Or do you want to keep your long underwear on, an' I'll just open it up where I need to? 'Tis cool in here if you ain't got clothes on, I reckon, though I'm planning on lightin' a fire inside you."

Oscar sighed and gazed down at himself, where I'd splayed his union suit wide to reveal his underbelly and other parts. "I like it like this, Jimmy. I reckon if I gotta turn o'er, you can get at me there, too."

I smiled, nodding. "I surely can. Whoever invented this here type of underwear knew what they was about. Although, if and when we get to that point, I'll probably just pull it all down and to hell with it."

"Yeah," Oscar said. "And, Jimmy? I'm already burnin' up for you."

"Oh, I know it." I tilted my head, gazing down at him. "You okay if I just get your arms out of it? I like to see those slim muscles you got and the veins that bulge under your skin." I licked my lips.

Oscar seemed surprised and pleased by this information. He was self-conscious of his slimness, although mostly he liked feeling delicate and breakable. He was stronger than he looked and tough as a wildcat.

"Yeah, okay."

"I'll keep your legs covered, though. I like the way they look in the long johns, especially when the rest of it's all askew. Don't know why. Seems more…indecent, I suppose."

Oscar nodded, his mouth open, his eyes big and cock hard.

I helped him out of the sleeves and left the garment underneath him. He did look indecent, and unwrapped, and…ready for whatever I wanted.

I picked up a piece of the cord, letting its end trail across his skin, watching him twitch and sigh. Then I wrapped it around his ankle and secured the other end to the foot of the bed frame. I'd cut and measured the pieces so they'd reach. I repeated that process with his other leg.

"There. Now you can't get away."

"I don't even want to."

"Hmm. Not *now*. Just wait. I'm gonna get you so worked up you'll be tryin' to, I reckon."

"Oh fuck," he said, his chest going up and down again with his quick breaths. "Now you gonna tie up my nubby, Jimmy?"

I smiled a slow, devilish smile. "I surely am. So, you need to stay still. I'm gonna have your bits in my hands, and I need to concentrate."

"Okay. Okay."

"Keep them hands up there, above your head."

"Yes, sir."

I picked up another length of cord, leaving one on his belly. This one was a tad shorter than the others. I reached down and took his balls in my hand.

"I'm gonna be as gentle as I can be. But use your stop word if it gets too much or you get nervous. This is supposed to be fun."

He wrinkled his forehead in apparent consternation as I slid the leather cord beneath his testicles.

"It's meant to be a little scary, I reckon, but mostly fun. You know I won't hurt you? That I'll be careful?"

"I know it," he whispered, watching me with a reverence that was good for my ego.

As I wrapped the cord around the top of his sac and pulled it snug, he hissed.

"There's gonna be a bit of…discomfort—and maybe some pain." I glanced at him with a smile. "The fun kind. But if you feel anythin' worse, you let me know."

"I will."

"Good. Because I don't want to hurt you too much. Just enough to make things interestin'."

Oscar shivered as I used a piece of the cord to divide his testicles then tied it snug to keep them that way. "How did I ever end up with someone like you? You know just what I like. You know things that even I don't know about me," he said.

My heart filled at them words, and I nodded, proud of it.

"I guess I just know how your mind works, how you like to be helpless and under my hand, because you know that I love and cherish you."

"I do. I do."

"And I got a good imagination. When I saw this cord hanging up in the cobbler's shop, all I could think was how good t'would look against your skin."

"And does it? Does it look good?"

I examined his balls, running my fingertip o'er where the skin was tight and sensitive as he gasped, then winked at him. "Oh, it does. It looks so good. Your balls are my prisoners now. I got them right where I want them. Now I just need to tie up your dick."

Oscar moaned and shuddered. "Oh God."

I took the end of the last piece of cord and pulled it slowly, so it dragged o'er his belly and down his crotch. Then I used it to wrap around his standing cock, as snug as I could make it but not so tight that it would cause him any harm. He was so hard already that it probably wouldn't do that much, but it sure did look nice. And I was able to make it so his nubby bulged out a bit. When I was done, I stood and stepped back.

"How does that feel?"

"Oh. God. It feels…so…so…naughty."

"Yeah, it looks naughty, too. Very naughty…just like you."

"Oh fuck."

I put my knee on the bed, below his spread thigh, and loomed o'er top him, my gaze drifting along his pale, quivering body. He blinked up at me, twisting his hands together above his head, his mouth wide open as he breathed hard.

"You like to be naughty, don't you?"

"Yes," he breathed.

"For me."

"For you. I can be *so* naughty for you, Jimmy."

I grinned, my gaze moving o'er his soft, slim neck and his sweet face, his arms and the tufts of dark hair in the hollows of his armpits.

"Oh, I know. But I reckon you've never looked as naughty as you look right now. 'Cept when I had you bent o'er my saddle that time, maybe…"

"Oh…" Oscar moaned.

He remembered.

Soon after deciding to bring him with me on my journey to Whitehorse, when we'd been camped under a cold, starless sky, I'd stripped him, put him o'er my saddle and given way to the feelings I'd been fighting. It had been a revealing moment for the both of us, and I thought about it fondly to this day. I reckoned, so did he.

"You sure look naughty now, though, with your little nubby all wrapped up snug in those soft cords." I trailed my fingertips o'er his chest and belly, then tickled them along his captive cock as he cried out and squirmed.

"Oh! Oh, fuck!"

"How does it feel?"

"Oh *God*. So good. So *good*, Jimmy."

Chapter Ten

Christmas Eve in the Country

I traced my fingertips o'er his testicles again, where they bulged between the cords, and he gasped.

"I bet you feel that real good," I said.

Every sensation would be heightened by the constriction. Oscar enjoyed a bit of pain, sure enough, but I was starting out slow and I'd be careful, whatever I did.

I'd spent time in the gang learning to restrain people securely, without causing damage or inflicting more discomfort than necessary. The others might not have cared, but I did. And even the cold-hearted among them knew that the fewer people we killed or severely injured, the less the law would come looking, so they let me take care of the prisoners. I did my best for them and hoped they'd be released before Spook got bored and looked to them for entertainment. A flash of guilt hit me, but I shoved it aside. I was deep into wanting to do this to Oscar now, and I couldn't bear to be distracted by wayward regrets from my past. T'was only a bit of cord, and Oscar wanted me to restrain him.

I'd never imagined using my skills for anything like this, but they sure came in handy. I suppose t'was good I'd picked up a few things while I was living that life. I'd learned to shoot, to hunt and even to cook—or, at least how to skin and roast game—and to tie knots, ride and even how to tend to wounds. We didn't have no access to doctors when we were in the gang, so we had to make do. If someone got hurt bad enough that we couldn't heal them, or if the wound got infected, they died. We'd left injured people behind, and I was sorry about that. But what else could we have done?

I shook my head to clear those memories and the emotions they brought with them. That part of my life was over. But I'd be damned if I would regret the skills I'd acquired simply because they were attached to an unsavory business.

I peered at Oscar's cock, wrapped up as t'was in soft leather, bulging out between the tight strip of cord, and I took a deep, steadying breath. His dick, that he liked to think was small and dainty, looked mighty impressive at the moment.

"Look at this little thing," I said, patronizing him because I knew he wanted me to. I stroked my fingertip along its underside, bumping o'er the leather and the swells of flesh. "Little dick trying to be a big one, bulging all out of its strings."

Oscar gasped and went pink and rigid all o'er. "Oh, fuck."

His arm came down, but I caught his wrist.

"Oh no you don't. Keep your hands up there," I said.

He moved his arm back and panted, gazing at me in desperation.

"Now you keep 'em up there, you hear? Don't move 'em."

"Yes, sir."

I could barely hear them words, he was so quiet. I held his gaze and bent down, edging my face closer and closer to his groin until I tilted my chin and licked the head of his cock.

Oscar stiffened and cried out, a surge of fluid pulsing out to meet my tongue, showing how much he was enjoying himself. He didn't spend, which was good, because I needed to torture him a little bit longer.

I had plans.

I licked all o'er and around the sensitive tip and tongued and dipped into his foreskin, where t'wasn't held fast by the cords.

Oscar moaned and panted, then keened like he couldn't stand it. But he didn't say his stop word. I licked down along the bulging skin and across his tight, captive balls, my tongue bumping o'er the leather cord, while he made horrible, beautiful sounds of distress and pulled against his bindings, making the wood of the bed frame creak.

"Jimmy! Jimmy!" he panted. "Oh fuck. Jimmy!"

I lifted my head.

"You want me to stop?"

"No — yes — no — I don't know. No. No. *Keep goin'*."

I smiled and worked up some spit in my mouth as Oscar's eyes widened, his gaze fixed on mine. I let a wad of saliva slide from my lips and drop, landing smack on the head of his cock.

"Ah!" he said. "Oh…"

I did it o'er, and o'er, until his cock was soaked with my spittle and his juices. Then I made pretty designs with my fingertip all along it, bumping o'er the cords, urging all kinds of desperate sounds from his wet, parted lips.

His whole body shuddered, and his arm came down again. I grabbed it just in time.

"*Oscar.*"

"But I can't keep still."

I raised my eyebrows. "Do I need to use a cord on your wrists? Splay you out like a hide strung between two poles?"

His mouth made a silent O as his breaths came harsh and quick. "Yes!" he said. "Do that. Do that, Jimmy. *Please!*"

"All right," I said. "Because we ain't even close to being finished here."

He stuttered a moan that sounded like a plea, and I took it inside me and let it stoke my own fire. He watched as I stood and got more cords from the table. T'was a good thing I'd bought enough to restrain him properly *and* have fun with his nubby.

I took his wrist and wrapped it with a piece of the cord, then secured it to the head of the bed. I did the same with the other, my dick hard and aching. I wanted to get into him soon, that was a fact. I wanted to fuck him as he was—tied down with his cock and balls in leather cords, at my mercy—because it touched something inside me that wanted him quiet and conquered, because he'd given me permission and continued to do so every minute he didn't use his stop word.

He watched me with glazed eyes and a slow-blinking disbelief as I finished securing him.

"How's that?" I asked when I was done.

"Perfect," Oscar said, pulling at the bindings. "It's…perfect."

I smiled. Nodded once. "Good. Now you can't touch yourself or save yourself, unless you use your word. Understand?"

"Yes, sir. Oh, yes, sir."

I stood there just looking at him laid out there for me, hardly believing how fortunate I was to have him.

"W—what are you gonna do now?" he said, pulling against his bonds, his cock bulging and leaking futile drips in its leather prison.

I gave him a slow smile and moved back to my position between his legs. I picked up the jar of saddle grease and showed it to him.

Oscar gasped and twitched. "Oh. Fuck."

I nodded, with an evil smile. "Oh yes. There's a sweet little hole down there just waiting for my attention."

He whimpered as his forehead creased and closed his eyes. "*Yes.*"

"I'm gonna start with my fingers," I said. "Get you nice and slick and ready."

He whimpered again, a long sigh following.

I took the top off the jar and scooped up some grease onto my index and middle fingers.

"Then I'm gonna fuck you, Oscar Yates, until your cock figures out a way to spend while it's all tied up like a Christmas turkey."

His eyes flashed open and his lips parted as his cock surged, more moisture oozing out the shiny tip that was full out of its hood by now, looking vulnerable and sweet.

"Jimmy…" he whispered, squirming in a delicious way.

"Yes, Oscar?"

"Please. *Please.*"

"All right," I said, rubbing my slick fingers against his soft hole and pushing them inside him.

He arched his back as I slid them fingers all the way into him, accompanied by his soft cry of submission. I stroked him on the inside as I pressed to find his spot, that little bundle of nerve endings that drove him crazy.

Sure enough, Oscar shuddered and groaned when I found it.

"Oh God." He moaned. "Right *there.*"

I brushed my fingertip o'er it a few times, then withdrew them and spread grease o'er his hole and between his cheeks, making him nice and slippery.

When I breached him again, t'was with three fingers, and Oscar arched his back as I pushed them in deep.

He cursed and panted as I twisted them, opening him up so's I could fuck him and do it well. He looked so beautiful, giving himself up to me and what I was doing. I couldn't hardly look away — and why would I want to?

All of a sudden, I couldn't stand it. I had reached a point of desperation so urgent that it took me by surprise with its severity.

I scrambled with my trousers and my long underwear, getting my dick out and slapping some grease on it, almost spending from the friction and the sight of Oscar below me, spread out on our bed and waiting — waiting for *me.*

I put a knee up on the mattress and found his hole with my fingers again, guiding my dick with my other hand. I flashed back to the first time I'd ever fucked him — in the dirt of our camp, in complete and utter torment and guided by some force outside of my control. And I drove my cock into him now with the same sense of possession, like I couldn't do anything else. I'd stopped trying to resist.

Oscar made a sound like supplication as I shoved in all the way, till I could feel his tight, captive balls against my belly.

"You like that?" I whispered. "You like having my cock inside you, all the goddamn way?"

"You know I do. You know it." He swallowed and licked his lips.

I made a sound, a groan, as I retreated and thrust into him again, his insides velvety smooth and hot, so hot, around me. I was gentle but I was relentless. I pierced him again and again with my cock that was so hard and aching for release. But I held off, because I wanted him to go off before I did.

His sweet cock, his *nubby*, all tied up with the leather cords, pulsed and dripped, and I quickened my movements just a little in order to set him off. He started to pant and cry out, and I knew it would be soon. I craned my neck down to watch and snapped my hips, raking o'er his special spot again and again.

Oscar made a choking noise and an animal sound as he went rigid, his cock shooting spatters of white onto his belly as I kept fucking him, draining him, making him mine, giving him that pleasure as if it were my sacred duty.

"*Argh! Ahhhh!*" he screamed as he spent and spent and spent. I kept up my rhythm until he'd finished, then went fast again as my need ramped up. He was sensitive, no doubt, but t'wasn't long before I got there, garbling curses and praise and deep-throated groans of bliss into his neck as I emptied into him.

"Oscar. Oscar."

T'was all I could say as we lay there, wrapped up together, our breaths slowing and our bodies relaxing, our brains coming back to earth. I peppered his face with kisses until he laughed and pushed me away.

* * * *

On Christmas Eve, we got our morning chores done, made sure Poke had enough to eat and drink, added wood to the stove to keep our house warm while we were gone and set out for the Trelawneys' place. I'd convinced Oscar to put some of his candy aside as a gift for Irene and Clarence, because it would be a kind gesture. But I had to promise to let him buy more the next time we went to town. Oscar drove a hard bargain when it came to sweets.

We'd been blessed with fine weather. T'was a tad on the windy side, but the sun was shining, and we bundled up. I'd taken a brace of partridges to Irene the day before, so's she could pluck them and figure out how to cook them for our supper. She'd been delighted, and even Clarence had given me a nod of thanks for the contribution. I reckoned he'd appreciated being saved the trouble of going out himself.

When we broke through the cover of the trees, we saw Clarence standing on the porch. He stepped down to greet us.

"Merry Christmas, Jimmy. Oscar."

"Merry Christmas. We're happy to've been invited," I said.

"Oscar, you go inside. Irene's excited to see you."

"Yes, sir!"

The barn was more spacious than ours, with four good-sized stalls. Clarence's bay gelding and Irene's chestnut mare were there, but they didn't seem to have any other animals. The place smelled of fresh hay and manure and leather.

While we worked to unsaddle and stable Dixie and Onyx, I glanced o'er at Clarence.

"Thank you kindly for having us o'er on Christmas Eve, Mr. Trelawney. Oscar and I don't have no family nearby, and we were just gonna be together."

Clarence eyed me curiously. "Call me Clarence, or I'll never hear the end of it from Irene. You come from Whitehorse? You got family there?"

"No, I— I was there on a job when I found Oscar," I said, uneasiness gnawing at me. Any time people asked me personal questions, I felt defensive and like I had something to hide—probably because I did. Oscar knew about my life as an outlaw, but I didn't want everyone to find out. I'd come up with a cover story about growing up in Alberta and losing my parents— which was close enough to the truth—and being brought out to the Yukon by a relative who'd set me up hauling supplies. But every time I had to explain, I felt like even more of a liar than I was already. T'was bad enough that Oscar and I had to keep the truth of our relationship a secret, but I felt I had to keep my outlaw past hidden away, too. The difference was that I was shamed and remorseful of that part of my life, but I was proud of what Oscar and I were together.

Carson Moore and Tim Jensen were one thing, but the Trelawneys were our neighbors and I hated to lie to them right off the bat, when they'd been so kind and welcoming.

Clarence grunted and continued to help with the horses, but I felt like I should try to make conversation. I was trying to think of something to say when Clarence spoke again.

"What do you mean, you *found* him? Was he lost?"

I looked o'er there, trying to see Clarence's face under his hat, and I reckon I saw his lips twitch, like he was making a joke, and t'was so surprising I didn't say anything for a moment. Then I nodded.

"I reckon he was real lost, yeah," I said, wondering how much I should reveal. I kept it simple. "He was down on his luck, and he looked like he could use a friend. So, I offered to help him by bringing him to his uncle here in Port Essington."

They say when you're telling a lie you should keep it as close to the truth as you can, so that's what I did. I didn't want to tell Clarence that Oscar had been scraggly and starved and offering himself for cash outside a cathouse. Oscar wouldn't thank me for that, and I reckon Clarence didn't have to know about any of it—and neither did anyone else. That was a secret between me and Oscar, as much as the true nature of our friendship.

"Hmm. So, you traveled from Whitehorse to Port Essington together?"

"Yes, sir. I reckon we got to know each other pretty good on that journey. We're close friends now, and he's letting me help him build on the property and make a home here."

Clarence nodded. "I see."

I wasn't really sure he did, and I hoped he didn't see anything that looked suspicious. Maybe I should change the subject.

"How long have you and Irene lived here?" I asked, hanging Dixie's bridle up on a hook and putting her rope halter on. I led her into the stall and shut the door with a click of the latch.

"Oh, we been here for about six years now, I guess," Clarence said.

"You like it? Living here in Port Essington, I mean?"

Clarence shrugged. "Sure. I guess." He eyed me carefully. "Winters can be hard."

"Yeah, I can see that."

"Maybe this one won't be so bad."

"No?" I said, wondering what he meant.

Then, of all the miracles, Clarence nodded and gave me a smile. "We got neighbors now. I reckon me and Irene could use some socializing, before we go and disappear into ourselves completely."

I grinned with relief and gave a little laugh. "I reckon you're right. There ain't nothing better than other people to share the dark months with."

I'd spent my winters in the company of some unsavory people, and I was very glad to have Clarence and Irene.

"Do you mind if I ask how you make a living out here? Oscar and I are gonna need to figure something out this spring. We've got enough money to get through this winter and build a proper house, but after that, things are gonna be tight."

"Sure. I reckon there's work in town, at least o'er the summer months. I work at the blacksmith from April to the end of October. And Irene is a dressmaker. She runs a mail-order business." Clarence sounded mighty proud of his wife.

"That's wonderful."

"She's an excellent seamstress," Clarence said. "She advertises in all the best catalogs and quarterlies."

"Well, that's quite something. Good for her," I said.

"You get her to show you her work room. 'Tis filled with fabrics and dress forms and all sorts of ridiculous trimmings. But it pays well, and she enjoys it, so…" He shrugged and threw me an indulgent smile. "She brings in more than I do right now, so I can't complain."

I didn't know about that. I figured lots of men would complain about their wives making more money than they did, but Clarence didn't seem to care. I was glad he didn't hold it against her, like some would have done. Seemed like a pretty nonsensical outlook to me, and I suppose Clarence thought so, too. If Irene's hard work benefited him, what did he care about outdated standards of acceptability?

Clarence didn't say anything else until we'd finished with the horses. Then he looked toward the house and nodded.

"I s'pose we'd better go rescue your friend. Irene's probably talkin' his ear off about all sorts of nonsense."

I laughed. "I reckon Oscar's probably keeping up with her. I've never known a more talkative man than him."

Clarence smiled as we made our way across the snowy yard and onto the porch, and the door swung inward. T'was Oscar.

"Where the hell have you been, Jimmy? You gotta smell this stew. Irene's been telling me what all's in it and, by gosh, I can't wait to try some."

"Well, you gotta let me in, Oscar, if you want me to smell it. You're blocking my way you're so excited to tell me."

"Sorry… Sorry," he said, moving back and letting us in. "Come on in. Can you smell that? My mouth's been waterin' since I got here."

Irene, who was standing at the cookstove stirring something in a pot, laughed. "It's nice to have someone so excited about my cooking!" she said.

Clarence, who was taking off his boots, harrumphed and gave Irene a stern glance. "My excitement ain't good enough, woman?"

Irene snorted. "Excitement? Clarence, you have never been excited about a pot on the stove in your lifetime. I'm lucky if I get a 'thank you' when you're done eating."

I glanced at Clarence, who took off his hat and his coat and hung them up, and he didn't look at all upset at Irene's words. I reckoned they must be true, then.

"Well, I cannot argue with you about that. Sometimes, what's in my heart ain't plain to see, that's true."

They exchanged a look, the two of them, and Irene's eyes softened.

"Well, you're lucky I can see it most days," she said in a quiet voice, glancing at Oscar and me like she was saying something private but plain, and it showed the kind of folks they were.

I'd only ever seen Clarence all wrapped up in his winter gear. I looked him o'er while trying not to be obvious about it. Now that he'd taken off his coat and scarf and hung his hat up, he seemed a bit small for a man, but I guess his gruff attitude more than made up for that. Oscar was on the small side, too, and I didn't hold that against him. Clarence didn't seem as delicate as Oscar, but he wasn't big and muscly either. He was dressed in plain, rough trousers with wide leather suspenders, and a tucked-in blousy red shirt, buttoned right up to the nape of his long neck. His hair was sandy brown and clipped real short.

But Oscar was staring at Clarence, and I elbowed him to get him to stop.

"Where's this stew you're raving about?"

Oscar turned and grinned, taking me o'er to where Irene was stirring a thick, savory mixture in a copper pot. "Don't that smell good?"

I bent close to take a whiff and felt moisture pool in my mouth. "My goodness, but that smells wonderful, Mrs. Trelawney."

"Now, Jimmy, you call me Irene. We're neighbors."

"All right. Irene. That smells mighty good."

She smiled at me, and I about lit up inside. She had that same spirit of happiness that Oscar did, so that when they were pleased about something, the whole world knew it, and those who were close to them were blessed.

"It's thanks to those birds you brought me yesterday. I had a recipe for turkey stew, and I figured t'would work with partridge. I suppose we'll see, when it's ready."

"Irene let me have a taste," Oscar said. "And it's heavenly."

"There's biscuits in the oven, we bought some butter in town and I made bread yesterday. And there's fruitcake and plum pudding for dessert," she said, beaming. "Oh, and sweet potato pie!"

"My God, Irene, you'd think t'was the Queen coming o'er," Clarence grumbled.

"Clarence, it's Christmas! Of course, I'm going to make a feast. This is the first we've had visitors on Christmas Eve since we set up in Port Essington!"

Chapter Eleven

The Trelawneys

Oscar's wide smile stretched across his sweet face as I laughed, feeling so very welcomed and looking forward to a tasty meal. My heart warmed and expanded as I gazed about me at Irene and Clarence's house.

T'was a more substantial home than ours and, since they'd lived here so long, t'was real homey. The furniture seemed handmade out of fine woods, with covered cushions in attractive fabrics. A wide rug of blue and gold was laid out o'er the floor, and a piano sat with a majestic air in the corner by the fireplace. The main floor seemed to be one large space, with a small kitchen visible toward the back that seemed well-appointed, with a wide wood counter and an iron cookstove like ours. In between the sitting area and the kitchen, Irene had laid out a large dining table with fancy plates and cutlery, and even a centerpiece of winter greenery and berries.

"I wanted a Christmas tree, but Clarence said t'was too much work."

Clarence rolled his eyes.

"Maybe next year." Irene smiled.

"Sure," Oscar said. "Next year, me and Jimmy'll help you get one."

Clarence clicked his tongue. "I could get her one if I felt t'was worthwhile. But I reckon it'll only make a mess and take up space we ain't got."

Irene turned to Clarence then, who'd come closer to the dining table where we were standing, and I swear she stuck her tongue out at him like Oscar had done to me more than once, then she threw her dish towel at him.

Clarence caught it with a gleam in his eye and the tiniest inkling of a smile. I reckon t'wasn't the first time this had happened.

Oscar and I exchanged a look. I felt more at home here than I had anywhere in my lifetime, and I could tell Oscar did, too. He seemed to find Clarence and Irene's gentle ribbing just as amusing as I did, because it reminded me of the two of us, and the way we liked to chide each other. T'was too bad we couldn't say so.

Clarence threw the dish towel back to Irene, and she caught it with a smirk.

I cleared my throat and gazed down at the polished wood floor, in case I let my true feelings for Oscar out by mistake. I was surprised when Clarence slapped an affectionate hand on my back.

"You smoke, Jimmy?"

When I turned, Clarence was filling a pipe with tobacco.

"Nasty habit," Irene muttered but she didn't look too mad about it, since she was smiling as she returned to her stirring.

"You told me you like the smell of it," Clarence said gruffly, patting down the leaves and adding more in the bell of his pipe. "She does. You watch. She'll be sittin' there sniffing like t'was perfume."

"All right, now," Irene said. "Oscar, you want to help me with something?"

"Sure," Oscar said, leaving me with Clarence, who gestured for me to follow him into the sitting room.

"I don't," I said. "Never took it up."

Clarence sat down in an armchair by the window and picked up a book of matches from the little wood table beside it.

"Just as well," he said, taking a match out and striking it. "'Tis a nasty habit."

He lit the tobacco and sucked on the tip of the wooden pipe, making a red flair in the bell as the leaves caught. I smiled at the good-natured way he had about him, now that he had relaxed in my presence.

"It ain't so bad," I said, remembering how the men in the gang had liked to spend their time. But I didn't want to think about that right now, in this cozy and friendly place with people who cared about other people and didn't wish them harm.

I realized then that Oscar, sweet Oscar, had led me here, to this place. I'd escaped the gang, sure, and made a kind of a lonely life for myself. But if I hadn't come upon Oscar in Dawson City and brought him with me to Whitehorse, I'd have never had the chance to follow him here, where we'd found a welcome and a place of friendship.

It hit me all of a sudden that Oscar, in a multitude of ways, was the reason I was so happy now, in this moment.

"You all right?" Clarence asked, his eyes narrowing as he puffed on his pipe.

"Yes, I—" I cleared my throat and tried to quell the emotion that had risen inside me at that sudden realization. "I guess I just been thinking how lucky me and Oscar are, to've found such a friendly place to call home."

"Hmph. Not everyone in town's so friendly," Clarence muttered. "But I s'pose you're right, that it's mostly a good place. I reckon all towns have got a few nasty folk in 'em."

I gazed at Clarence with concern and wondered who had been nasty to him. But I figured he was right. I wouldn't expect there not to be ornery people. But we hadn't encountered any as of yet, and I hoped it would be a while before we did. Anyway, now that we were friendly with Clarence and Irene, they could let us know who we could and couldn't expect kindness from.

Port Essington was a better and more promising place than I'd ever been, truth be known. T'wasn't a burned down house where my parents had died, and t'wasn't the wilderness in the midst of a group of bloodthirsty hoodlums.

"You wanna try?" Clarence said, offering me his pipe. "'Tis good for relaxin'. I reckon it won't do you no harm, and 'tis Christmas Eve."

I felt honored that he'd offered it to me. So I took it, put the pipe to my lips and breathed in a lung-full, just as Oscar came around the corner from the kitchen.

My lungs burned and I coughed, pulling the pipe out of my mouth and trying to hold it steady as I choked and sputtered, an embarrassment to men everywhere. My cheeks were hot as I passed the pipe back to Clarence, who watched with an amused smile.

"Clarence, don't poison our guests, for heaven's sake!" Irene hollered from the kitchen.

Oscar was watching me with a strange expression as I tried to catch my breath.

Clarence offered him the pipe. "You want a pull, Oscar?"

"Well now, I don't mind if I do," Oscar said, taking the pipe so casually from Clarence that my eyes widened. He held my gaze as he lifted it to his lips and took a few inhales, puffing the smoke out of the side of his mouth like he'd done it all his life. Hell, for all I knew, maybe he had.

"There you go. Oscar's smoked a pipe before," Clarence said with some satisfaction.

"'Course I have. I won one in a card game in Dawson City once. Learned to smoke it. T'was a fine thing when I could get my hands on some tobacco." He took it from his mouth and examined the bell. "This is a good blend you got, Clarence. It's real smooth. I can feel my bones relaxin'."

My coughing fit waned, but I stared at Oscar, hardly believing what I was seeing as he took a few more pulls and passed the pipe back to Clarence.

"Thank you, kindly."

"You're more'n welcome, Oscar Yates. We just need to train Jimmy up." He grinned and looked o'er at me as Oscar laughed.

I held up my hand. "No, thank you. I'll stick to whiskey."

"Oh, hell, I didn't offer you gentlemen a drink. Excuse my manners," Clarence mumbled, resting his pipe on a plate and getting up. "I got whiskey and gin and even a bottle of Jamaican rum, if anyone wants some."

Now that was a better offer than a pipe full of foul grasses. I hadn't had a tot of gin in ages. Oscar and I'd bought more whiskey to keep at the house—hopefully enough to see us through until spring, and we had a dram now and then.

"I'd love to have a bit of gin, please, if you don't mind. That would hit the spot real nice."

"Clarence, are you gettin' the rum out?" Irene yelled.

Clarence rolled his eyes and smiled, like he'd been expecting it.

"Never you mind. It's for our guests," he said, eyeing us and lifting his hand with three fingers raised. As we watched, he folded them in one by one, and as soon as he'd folded the third finger down, Irene came around the corner, wiping her hands and narrowing her eyes at her husband.

"Clarence Trelawney, if I gotta stand over this hot stove making food for you men, you're gonna pour me a tot of that fine Jamaican rum. You hear me?"

Oscar and I raised our eyebrows at each other and tried not to laugh at how serious Irene was in her outrage.

"Calm yourself, woman. I'll get you some. Geez, I was only joking."

Irene pushed a bit of hair out of her face and blushed, glancing at Oscar and me.

"I do apologize. I really thought he was bein' stingy with it. I only like a little, now and then. I know it's not really proper, but..." She shrugged. "I don't really give a good goddamn."

Her gaze went back and forth between us to see what we'd make of her words and her desire for the drink.

Oscar's face broke into a broad smile. "Come on, Irene. Sit with us. You can take a break from cooking, can't you?"

She smiled, relief showing on her kind face. I didn't reckon Irene was more than a few years older than Oscar, and she was mighty fine looking—plump and pretty and full of contentment. I liked the fight in her, too. If my needs had lain in another direction, I might feel more than a passing appreciation for the way she looked. But seemed like women—even nice-looking ones like her—didn't affect me much at all anymore.

Because now I knew the delights that a man could provide… I wondered if I'd find my cock hardening for fellas besides Oscar. So far, it hadn't happened, but it might. Just because I had a home with Oscar didn't mean I was blind. I figured at some point I might start feeling something physical for another man, but I wouldn't act on it, especially since t'would be dangerous to admit who I was to anyone but Oscar, but also because he had my heart and I'd never betray him in any way.

But I liked Irene a lot and that was a hard fact. Even Clarence was getting to be more appealing.

"I reckon I can. Just let me settle things in the kitchen. Clarence, get me a drink, please."

"Of course, my darling." He winked at us. "I just like to give her a hard time. But she enjoys a dram as much as anyone, and there ain't no reason to deny her." He glanced back and forth between us. "Irene and I don't have a whole lot of respect for the expectations of wider society, when it comes down to it. We do what we want in our home."

I nodded. Now that was an attitude I could get behind. "I reckon that makes sense. We ain't got no problem with it, do we, Oscar?"

"No, sir. No problem a t'all." Oscar's eyes widened. "Oh! I almost forgot. I brought a little something for you."

He reached into his pocket and pulled out the paper bag of candy he'd separated from his stash. Now he seemed proud as he offered it to Irene.

"T'isn't much." He shrugged.

Irene took the bag with a smile and peered inside. Her eyebrows flew up and she grinned wider, gazing at Oscar. "Oh, thank you! I haven't had candy in ages."

"Oscar got some that day we saw you in town, and he saved a bit for you. T'was very difficult for him, I reckon, so you should feel honored," I said, winking at Oscar, who nodded.

"Well, t'was hard not to eat it all, that's true. But I wanted to have something to bring today."

The four of us sat down then, in the Trelawneys' cozy sitting room, drinks in hand, and chatted about all sorts of things. Turned out Clarence and Irene had come west from Saskatchewan, figuring to set up in some small town on the coast, and finally found themselves here in Port Essington. They liked it, for the most part.

My mind wandered, and I found myself thinking it a bit peculiar that they had no children, after being married so long and seemingly happy together. I didn't want to ask, in case Irene was barren or Clarence had had some sort of accident to make him unable to reproduce. Those were personal things, and I figured, if they wanted to tell us, they would. But for now, we needed to take them the way they were and not question things.

To be honest, I was relieved there were no little ones running about, and we could enjoy the peace of a winter's day with the smoke from Clarence's pipe making a pleasant smell, along with the oranges Irene had sliced and placed in a bowl for snacking. The taste of the gin on my tongue and the sight of Oscar and Irene relaxing with glasses of rum as the sun shone on the snow outside the window was giving me all kinds of feelings of satisfaction that I didn't know hardly what to do with. Once in a while, I'd catch Oscar's gaze, and we'd share a small moment of connection before looking away to the crackling fire in the fireplace or the table with the dinnerware all laid out for the much-anticipated meal.

I tried to make conversation.

"Where did you get these oranges?" I said, taking a slice and biting into its juicy center. "We didn't notice any at the store, else we might have got some for ourselves."

Irene glanced at Clarence. "Well, we know a few people in town who get particular items shipped from afar, and they were kind enough to sell us some. Aren't they nice to have this time of year? They're so tropical and make me think of palm trees and beaches." She sighed.

"You ever been down south?" Oscar asked, taking an orange wedge and popping it into his mouth. I tried not to watch as a tiny bit of juice squirted o'er his bottom lip.

"Excuse me," he said, wiping it with the back of his hand. "Oh, shoot, I prob'ly should have used a napkin," he said, looking about for one. "I'm so sorry."

His face had gone pink, and it seemed he thought he'd committed some horrible offense of decency.

But Irene simply laughed and offered him another wedge. "Don't be silly. This isn't a royal visit, Oscar."

He chuckled and took the wedge. "These oranges taste like sunshine."

"Don't they?" Irene agreed. "I've used some of the peel in the stew, to give it a lift."

"That stew smells better n' better as the time goes on," Oscar murmured, putting his stocking-covered heel up on the chair as he leaned back, then reconsidering and putting his foot back on the floor and sitting up straight.

Irene narrowed her eyes. "Oscar, sit how you like. This isn't a palace. I like to see my guests relax and enjoy themselves. At least, I s'pose I do." She made a funny face and laughed. "It's been so long since we had any that I can hardly remember."

Clarence shook his head at her, then turned to us. "You've made my wife very happy by coming o'er." He sucked on his pipe and puffed out more smoke. "And me."

When the sun had dipped and the light inside was fading, Irene lit some oil lamps and set alight some candles on the table.

"Clarence, will you help me serve?"

"Of course."

"Jimmy and Oscar, you sit yourselves down at the table. The food's coming out."

"I can help," I said as I got up from my chair.

"We'll help you bring—" Oscar spoke at the same time as me.

"No, no. You two are our guests. Sit yourselves down at the table and let us host. Please," Irene said.

We glanced at each other, shrugged, and found spots across from each other at the wood table that had been decorated and laid out so nice.

"These plates are so fine, Jimmy," Oscar said, examining the china. T'was real china with a nice sheen on it—white, with green vines swirling on the edges. I didn't think I'd ever seen dishes so pretty.

"They are nice," I admitted. "I know Irene keeps saying we ain't in a palace, but compared to our place, it sure seems like one."

Oscar grinned. "I know it."

Clarence brought out a plate piled high with biscuits and a dish of fresh butter, then a basket filled with fresh sliced bread. Irene carried the big pot of stew and placed it in the middle of the table on a piece of thick cloth to protect the wood.

"I told her I'd carry it, but she wanted to bring it," Clarence said, rolling his eyes.

"You think you're stronger than me?" Irene said with a grin. "Who's the one that does all the laundry and the cleaning every week?"

"All right, all right," Clarence said. "You're as strong as a horse, Irene. That's why I married you, in fact. T'weren't your glamorous looks a t'all."

Irene laughed and returned to the kitchen, coming back with a ladle as Clarence sat down and placed his napkin in his lap.

"Pass your bowl, Jimmy," Irene said, holding out her hand.

I did so, then placed my napkin in my lap and watched Oscar do the same.

"Everythin' smells so good!" Oscar commented.

I'm sure his mouth was watering. I hardly knew if he'd ever enjoyed such a bounteous meal, but something told me he hadn't. And I was so grateful to Clarence and Irene all of a sudden that they had given him this experience. As for me, growing up when my parents were alive, we'd had some meals like this, and t'was a nice reminder of how good it could feel to be surrounded by care and prosperity. I'd lived awful rough for all those years with the gang, and that made me appreciate everything I had now, true enough.

Once we'd loaded up our plates, Irene and Clarence folded their hands together and closed their eyes. Oscar was reaching for the butter knife when I touched his calf with my toe under the table and motioned to them. Oscar brought his hands together and bent his head, as did I.

"Dear Lord," Irene began, "we thank you for this bounty and for our new friends — Jimmy and Oscar — who've started a life here in Port Essington. And we thank you for keeping us healthy and for giving us what we need. Amen."

"Amen," I repeated, at the same time as Clarence and Oscar said it.

"Help yourselves, gentlemen. Clarence," Irene said, taking a biscuit for herself and pulling it apart, steam rising from its center.

I don't know when I'd ever had a more pleasant meal, to be honest. Clarence and Irene joked with each other, and Oscar and I soaked up their happiness. T'was strange we'd been so wary of them at first, when they were two of the nicest people I'd ever known. I think Oscar felt the same.

The biscuits were light and fluffy, the butter rich and smooth. The stew was savory and fragrant, with a citrusy, fresh taste from the orange peel. I'd have to remember that trick, if we ever had oranges ourselves. I'd have to ask Irene to hook me up. Maybe her friends would sell us some.

By the time we were done, darkness had fallen, and the house was lit with the soft glow from the oil lamps and the flickering light of the fire.

Irene brought out fruitcake with some kind of almond paste icing that I licked off my fingers t'was so good and a pecan pie that Oscar seemed to favor. Then the plum pudding on a plate, that she doused with brandy and lit with a match. The blue flames danced o'er it as Oscar and I exchanged a glance and smiles. Irene was an excellent cook and an even better baker, and Clarence was a lucky man. We were fortunate to have them living so near to us.

When we'd finished, we went to the sitting room with small cups of coffee and sat on the settee and in chairs in front of the fire to let our meal settle. Once our cups were drained, Irene poured me some more gin and some rum for herself and Oscar, while Clarence had some whiskey and filled his pipe again.

T'was the most pleasant thing in the world to sit there, in the warmth from the fire, full of food and drink and surrounded by goodwill. It seemed as though God was smiling down upon us, as much as I felt like I needed to make reparations for all the questionable things I'd done. For the first time in a long while, I thought maybe God might forgive me, or at least, figured I was worth saving.

"Oscar, will you sing for us?" Irene said, once we'd all helped to wash and dry the dishes.

I scooped my pocket watch from my vest pocket and glanced at it. T'was nigh eleven. It would only take me and Oscar about ten minutes to ride home, but I reckoned we should take our leave in the next half hour or so. We didn't want to overstay our welcome.

I glanced at Oscar and waited to hear what he'd say.

"Well, I — I don't know. I ain't sung in a while."

"I heard you singing on Tuesday," I said.

Ever since I'd made a point of praising his voice when we were in town, Oscar had been more free with it, singing around the house or sometimes to his horse when we were in the stables. But I reckon he was shy about it still.

"Oh, please?" Irene said, sitting down on the piano bench and raising the wooden fallboard to expose the black and white keys. "I love to play, and I don't usually have anyone who can sing with me. Clarence, bless his heart, can't hold a note."

Clarence laughed. His cheeks were rosy from the drink and the heat from the fire. He made a face. "You don't wanna hear me try."

Oscar frowned. He gazed between me and Irene. Then he rolled his eyes and stood.

"Fine."

A warm flush of anticipation flooded me. Irene and Clarence had never heard Oscar sing, but I had. And I knew that if he didn't let his shyness bother him too much, they'd be awful surprised and pleased by the quality of it. I held that cherished secret close to my heart, but I wanted to share it with these kind folks. I wanted Oscar to share his talent with all of us.

"What should I play, Oscar? I know lots of spirituals and folk songs," Irene said.

"Can you play *Amazing Grace*?" Oscar asked, moving to stand beside the piano bench. He looked so fine in his best clothes. We'd dressed for the occasion, and to make a good impression on our new neighbors. Oscar had loosened his cravat and unbuttoned the top button on his shirt, which made him look like a gentleman comfortable in his surroundings. I settled back to enjoy the show.

He shot me an amused glance, then pointed his index finger at me and raised his eyebrows. "This is your fault, Jimmy."

"What?"

He frowned, but I could see he was teasing. "If you hadn't said anything about my singin' — "

I held up my hands in surrender. "Well, excuse me for wantin' you to share your talent with our neighbors. You got a gorgeous voice, Oscar. Truly."

"Fine," he grumbled, trying to look annoyed instead of pleased. He didn't quite succeed.

Irene began to play, and after a few bars, Oscar started to sing.

"Amazing grace, how sweet the sound
That saved a wretch like me."

We shared a glance as I recalled how we'd first met outside a cathouse in Dawson City, where a starving and wretched young man had been wanting to debase himself for coin, but instead had fallen into my dubious care.

"I once was lost, but now am found,
Was blind, but now I see.
T'was grace that taught my heart to fear,
And grace my fears relieved.

How precious did that grace appear,
The hour I first believed.
Through many dangers, toils and snares,
I have already come.
'Tis grace has brought me safe thus far,
And grace will lead me home."

Our eyes held and I reckon we both understood how fortunate we were to be here, safe and sound, with good people, when we'd come to so much trouble on the way and when it'd been pure chance that Oscar had been placed in my path.

Or had it been more than that? A thought occurred to me as Oscar's angelic voice rose to the rafters, and the shock on Clarence and Irene's faces transformed into awed appreciation of his pleasing tones.

Had God put Oscar in my path so I could make absolution for all the things I'd done? Was Oscar himself the way God would forgive me? Because I'd taken such good care of him and continued to cherish and protect him?

Some would argue that there wasn't any goodness in what had sprung up between Oscar and me so long ago in Dawson City, but I knew that there was. I knew it with the same conviction I knew the sun would come up each day and set each night.

And sitting here on the settee in Clarence and Irene's sitting room, listening to Oscar sing, I felt God working through him to show me that I was still his child, even though I'd been led astray by cruel and heartless men for so long, and that I had every chance at happiness in this town.

A hushed silence filled the space as the last notes of the song drifted away. Then Irene said, in reverent tones, "That was beautiful."

"T'was heavenly," Clarence agreed. "Thank you."

T'was tragic, in a way, that I couldn't show how much Oscar's performance had affected me, but I smiled like a proud parent instead of running o'er there to grab him in my arms and kiss him.

"Do you know this one?" Irene said, as she started playing a lively tune.

"I think so," Oscar said as Irene began to sing. He joined in with her, and I watched them having such fun together. Irene had a lovely soprano and matched well with Oscar's tenor. They performed several pieces, Irene finding songs that Oscar knew, and by the end of it, they were fast friends.

When it got close to midnight, I thanked Clarence and Irene for their hospitality, and Oscar and I got ready to leave. I told Oscar to stay inside with Irene while I went to saddle the horses, and Clarence came along to help.

"I want to thank you for bringing Oscar over tonight. You've given me and Irene a Christmas to remember," Clarence said, as we worked to tack up Onyx and Dixie.

"Clarence," I said, my emotion still high from Oscar's hymn and my stifled reaction. "It's us who should thank the two of you. We never imagined such a fine welcome as this. I'll remember that meal and your company for a long time. Oscar and I, we ain't had such good Christmases lately, and I hope this is just the beginning of lots of 'em."

Clarence regarded me with a contemplative smile.

"Now, Jimmy, these winters in BC are long and lonely. I reckon we'll have you and Oscar over whenever you like. Irene and Oscar seem to be good friends already. I've got a checkerboard and chess pieces we can get out on a Saturday or Sunday. So please, think of our place as your second home."

"Thank you, Clarence. I surely do appreciate it."

Riding home in the starlight, with the lantern in my hand and the puff of our exhales hanging in the night air, I felt warmed by the memories of the Trelawneys' cozy home. Oscar kept Onyx close by so he could share the light from the single lantern.

We'd just come out of the trees near our place when he pulled Onyx to a stop.

"Jimmy. Jimmy, stop. Look," he whispered.

I pulled Dixie up and glanced beside me. Oscar sat still in his saddle, staring at the night sky, his head tilted right back, hands loose on the reins as Onyx shuffled from one hoof to the other.

"I don't think I've ever seen so many stars," he said, his voice hushed and reverent.

I lowered my lantern and gazed upward at the broad expanse above us, rife with sparkles and twinkles of starlight.

"Makes me think of the Christmas story from the Bible," I said.

"Glory to God in the highest Heaven, and on Earth, peace and goodwill toward men," Oscar recited, his gaze moving from the heavens to meet mine. "I remember that pretty well, though I've lost most of my other Bible teachings." He shrugged.

I blinked back sudden emotion. "I reckon that's the important bit."

"Yeah," he said.

We stared at each other as we sat our horses under the stars and thought about the meaning of this special day. Then Dixie snorted and jingled her bit like she was saying, *Come on now. I'm cold. Let's get home.*

"All right, all right," I crooned. "Let's go, then."

By the time we'd got the horses sorted out, watered and cozy in the stable, and had stomped the snow off our boots and hung up our coats and hats, we were plumb exhausted, what with all the good food and the liquor. We added wood to the stove then pulled off our trousers and shirts and got into bed in our union suits, snuffing the lantern and snugging up in the darkness.

"You reckon it's Christmas Day yet, Jimmy?"

"My pocket watch is in my vest still, but I'm sure 'tis."

"Merry Christmas, then," Oscar said in a sleepy, slurred voice.

"Merry Christmas, my love, my heart," I whispered, kissing him on the cheek as he gave me a drowsy glance then drifted to sleep. I followed shortly, blessed to be warm, cozy and well fed in the middle of the deep, dark winter.

Chapter Twelve

Merry Christmas

T'was almost eleven when we woke the next morning to a bright Christmas Day. I went to feed the animals and turn them out, while Oscar loaded wood into the stove and got out what I'd need to make him breakfast.

"You making me flapjacks like you promised, Jimmy?"

"Did I promise you flapjacks?"

Oscar frowned. "You said you'd make me flapjacks for breakfast on Christmas Day. You *did* promise."

"Oh, that's right. I remember," I said. "But I want to give you something first."

Oscar's lips curled in a saucy grin. "Oh, I see. Well, I ain't got no objections to a quick tumble."

I rolled my eyes. "That ain't what I meant. I got you a present."

I opened the drawer and took out the small parcel I'd had the clerk in the store wrap up for me.

Oscar's grin had vanished, and he peered at me with astonishment. "A present? For me?"

"Yes," I said, my breaths quickening, hoping he would like it.

His eyelids fluttered as he gazed at the brown paper tied closed with a bit of string. "I ain't got nothing for you, Jimmy. I didn't know we were gonna get each other presents."

"Oscar," I said, sitting down on the edge of our bed and taking the fingers that toyed with the white string in my hand. "All I want is a kiss if you like what I got you."

The grin came back, a little less saucy and more thankful. "Well, I can give you more'n a kiss…"

"Oscar, just open it, will you?" My heart beat a tattoo in my chest.

Oscar pulled his hand away from my gentle hold and pulled the string. The paper fell away from a navy cardboard box about the size of Oscar's palm. The words 'Waltham Watch Co.' were pressed in gold on the top.

Oscar's big brown eyes flashed upward for a second, then he carefully lifted the lid and gazed at what was inside as I held my breath. He stood still as a stone, staring at the contents of the container. The finest tremor of this fingers caused the box to shake.

"Fuck, Jimmy," he whispered, blinking quickly.

"That's yours. A pocket watch of your very own." I ran a nervous hand through my hair. "Every man should have one."

He nodded, but he didn't look up.

"It's fourteen carat gold. I figured you oughta have something gold, to make up for all them years you spent without in Dawson City—so near to all them riches but never havin' any of your own."

Oscar opened his mouth to say something but nothing came out. He glanced up and held my gaze. I was almost felled by the raw emotion in his eyes. I had to look away so's I could keep my composure.

"It's our first Christmas together, after all," I said, trying to explain why I'd got him something so extravagant when we were living off canned beans and bread for the most part and trying to save money.

He finally got his voice to work. "It's beautiful. Thank you."

His eyes gleamed with appreciation and emotion. My face flushed with pleasure at his words and the look he was giving me, like he truly couldn't believe what he held in his hands.

I pointed at the small device.

"It's a hunter style, with a double case. I had the back of it engraved. Go on. Take it out and have a look."

I was eager for him to examine it and see the fine work of the pricey token. I'd picked the prettiest one I could find that didn't have flowers and such all o'er it. This one had intricate designs of filigree on the front instead and had seemed to call out to me as something Oscar might like.

He lifted it with great care from its nest of snow-white silk and drifted his fingertips o'er the cover and along the edge.

"That's called a pie-crust edge. Fancy, ain't it?" I chuckled. "Figured with your sweet tooth, that made sense."

The fitting around the watch face was designed with ridges that imitated the bumps of a pie crust. T'was elegant and pleasing to the touch — another reason I'd chosen this particular model.

"Jimmy, it's so fine. It's too fine for the likes of me," Oscar said in a hushed tone.

I clicked my tongue, hating to hear him talk that way.

"Nonsense. It's yours. Turn it o'er."

Oscar did as I'd told him, as he liked to do when we were together and feeling close, like we were now.

On the back of the gold case, *Oscar Theodore Yates* was engraved in stylish lettering, and underneath it, *Port Essington, BC, 1906*, so he could remember the date he'd received it. I'd persuaded him to tell me his middle name some time ago, expressly for this purpose. I'd wanted to give him something of his own that he could be proud of, and a pocket watch was useful besides. We only had mine between us at the moment, and I figured he could use one. Why not make it a special gift?

He traced the outlines of the lettering with his thumb, and I admired the work and didn't notice for a moment that tears were streaking down his cheeks.

"Oh, I'm sorry. I didn't mean to make you cry," I hastened, wringing my hands and wondering what I should do.

But he shook his head and gave me the most honest, heartfelt look as he smiled wide, his cheeks glistening.

"'Tis the most precious thing I've ever been given," he said, beaming, "except when God gave me you, Jimmy."

Moisture began to prick at my own eyes, and I blinked to keep it at bay.

"Do you like it? Truly?"

Oscar laughed and nodded, placing the box on the counter and snaking the gold chain between his fingers, flipping open the cover and looking at the face with the numbers and delicate hands.

"I ain't never had anything engraved with my name on't. 'Tis truly special," he said, working his lower lip with his teeth.

"I'm glad you think so. I wanted it to be special — as special as you are to me."

He nodded and laughed again, handling the small pocket watch with reverence. "Golly, how am I ever gonna top this? Now I gotta get you something spectacular for next year."

I scoffed. "I got everything I need right here," I said. "I already got a pocket watch — and I got you. I reckon I don't need anything else to be truly happy."

Oscar glanced up again, and this time his smile was coy and saucy, as it often was. "Well, I reckon I can give you lots of particular attention then, in return."

I blushed. "That's not required. 'Tis a gift."

"Oh, I know it ain't required. But you gotta let me thank you in some way. And, you know, that's the way I like best. And, so do you," he said, giving me an intense look to let me know he meant it. Then he sighed. "But first, I want some flapjacks." He lifted the watch and showed me the time. "'Tis almost noon, after all."

I grinned. "Will you help make the batter?"

He shrugged. "Sure."

Oscar put the pocket watch on the bedside table, nestled back in its box, and we set about making flapjacks. I had a recipe in my little booklet, and t'wasn't complicated. We had eggs and a bit of milk that I kept in the cold storage cellar. Oscar mixed the flour and salt together while I beat the eggs in a bowl. Then we mixed them. By then, the iron skillet was hot, so I helped Oscar pour three little bits of batter that spread out and started bubbling at the edges.

"That smells so good!" Oscar said with excitement. Then his face fell. "Wait. Do we have syrup?"

I frowned. "No, they didn't have any at the store, and I forgot to ask Irene if she had some. But we've got brown sugar and butter. And I even have a lemon if we want to squeeze some on it."

"Oh, that sounds all right."

T'was more than all right. The room filled with the smells of fried batter, then sugar and butter and lemon. We ate slowly at our little wooden table on our tin plates, with tin cups of water for drinking.

"Oscar, you're makin' a mess of yourself," I said, pointing at a smear of butter and sugar on his cheek.

He gazed at me calmly for several seconds, then scooped some butter off his plate with a finger and sucked it into his mouth. It slid out with a pop, and my dick sprang to attention.

"Oscar," I breathed.

"Yes, Jimmy?"

"You aimin' for a Christmas Day spankin' and fuckin'?"

Oscar's lips parted and he grabbed the edges of the table, his chest going up and down. "I am now. I was thinkin' that nothin' could beat getting such a special gift and having homemade flapjacks for breakfast, but I reckon that could."

The noise of our breaths sounded in the relative silence while we gazed flames at each other. Then Oscar jumped up from his seat and ran to the bed, with me close on his heels. T'wasn't far, of course, and we landed in a heap as I fumbled to grab his wrists and wrestle him still beneath me.

"Now, now. You need to behave, Oscar Yates."

He giggled. "Oh, I will. But I wanted you to chase me. Too bad you ain't got your lasso."

He was referring to something we'd done on the last night of our journey before we'd reached Port Essington when we'd felt playful and bold, and I'd thrown my lasso o'er Oscar and pulled him off his feet. I'd then bound him all up with rope until he couldn't move or do anything else but submit to be cherished...and fucked as slow as molasses. I shivered, remembering it.

"Too bad. 'Tis in the stables, though."

Oscar frowned. "If t'were summer, I'd tell you to go get it. But I reckon I don't wanna wait while you get your coat and boots and all that."

"Anyway, I don't wanna lasso you right now. I do wanna smack your ass until you spend o'er my knee, though."

He narrowed his eyes. "I thought you wanted to spank me *and* fuck me."

"Well, I changed my mind. I thought it might be nice to remember that first morning in the hotel in Dawson."

"We'd better get undressed then. I reckon we don't want our union suits gettin' all messed up."

T'was a mild day for late December, so the inside of the little kitchen-house was cozy warm. We stripped to our skins, leaving the dirty dishes on the table. I sat against the headboard of the bed and pulled Oscar across my thighs.

"You been a good boy for Father Christmas?" I asked as I ran the palm of my hand o'er his plump behind. The flesh goose-pimpled up right quick, and t'wasn't from cold.

"Oh, no, I ain't. I been plumb naughty."

I couldn't help laughing, but my mirth turned into a groan when Oscar pressed his hip against my rising cock.

"Oh, I know it. I just wanted to make sure you owned up to it," I panted.

"I know I been naughty," Oscar said. "And I mean to keep on bein' naughty."

"You do, do you?"

"Yes, sir."

"Why?"

"'Cause 'tis such fun and keeps me from gettin' bored."

My eyes widened. "Keeps you from gettin' *bored*?"

"Yeah."

"Well, now. I gotta whole long list of chores I can give you to keep you from boredom, son."

He turned his head and frowned at me. "No thanks."

"No thanks?" I said, shocked at his cavalier attitude.

He stuck his tongue out, and that was that.

"Oscar Yates, you put that tongue back into your mouth. I'm gonna spank you now, and you better not make a sound, else I won't let you spend, and I'll leave you achin' and wantin' all this long Christmas Day. *And* I'll make you do some of them chores you dislike so much."

"Aw, Jimmy, don't do that," he said, his breaths loud and fast, belying his protests.

"You gotta stay quiet, e'en if I do *this*." I sucked my middle finger into my mouth, then slid it out and ran it down between his buttocks, along the cleft there. Oscar groaned and parted his thighs as I found the wrinkled round of muscle guarding his insides.

"Oh..." he moaned.

I rubbed his hole as he trembled and groaned, then I teased the tip of my finger inside.

"Fuck! Gawd! *More.*"

I grinned, though he couldn't see my face, and obliged him, pushing my finger in up to the knuckle as Oscar keened, panted and cursed again.

"Just take it and be quiet," I said, as I pumped my finger in and out of him, going deep then shallow, in a way I knew would feel good and drive him crazy.

He stifled a moan as he gripped the sheets and rocked against my finger. "Oh. Oh."

"*You* are a *very* naughty boy," I said in a matter-of-fact tone of voice. "And I ain't got nowhere else to be. So I'm gonna do whatever I please until you beg me to let you spend. Got it?"

"Yes. *Yes.*"

He spread out across my lap and widened his legs to accommodate my fingering. I grabbed the jar of saddle grease from the bedside table and slicked up three fingers, then took my time working them into him as he struggled to be quiet.

"How do you like that?" I said, once I had them deep inside. Oscar's face lay sideways, pressed against the mattress, his eyes closed and lips parted as he made the quietest sounds of pleasure. "You can answer me."

"Oh, I like it," he said, his voice barely audible. "You gonna spank me soon?"

"Maybe." I smiled. "Or maybe I'll just do this all fucking afternoon."

I repositioned my fingers to brush against his special spot, causing him to make a choking noise, but that wouldn't do. He was getting entirely too much pleasure from this. I removed my fingers with the delicacy of a cad and wiped them on a cloth.

"If you're a good boy, stay still for your spanking and hold off spending, I'll do that again. Or I'll fuck you, and make you shoot clear across this room."

"Oh," he whispered, "I don't know."

"Well, I don't care if you spend while I'm spankin' you or if you wait 'till I do something better. But even if you do spend, I still might play with you, and I still might stick my cock in you so's I can take my pleasure. I reckon that might not feel so good if you've already spent, so—"

"I don't care. I *want* you to!"

"Really?"

He squirmed o'er my lap, and he must have felt how this was affecting me.

"Yes, oh yes! Use me. Use me for your own pleasure. I love that."

"Hmm. All right."

"Oh *God.*"

"You be quiet now. Don't wanna ruin the peace of a beautiful Christmas Day with your caterwauling, just 'cause you're gettin' a hidin'."

Oscar moaned real loud then stifled it with a fist between his teeth. He glanced back at me, his eyes frantic.

"Ready?"

He nodded, then turned into the mattress, his fist still in his mouth.

I gave him a good one—a Christmas Day spanking that left him pink and desperate—and humping my leg like a randy elf. T'was hard for him to stay quiet, I could see that, and I let them little moans and grunts go, because I reckon t'was impossible to be completely silent when someone was spanking your ass like I was.

He came close to spending a few times, but he held off. And when I was ready, I slipped out from under him, slicked up my cock with saddle grease and went right into him, fucking him hard with a frantic passion I could hardly contain. I spent with a god-awful groan and plowed him until I was empty. I didn't know when or if he'd spent, to tell the truth. And truly, in that selfish moment, I didn't care.

I rolled off him and lay there, catching my breath, staring at the ceiling, seeing stars and praying to God that neither Clarence nor Irene had happened by to wish us a Merry Christmas. We really did need to get some curtains.

Oscar was silent and still, but I could see his back moving, so I knew he wasn't dead.

"Oscar."

He didn't answer me.

"Oscar, what're you doin'?" I asked.

"Layin' in a lake of my own spunk. What're *you* doin'?"

I gasped a laugh and hauled myself up onto my elbow, then ran my hand down along Oscar's spine until it rested at the top of his buttocks. In between was shiny with grease and a bit of my spend that had leaked out.

"You look freshly fucked."

"Hmm, I wonder why?"

"You gonna stay like that all day?"

"Maybe."

"C'mon. Get up, and I'll clean you off."

"That's only fair, I suppose."

I pumped a bit of water at the sink and cleaned myself, then took a cloth o'er to Oscar and tended him with such tender care that he shook his head at me.

"I ain't no china doll, y'know."

"I know. But I like to be careful, just the same."

"Uh, you just fucked me so hard I thought I was comin' apart."

I grinned. "Well, sometimes I like to cherish you and other times I like to wreck you. You seem to enjoy both so…"

He sat up and took my face in his hands. "I do, Jimmy. I surely do. You treat me so good. This is the best Christmas I've ever had. I know I don't have much to compare it to, but t'was a magical day."

"Yes, t'was. We make magic together."

He smiled. "Sometimes I think we could power a whole town with the force of our connection."

I laughed. "Maybe so. 'Tis potent enough."

Oscar noticed the open box with the pocket watch in it. He curled himself o'er so he could reach for it with this right hand. He scooped the gold trinket from its silk pillow and rolled himself back.

"This is so pretty, Jimmy. I love it," he said, playing the chain through his fingers and touching the gold case. He turned it o'er and ran the tips of his fingers along the engraving of his name.

"Oscar Theodore Yates." He grinned. "That's me."

"That's you."

He frowned. "Shame you couldn't put some kind of romantic declaration on it."

I smiled. "And what kind of romantic declaration would you have wanted?"

We both knew t'was impossible, but t'was fun to speculate.

"Hmm." He gazed at the roof, thinking. Then he brought his coy gaze to mine. *"One spank was never enough?"*

174

I threw back my head and chortled. When I'd gotten a hold of myself, I looked at him.

"Now that might raise some eyebrows, and 'tis true enough—but not really an appropriate sentiment for the back of a pocket watch."

"Well, if I can't have that, I'd just as soon only have my name." He gazed on the etched gold with a fondness that clearly came from somewhere deep inside him. "Truly, Jimmy, this is so special. I'll treasure it always."

"I'm glad. You deserve all the gold and trinkets in the world, Oscar. I'm glad I could give you at least one."

Chapter Thirteen

An Unexpected Encounter

A week passed before we decided to ride out to Clarence and Irene's again. The weather had turned on Boxing Day, with frigid winds from the north and more snow, so we'd stayed home and wiled away the hours making love and going o'er Oscar's letters. T'was not a bad way to spend a week, but we missed our new friends.

Oscar's reading and writing was coming along fine, and I was proud of him. Now and then he cursed whoever was behind such a complicated system, but mostly he bent his head to it without complaint. I'd started giving him some figures to do as well, which he seemed more inclined to than the language. He was good at counting and figuring in his head, and he simply needed the skills to put it on paper. But he was getting there.

I was mighty proud of myself, too, for my patience. I'd never figured myself for a teacher. But to do something for Oscar, to ensure he could make his way in society even if I wasn't around to help him? Well, that was an honest and worthwhile use of my time. I reckon my mama would have been proud of me, even if she might not have understood the love between Oscar and me. I don't suppose she would have begrudged me having it. She'd have been more appalled by the fact I'd spent so much time with ruffians and murderers, a fact that I was growing more and more ashamed of. Now that I'd seen my share of goodness in the world, I don't know what had possessed me to find my way with the likes of them. Immaturity and ignorance, I supposed — two of the most dangerous things a man had to deal with. At the time, it hadn't seemed like a choice I was making but rather a circumstance that had been thrust upon me in the name of survival. I was wondering more and more if that were true or simply a justification I'd used to ease my conscience. T'was true that I'd not had many opportunities to prove myself to anyone but those low-life's, but perhaps I should have searched some out instead of going along with them and believing their lies and subterfuges.

All of that was done and buried. I shook myself off from my reverie and picked up my hat.

"You wanna ride out to the Trelawneys' place?" I asked.

Oscar's head shot up and he threw down his pencil.

"Yes, sir, I sure do. I've had enough of this figuring for today."

"You have, have you?" I asked in a sardonic tone, raising one eyebrow.

Oscar shrugged. "I been working hard on it all morning. I reckon I deserve a break."

I sighed. "I suppose we both do. Now tidy up your work, and we'll head out."

As we rode through the peaceful woods, we listened to the horse's grunts and heavy breaths, the thud of their hooves on the snow accompanied by the occasional snap of a branch or twig, and the noises of woodland animals. Seems we weren't the only ones who'd decided to venture forth after the bad weather.

"'Tis a beautiful place, ain't it?" Oscar said, gazing about him from under the brim of his hat. "Sometimes I can't rightly believe how lucky we are to live here."

"Me neither. We've fallen on someone's kind graces, and that's a fact."

Oscar smiled at me as the air was split by a low growl and a sudden scream.

"Jesus, what the fuck was that?" he said, his smile disappearing as he struggled to control his horse.

Dixie shifted under me, too, unsettled and alarmed.

We were almost at the spot where the trees opened up onto Clarence and Irene's place, and a shiver traveled down my spine.

"Oh fuck. Come on!" I got control of Dixie and spurred her toward the sounds. We broke through the trees and into the clearing and faced a dismal sight.

A huge brown bear stood on all fours o'ertop of someone—Clarence, I reckoned—who lay in blood-drenched snow between the barn and the house. Movement drew my gaze to the door of the house as it opened, and Irene stepped onto the porch in a brown and red dress with a rifle on her shoulder.

All I could think for a god-awful second was that if Irene missed and only made that bear madder, she was gonna be next—or we were.

I pulled Dixie up and grabbed my rifle from the holster of my saddle, lifting it to my shoulder as a flash and a bang sounded ahead of me, then another.

The bear turned toward Irene and made a move to go after her, but I pulled my trigger and lodged a bullet in its neck, beside the one that Irene had already put there.

The bear screamed in pain and fury and turned as if to come for us. It took one step then fell to the snow as its lifeblood leaked out onto the white drifts like tipped paint on a snowy canvas.

"Clarence! Oh God! Clarence!" Irene hollered as she lowered her gun and ran forward.

I slid off Dixie and ran to Clarence. Irene had dropped to the snow, her hair loose and wild, her movements sure and quick as she checked him.

"He's alive, Jimmy!" Irene said as I approached. "But he's hurt."

She'd kneeled down in the snow and laid a hand on Clarence's cheek as she examined the rest of him.

"It's my leg. My thigh!" Clarence groaned, his lids fluttering as he tried to remain conscious. "Bastard got me good. Would've taken my balls if I had any..."

Irene glanced at me and said, "Shhh, it's all right. Jimmy and Oscar are here."

Clarence seemed to see me then and smiled weakly. "Good timing," was all he said before he passed out.

I was too busy attending to Clarence's wound to pay much attention to his words, and I figured he was in shock and might have said some things that didn't make sense. I didn't have time to analyze it or wonder what he'd meant. I pressed down on the bloodied cloth of Clarence's trousers to stay the bleeding.

"We need to get him inside."

"Is the bear dead?" Oscar said, holding Onyx's reins as he stood beside me and stared at the pile of brown and red fur with trepidation.

I followed his gaze and nodded. "Yep. He won't cause us any more trouble. Reckon he's caused enough." I looked at Irene. "I need a long cloth so's I can wrap his wound and stop the bleeding, then we'll get him into the house."

"All right."

While Irene was getting what I needed, I glanced at Oscar.

"You all right?"

"Well, my heart's goin' like a scared jackrabbit's, and I almost shit myself. But sure, I s'pose."

I gave him a grin. "I feel the same. Don't worry about it. We should be thankful Irene's a crack shot. She got him twice and he probably would've died without the bullet to his neck, although it didn't hurt. Well, it hurt him." I gestured to the bear.

"Fuck, Jimmy. Is Clarence gonna be all right?"

"I hope so. We need to get him inside and warmed up—and he needs a doctor."

"We got a doctor in town?"

"Yeah."

"How do you know?"

I stared at him. "Because I needed to find that out in case you got crushed by a tree or cut your hand off learning to chop wood."

Oscar's cheeks reddened. "You make it sound like I'm feeble as a girl."

"Girls ain't feeble. They're just not allowed to show their strength half the time. Anyway, I thought you liked feeling like that."

He blinked at me. "Between the sheets maybe, but not for regular everyday stuff."

"I just…needed to know who to go to if we needed more medical know-how than I've got to hand."

I took a chance and lifted the soaked fabric of Clarence's trousers where the bear's claw had torn it. I wanted to see how bad it looked. T'was right at the crease where his thigh met his groin, and while I was trying to get a look at the wound, Oscar pushed at my shoulder.

"Jimmy."

"What?" I examined the deep cut, trying not to let my dirty fingers get too close. I wasn't really paying attention to much else.

"Um, he ain't... There ain't no... I mean, I think Clarence ain't a fella."

Oscar's words seemed like nonsense, and I couldn't get what he was saying, so I turned to stare at him, my forehead wrinkled with confusion.

"What?"

Oscar pointed near to where I'd pushed back Clarence's trousers.

"There's no cock. That there's a cunt. I ain't seen that many, but I'm pretty sure."

The door opened, Irene rushed out and I only had time to glance at where Oscar was pointing before he stood and turned away, pretending to attend to his horse.

"Here, Jimmy. Will this work?" Irene said, shoving a torn length of sheet at me.

She glanced down to where Clarence was exposed and tried to cover him up while I pretended not to notice.

"Yeah. Thank you."

"I'm the one who's thankful, Jimmy. Thank God you and Oscar were here."

"You killed that bear, not me. He was already a goner when I shot him. Where did you learn to shoot like that?" I said, hoping to distract her while I wrapped Clarence's leg.

The gash was high up on the inside of his thigh, but I was able to wind the cloth around a few times and snug it up into the groin in order to fasten it. I wanted to do that before we moved him or we'd risk him losing too much blood.

"Clarence taught me to shoot, and t'was fun, so I practiced quite a bit o'er the summer. This is the first time I've shot something bigger than a fox."

"Well, you did real good. Now help me get him inside."

"I put a blanket down on the settee. We can put him there."

"All right."

Oscar looked after the horses while I helped Irene get Clarence comfortable on the settee by the fire.

"He's gonna need a doctor," I said.

"Oh, Jimmy. I don't think —"

"You want him to die?"

Irene gave me a look that made my blood run cold. "Of course not. But Clarence ain't one for doctors. Can't you tend to him?"

"I know a little bit. But, Irene —"

"Jimmy, Clarence can't be seen by a doctor," Irene stated in a tone of voice that brooked no debate

I stared at her, and she stared back at me.

"Is it because —?" I started to say.

"Clarence is more of a man than any other person I've met. He's my partner, and he's the love of my life. I don't care what you saw, or what you're going to see while you tend to my husband, but a doctor might care, and I don't know that I want that kind of attention. I'm sure Clarence won't."

I gazed at Irene, and for the first time she seemed like an exhausted and frightened girl. I put my now-clean hand on her shoulder.

"All right. I'll do my best."

"Thank you, Jimmy," she said, covering my hand with hers for an emotional moment.

I got her to boil some water as I unbuttoned Clarence's bloodied shirt and slid it out from under him. There was some kind of linen wrapped tight around him, and I glanced up as Irene came o'er, hoping she could tell I had questions.

"He uses it to bind his chest, so he looks like himself and not something else. I told him I don't care, and that his chest is pretty flat anyways, but he doesn't like moving around without it bound tight."

I was glad I'd gotten to know Cal at the Angel and she could explain to me herself how a person might feel that they'd been born into the wrong body, because I would have been more confused than I was about Clarence. I'd been taken by surprise, but the discrepancy between Clarence's intimate parts and his true self didn't bother me one bit.

"I understand. I've only ever known a woman who had male parts, though. I didn't know about the binding," I said, in an apologetic tone.

Irene blinked. "You know a woman who has a—?"

Oscar had come in, and he heard Irene.

"A cock. Yep. And a pair of balls bigger than anyone. 'Cause she don't care what anyone thinks, and she's just herself. That's Caliope. Only we call her Cal, for short."

Irene's lips parted and she gazed between us, hardly believing what we were telling her. "My goodness. It's nice to know Clarence isn't the only one, though I didn't suppose he was."

"Is Clarence all right?" Oscar asked.

"He's got a wound that needs to be stitched up, but he ain't gonna die, I don't think," I said with a glance at Irene. "He's only passed out."

"You want me to go for the doctor?" Oscar said.

I shook my head, glad for a second that I didn't have to send him to town on his own, though he could have done it, *would* have done it.

"Irene doesn't want the doctor. There'd be too many questions."

"Oh. Sure."

"So, I guess I'm gonna do it," I said, puffing some air out between my lips.

Irene and Oscar looked at each other, then at me.

"You ever done that before?" Oscar asked, and I reckon Irene wanted to know that, too.

"Yep. Back when I was running with outlaws," I said, deciding that with Clarence lying here injured and a bear dead in the snow outside, the secrets of my past could be revealed.

Irene gazed at me with tenderness. "Oh, Jimmy, did you spend a lot of time with them?"

I nodded. "Too much. But I did learn how to tend to wounds. We didn't have much access to doctors where we were, and I reckon they wouldn't have helped the likes of us, anyway."

I loosened the bandage to show Irene and Oscar what we were dealing with. There was a gash about three inches long, from the bear's claw, and it started oozing when I took the bandage off, but t'wasn't the pulsing-pouring of a fatal wound. T'was only a flesh wound, thank God, and I reckoned I could sew it up well enough. The real danger would be infection.

I looked at Irene. "It's not too bad. He's lucky."

"Thank God."

"Well, it ain't gonna kill him. Do you have a first-aid kit?"

"Yes! That's where I got the dressing from."

I nodded. "Good. It should have sutures and a needle. Can you please bring it here?"

"Yes," she said.

"I need you to boil some water and soak the needle in it for five minutes. And I need some water that's been boiled and cooled to wash my hands with, and some good, unused soap, if you've got it."

"Yes, Jimmy, I can get all of that."

I put two fingers to Clarence's throat. "He's got a strong pulse, and that's a good sign. And maybe 'tis good he's still unconscious, because this ain't gonna feel too good. Though it might wake him when I'm doing it. Maybe get some willow bark tea ready?"

"Of course."

"I can help," Oscar said.

They went to get what I'd need, and I kept pressure on Clarence's wound. The bleeding had stopped but I knew t'would start again when I went to sew it up. While I was sitting there, Clarence groaned and opened his eyes.

"What...? Am I...? Where's Irene?" Clarence muttered, licking his dry lips and trying to sit up. I placed a hand on his shoulder.

"Stay where you are. She's in the kitchen, boiling water."

Clarence gazed at me and sank back onto the settee. His gaze went to where the bandage was wrapped around his upper thigh, then back to me.

"I, uh, you're prob'ly wonderin' —"

I shook my head. "Don't matter."

He stared at me, assessing. "Well, I don't think so — and neither does Irene."

"And neither do Oscar or me. You're a man as much as we are."

Clarence blinked and stared at the beams above his head. "Thank you."

"You best wait to thank me. I gotta try to sew this wound up, because Irene won't let me get the doctor."

"Don't want no doctor if I can avoid it. T'would only add more trouble."

"I know it. So I'm gonna do my best and hope we don't need to bother him."

Clarence nodded. "I appreciate it."

I laughed to lighten the air in the room a bit. "Well, you might not. 'Tis gonna hurt like hell."

Clarence snorted. "I ain't afraid of pain, Jimmy. There's much more serious things to be afraid of in this world. Pain ain't one of them. If I can't take it, I reckon I'll pass out again."

"You want a piece of wood to bite on?"

"No, I'll be all right, but I might yell."

"You prob'ly will."

He looked at me, then glanced to where Oscar was helping Irene in the kitchen.

"You and Oscar are awful good friends."

My eyes flashed up from where I'd been looking, and Clarence met my gaze and held it. An unsettled feeling roiled in my belly.

"Well…I reckon we got pretty close while we were travelin' together," I said, in a measured tone.

"Mm-hm. I think you two are gonna need to work on your subterfuge."

I stared at Clarence as Irene and Oscar came back to the sitting room.

"Oh, Clarence!" Irene said, grabbing his hand and kissing him. "You're awake!"

"Mmm. Jimmy and I were discussing how he and Oscar need to work on bein' only friends in public."

Irene's lips parted as she threw her gaze my way, and Oscar and I exchanged an anxious glance.

"Well, now," Irene said, seeming unsure and a little taken by surprise, "I reckon we can talk about that once you're all sewed up."

"Hmph. Might as well tell 'em we know, so's they can relax and be themselves while they're here."

I cleared my throat. "Know? Know what?"

Goddammit. Had we already revealed ourselves? We hadn't been in Port Essington more'n two months, and we couldn't hide it.

Irene looked down, then faced us with a kind smile. "'Tis obvious the two of you are more than friends — least it is to us. But only because we're used to keeping Clarence's secret."

Oscar put his hand on my shoulder.

"Jimmy found me on the streets in Dawson City. He gave me a chance at a regular life, and I'm thankful for it."

Irene's smile widened. "I'm glad."

I cleared my throat. "We ain't ashamed of what…what we have."

Clarence wrapped his hand around my wrist and managed a smile for a second, though he was in some discomfort.

"Good. 'Tis plain as day how much you care for each other. I reckon most people will only see two good friends. But Irene and me? We picked up pretty early on that there was more to it than that." His grip loosened, and he sighed. "We're glad to know you, and you can be yourselves around us."

"Thank you," I said.

"And we think you're mighty sweet together, too," Irene added, grinning at Oscar, who blushed but seemed pleased with these developments.

"I'd best get to work," I said, needing to remind them that we had bigger things to worry about than whether Oscar and I kissed each other goodnight. "The bleedin's stopped for the most part. I'm gonna need to wash the wound with the water, though, and maybe a bit of brandy would be a good idea. The alcohol will kill the germs. T'will sting, though."

"I know," Clarence said.

"But this gash won't kill you, and I can sew it up pretty well. The risk is gonna be with infection," I said, getting some strips of bandage out of the kit Irene had brought. "You're gonna have to keep it as clean as you can. And take it easy for a while, so's you don't rip the stitches I put in. No chopping wood or hunting for a week or two."

Clarence nodded. "Sure."

I examined the gash and decided how best to go about sewing it up.

Oscar stood watching, Irene holding his arm and squeezing his hand as she looked on with a face full of worry. T'was too much and making me more nervous than I needed to be.

"Why don't the two of you play another concert for Clarence and me while I tend to him? T'will take your mind off things and give Clarence a distraction."

I'd told them not to mind if Clarence passed out. I didn't think he'd lost too much blood but he'd lost some, and now with the pain and the stress of it, he might just black out—but maybe not.

It took about twenty minutes to get that wound sewed up closed. I wanted to do it quick because I knew t'would hurt, but I also wanted to take my time and do it right.

In the end, he didn't black out and he didn't make much noise, just watched Oscar and Irene at the piano and lost himself in the music, hissing a few times when the needle caught on his skin. It had been a good idea to have Irene play.

When I was done, I wrapped his leg carefully in the surgical dressings and fastened some clean cloths o'er top.

When I'd finished, washed my hands and Clarence was resting comfortably, the relief of all that stress made me giddy, and I walked right up to Oscar where he was finishing a song and took him in my arms, holding him close and letting his warmth melt me. Irene got up from the bench and went to see to her husband.

"Jimmy, I knew there was something special about Irene and Clarence. I could tell."

I nuzzled into Oscar's neck, enjoying his comforting and familiar scent after what had been a harrowing afternoon.

"Seems an awful strange coincidence that we ended up bein' neighbors. I can't fathom it."

Oscar shrugged. "Maybe it's God saying he gave us kind neighbors who will know who we are to each other, even though we have to keep it a secret from everyone else." He took my face between his hands. "I reckon God forgives all those things you done when you were lost from his flock, and this is his way of showing it."

I blinked in surprise, trying to shake my head, but Oscar held me firm.

"But—but—it ain't that simple..." I protested.

"Ain't it? You've shown kindness and care to me, you brought me here and you convinced me to make a go of my uncle's land, and all while Clarence and Irene were here, just waiting for us. Seems pretty simple to me."

I tightened my arms around my precious boy and buried my face in his shoulder, hoping he was right, that God had forgiven me and had given us his blessing.

Chapter Fourteen

Friendship

Before we left, I built up the fire in the bedroom, and Oscar and I moved Clarence in there. I told Irene to keep Clarence's wound clean and dry and to apply fresh bandages every day. If we were lucky, it wouldn't become infected and would heal o'er the course of a few weeks. But she had to keep him from moving about too much, which seemed like it might be a challenge.

Oscar and I went o'er every day. We brought Poke, put him out in the paddock with the others and did the chores that needed doing in the barn and the house. I chopped wood and looked after the animals, and Oscar helped Irene with the washing and the cleaning, so she'd have more time to look after Clarence. We'd bring our washing o'er, too, and Oscar and Irene would do everything together and hang it up to dry in front of the fire, where Clarence spent his days on the settee, so he could see something other than the bedroom walls.

The wound did get better, and it didn't become infected. Irene had enough bear meat to make steaks and stews and all kinds of delicious meals. Oscar and I slept at our small kitchen-house but spent most of our time at their place. Now that they knew about us and we knew about them, we were comfortable in their presence and could be our true selves, only feeling obliged to conceal the strange games we got up to in private. They didn't need to know about *that*, and they might not understand. I decided t'was good to have *some* secrets.

Oscar and Irene became even closer friends, whispering and plotting together and making fun of me and Clarence. T'was nice to see Oscar bond with someone like Irene, who shared his optimism and his ability to find amusement in just about anything.

Clarence and I, though not as free with our affection, developed a bond, too. Seemed like stitching up someone's leg right next to their important parts brought two people together, especially when they shared a secret not to be divulged to anyone.

"You really kept it hidden your whole life?" I asked him one day, when Oscar and Irene were changing the bed sheets in the other room.

Clarence grunted. "Sure. I didn't want nothing to do with womanhood, and I ain't thought of myself that way since I was a child. My folks didn't care one whit. When we moved to a new town, they called me Clarence like I asked them to, and said 'he', and folks have accepted me ever since. Although, if it ever got out that my privates don't match, t'would be awkward." Clarence sighed. "Strange how people can be, ain't it, Jimmy?"

"'Tis. I don't understand it, and that's a fact. Seems like people should be allowed to be who they truly are and dress the way they like, even if 'tis just for fun but especially if 'tis because that's how they see themselves." I chuckled, remembering. "That girl we know at the cathouse in Telegraph Creek—Caliope—why, she dressed Oscar up in stockings and a basque and made him all pretty for me one time."

Clarence raised his brows. "My goodness." He glanced toward the bedroom and lowered his voice. "I bet he looked mighty fine. I can almost picture it."

I felt heat light my cheeks, remembering how I'd responded. "Yeah, well, he did look fine…and tempting. I—" I cleared my throat, going even redder. "I took him to bed right then and there, and I reckon we both had fun."

A gleam shone in Clarence's eyes. "I reckon you did."

"Everyone at The Angel knew what Oscar was to me, and they didn't bat an eye. I suppose they was all doin' things they weren't supposed to, living outside the law and society's expectations, so they didn't figure t'was all that strange."

Clarence frowned. "It ain't strange, but people make it seem so. 'Tis the most natural thing in the world to me and Irene, and I reckon to you and Oscar, too. I don't understand why most folks can't see that…or won't." He gazed at me with strong emotion. "I'm glad you came to Port Essington, and I'm glad you're our neighbors. Seems like it must have been fate or the work of God to throw us together, and I'm thankful."

"So'm I. You and Irene have been so welcoming. I ain't never—" I felt a lump in my chest. "I ain't never had real friends before, you know? What with bein' in the gang for so long. I feel like I missed out on a lot of stuff."

"I think you did. I'm sorry you had to live like that."

I nodded. "Yeah."

"And I'm glad you got away from that life, Jimmy. I think that God can forgive a lot of things, if you only make amends later."

"Maybe." I glanced up at him from where I was polishing some leather. "Do you really think so?"

"I do."

"Not sure I've made enough of them to cancel out all the terrible things I done," I said, confessing my fears.

"Jimmy."

I shook my head. "You don't know what I — ?"

"'Tis true, I don't. And I reckon I don't want to know. But it seems like you got caught up in that life because you didn't have many options, and you were taken advantage of by immoral men then stuck in a life that wasn't anything like you truly wanted."

I nodded, my heart heavy.

"But you can't do anything about the past. You can only change who you are now. And you've done that. Anyone can see it."

Laughter came from the bedroom, but Clarence continued.

"You know what I see?"

I lifted my eyes to him. "What?"

"When I watch you with Oscar and see you helping out around here?"

I shook my head slowly.

"I see a man who has witnessed a lot of inhumanity, knows what true cruelty and malice is and what it looks like, who wants to distance himself from all of it. I see a man who loves with his whole heart and would stop a bullet for his love if he had to — and has devoted himself to caring for others whenever he can."

I felt emotion build up inside me, because that was truly who I was trying to be, and I hadn't been sure I'd succeeded. I shrugged, afraid to speak, else I might start to sob. And I wasn't ready to share that part of myself with Clarence. I'd barely shared it with Oscar.

"You saved my life, Jimmy. And from what Oscar's told me, you've saved his life o'er and again. And by loving and cherishing him, you've brought that young man more happiness than he ever dreamed he could have." Clarence's eyes were bright with sincerity and emotion. "You've *made* amends. And you need to believe that God sees that."

I blinked fast and turned my head away, my hands balled into fists because I was trying so hard to control myself.

"Thank you," I managed to whisper, before the bedroom door opened and Oscar came out wrapped up in white sheets.

"Jimmy, look! Irene's made me into a bride!"

I wiped my eyes quick with a fist and grinned, looking at Oscar all fancied up like a maiden on her wedding day, if a white sheet could replace yards of satin.

"My, my, my," I said, my voice only a little shaky, "don't you look lovely."

Clarence laughed. "My goodness, you make a beautiful bride, my boy."

"Ain't I?" Oscar said, preening and posing. Then he stopped still and stared at me, with eyes big and round. "Would you marry me, Jimmy? If I was a girl?"

I blushed again, even though my cheeks were still flushed from my conversation with Clarence. "I reckon I would, though I can't imagine it."

Oscar laughed. "No, me neither." He sighed. "I wish I could marry you, even though we're both men. Seems unfair that I can't."

I walked o'er to him and took his hands, then kissed him sweetly and pulled back, gazing into his eyes that were as pretty and full of emotion as any girl's. "I reckon we are married, Oscar. In the eyes of God, at least, and that's what matters, ain't it?"

Oscar's lips parted and he nodded. "I reckon."

Then Irene clapped her hands together. "I just had the most marvelous idea!"

"Oh no," Clarence said.

Oscar and I held each other's gazes and listened as Irene continued.

"Who's to say we can't have a wedding?"

Oscar and I turned to look at her.

"What?" I said.

"Woman," Clarence began, "what are you saying?"

Irene walked o'er to Clarence and sat on the settee next to him, taking his hand. "I don't see why we can't have a little wedding, here in the house, for Oscar and Jimmy." She looked o'er at us. "If they want one."

We gazed at each other, Oscar and me, with shy smiles.

"What do you think?" I asked.

Oscar raised his chin. "I reckon you'll need to ask me properly."

I rolled my eyes. "I ain't got a ring—"

"I don't need a ring. But t'would be nice if you got down on one knee and asked me to marry you. Then I *might* say yes." He gave Irene a conspiratorial look. "Or I might say no."

"If I get down on one knee, you better not say no, Oscar Yates."

"Well?"

I sighed. I glanced at Clarence and Irene, but they didn't offer me any way out of this.

"Fine," I said.

I got down on one knee and took Oscar's hand in mine.

"Oscar Yates, will you make me the happiest man in Port Essington and marry me? Soon, mind you, because we been livin' in sin for a long time, and I want God to be on our side."

"I reckon God's been on our side since I met you," Oscar said. "And, yes, of course I'll marry you, Jimmy Downing."

He cupped my face, went down on both knees and kissed me full on the lips, slow and sensuous, with Irene and Clarence watching. I heard clapping, and I figured they must approve.

When he pulled back, he narrowed his eyes. "But I ain't wearin' a dress, though."

* * * *

A couple of days later, while I was stoking the fire in Clarence and Irene's sitting room after stacking more wood against the side of the house from a morning spent chopping, Clarence spoke up from his place on the settee.

"Jimmy."

"Yeah?"

"I was just wonderin'. Does Oscar know how to shoot?"

I frowned. "Well, yes and no. I got him a revolver that he carries around when I'm not with him — like, if he goes ridin' without me. But he ain't never learned how to shoot a rifle."

As I spoke, I realized t'was a serious oversight, out here in the middle of the wilderness, to not know how to shoot a rifle, when bears could attack you out of nowhere when you were walking from the house to the barn to feed your stock.

"Hmm," Clarence said.

"You reckon I should teach him."

"Well, all I know is, if I hadn't taught Irene to shoot a rifle, the two of us might not be having this conversation."

"True enough. I meant to teach him. I just forgot."

"How about I teach him?"

"You wanna teach Oscar to shoot?"

"Jimmy, I gotta do something or I'm gonna go stark ravin' mad, sitting here on the settee all day. You figure I can at least start walking outside a bit?"

"I s'pose. T'would probably be good for those muscles to get some movement."

Clarence inclined his chin. "I thought so. Anyway, if I'm teaching Oscar how to use a rifle, it won't tax my lower half too much."

I thought about it. "Well, walkin' in the snow is tricky, but I s'pose I can shovel a space for the two of you in front of the house and set up some targets. You got some empty bottles or cans around?"

"I'm sure we do."

"All right, then. It's a deal."

T'was a good idea. I had my hands full doin' all of Clarence's chores and looking after five animals. We'd brought Poke o'er so they'd all be together while we were spending most of our time here. It would be something for Clarence to do if he could tear Oscar away from Irene for a spell.

I made sure I'd finished the morning chores the next day before I shoveled a space in front of the house and set up some bottles on a turned-up log. I didn't want to be walking around the barn and whatnot with Oscar perfecting his aim.

The first lesson went pretty well. I was inside for most of it, shining up some of the horse tack and trying not to think about those other things we used the saddle grease for. T'was a peculiar thing to open a jar and immediately feel your cock rising. I mentally told it to settle down, and got to work, while Clarence and Oscar went outside and the lessons began.

The rifle cracked, and I glanced at the window.

Oscar stood beside Clarence, frowning. He held the rifle pointed at the ground and rubbed his shoulder, staring at the target.

Yeah, the kick was something you had to be ready for. T'was always a bit of a surprise when you first learned.

Clarence pointed at the log and smiled. Seemed like Oscar had hit one of the bottles on his first try. I watched him fire the rifle twice more. His stance was good, but he missed. Anyway, he'd get it.

"How is he doing?" Irene asked, glancing up from her sewing. She was working on the skirt of a very fancy dress that a lady living in Banff had commissioned.

"All right. I reckon he'll be as good as you some day."

"Oh, Jimmy," she said, resting her hand on the luxurious fabric, "I was so scared."

She'd gone white as a sheet, and I could see the leftover fear plain as day in her wide eyes.

"T'was a lucky shot, that one in the neck. And I was ready to shoot again, but then you were there, and you got him good. Thank God."

I put the bridle down and wiped my hands, then went o'er and touched her arm. "Coming face to face with that kind of thing can be traumatizing."

"Yes," she said, her voice barely more than a breath. She nodded at the window. "It's a good idea to teach Oscar. You never know what you might be up against out here."

"True enough." I followed her gaze and saw Oscar lift the rifle to his shoulder again. He seemed to be enjoying himself, though he'd be sore tomorrow.

"When we were coming into Port Essington," I said, "just about six miles out, maybe more, we were set upon by a pack of wolves."

I'd never told anyone about that. Only Oscar and I knew how close I'd come to losing him.

"Oh, Jimmy, what did you do?"

I sat down, picked up the cloth I was using on the leather and started rubbing the grease into the bridle strap. "Only thing we could, which was try to get to the trees and into some cover. I was planning to find a place we could turn and face them, with some protection at our back. But we didn't make it that far."

Irene put a hand to her mouth.

"They brought Oscar's horse down, and—" I took a shuddering breath. "When I saw him tumble off and the wolves attacked that horse, I rode o'er and grabbed him, though I expect he would have gone after those wolves if I hadn't. He was so mad that they were killing his horse right in front of him. But I pulled him up onto Dixie with me and rode like hell to the trees, and I ain't never been more thankful in my life."

"Oh, Jimmy," Irene whispered.

"That horse…Sprite was his name — well, he kept the wolves busy so that we could get to safety. Then they were so busy eatin' him they didn't bother us again."

I gave Irene a hard stare.

"But I'm telling you, I don't know what I'd have done if they'd got Oscar. I probably would have fought them with my bare hands and ended up dead as well."

Irene stared at me, her face pale. "It's plain to see you love him."

"I ain't —" I began, then swallowed. "I ain't never felt so much for another person in my life. Sometimes it scares me."

Irene gave me a weak smile. "I feel the same about Clarence. If anything had happened to him —"

We gazed at each other, long and silent for a minute.

"Well, we got each other now, don't we?" I said, trying to make light of the turn the conversation had taken, but making a good point. "The four of us. If anything were to happen, God forbid, there'd be people to lean on."

"Amen to that, Jimmy Downing. I reckon it's good to have true friends."

I nodded, and we were silent as we went back to our work.

"Now then, let's talk about something more cheerful," Irene said after a bit. "When do you want to have this wedding?"

I blinked. "I — Well, I don't know. Shouldn't we wait until spring? Maybe we could have a little ceremony out front of your place."

Irene frowned. "I don't know. I'd be mighty nervous doing it in plain sight, though it would be pretty. We don't get many visitors, that's true, but what if someone were to come across the two of you. I don't think I want to risk it."

"All right," I said. "I agree, 'tis safer to do it inside."

She smiled then. "That means we could do it as early as next week!"

"Now hold on a minute—"

The door opened and Oscar stomped his boots in the entryway. "Jimmy, I got a shooting arm as good as you now!"

I rolled my eyes. "I doubt that."

He frowned, moving forward as Clarence came in behind him. "Well, I hit lots of bottles. Didn't I, Clarence?"

Clarence laughed. "You did pretty good, son. You should be proud."

Oscar crossed his arms. "I am proud…but he's not." He jerked his chin at me with a scowl.

"What?" I said, raising my arms. "Sure I am."

He narrowed his eyes at me. "But you don't think I'm as good as you."

"Oscar, I been shooting rifles since I was eight years old and hunting since I was ten."

He put his hands on his hips. "Well, ain't you somethin'." He stood up straighter then and tipped the brim of his hat forward. When he spoke, his voice was low and lazy.

"Hello, my name's Jimmy Downing, and I grew up in the wilderness and ran with outlaws and now I'm the sharpest shooter in the West. Nobody can match me."

I couldn't help smiling, and Irene laughed outright as Clarence chuckled.

"Oh, you got him down," Irene said. "That's Jimmy, sure enough."

I hoped they were joking.

Then I saw a smile under that tipped-down brim and sure enough, Oscar peeked at me from underneath it with so much mischief in his gaze that I coulda bottled and sold it.

"That's very amusin'."

"Ain't it?" Oscar grinned and shucked off his boots, then walked o'er and flung himself onto my lap. I had to move the bridle I was working on and grumbled a bit as I made room.

"Maybe I ain't as good a shot as you, Jimmy, but I reckon I'll learn to be if I keep practicing."

"Hmm. Maybe."

"Awe, Jimmy. Come on and kiss me."

I felt the heat in my cheeks as Clarence cleared his throat and Irene giggled.

"Not in front of everyone."

"What? Why?" Oscar said, as if he couldn't make any sense of it. "'Tis only Clarence and Irene."

"He's right, Jimmy," Irene said. "We don't care what the two of you do together in front of us, so long as you keep your trousers on." She looked deliberately at Oscar. "Both of you."

"Well, hell, you ain't no fun, Irene." Oscar stuck his tongue out at her, and Irene did the same. They were two peas in a pod, for certain.

"Jimmy and I were just discussing the wedding," Irene said.

"Oh yeah? Well, there ain't gonna be one if he don't kiss me…right now."

"Fine."

I rolled my eyes, then cupped Oscar's chin and planted my lips on his, forcing his mouth open and giving him what he'd asked for, and more. When we pulled apart, he stared at me with an expression of surprise so comical that I had to laugh.

"What? That's what you wanted, right?"

He wiped his lips with the back of his trembling hand as he nodded. "Um, Jimmy, you reckon there's some things we need to attend to at our place this afternoon?"

I blinked. I knew just what things he was referring to, and I supposed we probably *did* need to attend to them.

I cleared my throat. "Oh. Yeah, that's true. I oughta— I mean, we need to—"

"The wedding?" Irene said, her hands on her hips and eyes raised, though I could see the amusement on her face.

"And I need my settee back, if you don't mind," Clarence said, moving stiffly into the room as Oscar and I scrambled to get up.

"Irene, could we maybe talk about the wedding tomorrow?" Oscar pleaded. I could see he was eager to be alone with me, and that made me a little desperate, too.

Irene rolled her eyes. "Fine. Go and have your fun. Clarence and I will pretend we don't know exactly what you're doing over there."

My mouth dropped open, and Oscar looked shocked.

"B-but...how c-can you—?" Oscar stuttered.

"I've heard things, you know. I reckon a lot more goes on behind closed doors than most folks would think. Also, I grew up on a farm. When a male animal can't get at a female for whatever reason, he improvises." She waggled her eyebrows, as if that statement weren't the most illuminating thing I'd ever heard. I'd never seen two male animals go at each other, but I s'pose it probably did happen.

"Uh, yeah, we're gonna go now," I said, getting my boots and coat on quick while Oscar did the same, except he kept turning to glance back at Irene.

"Will you be here for supper?" Irene asked.

"Try to," I said, then I pulled Oscar out of the door behind me, and we slammed it shut and headed to the paddock.

"How much you suppose she knows, Jimmy? About what we do together?"

I clicked my tongue. "God knows. But that woman ain't no fool. I reckon she can figure it out."

Oscar broke into hysterical laughter as I unlatched the gate and whistled for the horses.

Chapter Fifteen

A Country Wedding

Oscar barely let me get inside after we'd turned out the horses in the paddock at our place. He attacked me and started pulling off my coat and unbuttoning my trousers while I tried not to fall on top of him.

"Hold on. Hold on. We need to set a fire in the stove."

T'was barely warmer than outside, but we were so hot for each other we didn't feel it much. I reckoned once we got naked we would, though. I'd had the foresight to restock the wood basket by the stove before we'd started to spend most of our time at the Trelawneys', so t'was only a matter of throwing some logs in atop some kindling and getting it to catch. While I took care of that, Oscar lit the oil lamp on the bedside table, since clouds had come in and t'was dark and gloomy. Then he shucked all his clothes and took himself in hand, watching me while he stroked himself idly.

"That's very distractin'," I said, as I dusted the dirt off my hands and went to the sink. I pumped some cold water from the well to clean myself and wet a cloth for Oscar.

"Here," I said, throwing it at him. "Wipe your bits and under your arms. You're startin' to stink."

He caught it and gave me a look. "Yeah, well, you don't smell all that wonderful, either, 'cept I'm a sucker for a dirty man."

"I guess we oughta take Irene up on her offer to let us have baths at the house. I s'pose the embarrassment will be tempered by how nice it feels."

"I suppose so. T'would be nice to have a proper bath," Oscar sighed.

I dried my hands and walked o'er to where Oscar was sitting up, swiping the cloth under his arms and freshening up.

"Here," I said, holding out my hand. I'd already pushed my suspenders down and taken off my shirt, so I was only in trousers, socks and union suit that was open to my waist.

Oscar passed the cloth to me with his eyebrows raised.

"Now get on all fours and I'll clean the important bits."

Oscar whistled a breath in. "Okay."

He turned o'er and braced himself on hands and knees as I rinsed the cloth in the water and got some of the nice lemon soap on it.

"Spread your legs."

My voice sounded gruff, and Oscar obeyed me like he was born to it, presenting himself to be washed, which I took my goddamn time doing.

T'was a pleasure to tease him with the soapy cloth and at the same time make him presentable. Don't know who I'd present him to like this, except for myself, but that was reason enough to be thorough. Just because we lived in the middle of the wilderness didn't mean we were animals.

First, I cleaned his cock while he complained of the coldness of the cloth, then I wiped around his balls — slowly and carefully — both to tease him and do the job. Then I went and dipped the cloth again to get it nice and wet and I rinsed the soap off those same spots.

"Oh — Jimmy. Gawd."

His cock was harder than ever and didn't seem to care about the temperature.

"Mmm. Gotta get you shiny clean, boy."

"Fuck," he groaned. "Okay."

I went back to the sink and wet the cloth again, getting more soap onto it. I stood behind him, feeling the urge to say to hell with it and just fuck his dirty ass, but I supposed spending time with regular, respectable folks was having an effect on me...or maybe not.

"Spread 'em nice and wide, now. I want you to put your front down on the bed, reach behind you and spread your cheeks with your fingers so's I can clean you properly."

I was breathless with the sense of control and my shameless demands. Oscar's breath hitched and he shivered.

"Yes, sir," he said, and did what I'd asked.

My cock fought against the buttons of my trousers when he snaked his hands back and snuck his fingers between his ass cheeks, pulling the flesh apart to reveal his sweet pink crack and the tempting wrinkled circle that promised so much pleasure.

I sighed a curse and lifted the cloth in my trembling fingers.

"Now stay still."

"Okay."

His voice was barely a whisper, and I expected his eyes were wide, although I couldn't see them — mostly because I couldn't take my own off his pretty pink hole, which looked clean enough, really. But I figured t'was better to be safe, and hell, this was fun — and dirty, and completely reprehensible. I reckon we both loved it.

Oscar made sharp little gasps as he waited for me to start. His thigh muscles quivered with anticipation.

"Jimmy? What are you doin'?" he asked.

"I'm just lookin'," I admitted.

"Why?"

"'Cause you look so sweet and so damn filthy at the same time, holdin' yourself open for me. Your little pink hole is so pretty, Oscar. I love it so much."

He turned his head and gave a raspy little laugh. "I reckon you should put that in our wedding vows."

"Stop it."

"You gonna touch me or what? I ain't got all day."

I raised my eyebrows. "Oh, you ain't?"

"Well, I don't —"

"What if I wanna take all day with you? What if I wanna spend this whole dang afternoon running this cloth o'er every inch of you and following it with kisses? Hmm? What then?"

He moaned and closed his eyes. "Well, then I — I suppose I'd have to shut up and take it, wouldn't I?" He swallowed thickly.

"Yeah, I suppose you would. Now be quiet and let me do this."

"Yes, sir. I will. I'll be good, I —" He gasped and cried out as I drew the cloth o'er his hole with a rough swipe, then repeated the motion. "Oh, fuck!"

He clenched every time I did it and started rocking. T'was pretty obvious he liked it.

"Oh, Jimmy."

"Shh-h."

I used the soapy cloth to clean him up good and thorough, while he gasped and groaned and let me, until I couldn't stand it no more. I dropped the cloth and nudged his fingers aside so's I could hold him open, and I went at that pretty pink hole with my tongue and my mouth, tasting soap and water and Oscar, slurping and biting at him like the animal I'd claimed I wasn't.

I don't know if it made me a better man or a worse one that I'd never put my mouth to any of the whores I'd bedded. In fact, most of the time I'd only paid for them to use their hands or their mouths on *my* parts. On the odd occasion, if I'd had enough coin, I'd taken my pleasure all the way with one of them, but they had to be real pretty and real friendly for me to do that. I'd only ever done it if they had them French things that would make sure we didn't catch diseases from one another and that the girl didn't get with child. I was careful in my dealings, because the last thing I'd wanted was to complicate a woman's life, especially a woman who found herself working in a cathouse to make a living. Since Oscar was so young, I hadn't worried about catching anything from him, and since then, I'd learned he'd been careful, too. He'd only ever engaged in the act of sodomy with people he'd trusted and, like me, had focused more on the safer pastimes. The last thing either of us had wanted was to shorten our lives or make them more miserable than they were already, by contracting some god-awful disease.

Now that Oscar had turned me on to what I was truly into, it seemed I couldn't stop myself from wanting to eat him up, like I was the big bad wolf, and he was Little Red Riding Hood. I lapped at his hole, tongued it, shoved at it and made Oscar yelp and groan and shudder. I ran my nose along his cleft and rubbed my stubbled chin on him. I wanted to cover my face with his scent and claim him like that.

I trailed my fingers o'er his hips and down to grip his slim thighs, poking with my tongue and licking around his balls, even pretending I was gonna take a bite of them in order to give him that little bit of fear he craved, before I suckled them with the most tender care and teased him until he was a sweating, panting mess.

"Jimmy! Jimmy, oooh, Jimmy," he groaned, squirming in such a way t'was all I could do not to grab my cock and finish right there, kneeling on the bed behind him.

"You want me to fuck you?" I said. "Or you want me to suck on your little nubby till you explode and flood my mouth?"

Geez, I really hoped Irene could not imagine anything close to this, 'cause t'was right indecent.

"Oh gawd. Oh gawd."

"That ain't an answer."

"I don't know! Both, Jimmy. *Both*!"

"All right then. I'm gonna fuck you and fill you up with so much seed your belly's gonna swell like you're with child. If you can keep from spendin'" — I squeezed his thigh hard — "an' you better — then I'll suck on your nubby and make you spend that way, if you want."

"Fuck, yes. Yes, I do. *Please*!"

"All right." I slapped his ass. "Roll o'er then. And hold your knees."

Oscar gasped and got into position so fast I could hardly believe it. If I hadn't been so overcome with desire, I would have laughed. But when he lifted his legs and held them, spreading himself open like a wishbone, I could hardly think straight.

"Goddammit," I said, getting my trousers off and unbuttoning my union suit like a man possessed. "So many fucking buttons!"

"Hurry up," Oscar panted. "Please!"

Finally, I got it undone far enough I could get my dick out. I gave it a few pulls, just staring at Oscar and that hot, slick place I was gonna be in a minute. I grabbed the grease and got another dollop out, rubbing it all o'er my cock and trying not to groan.

"God, I always forget how big your dick is."

I grinned and raised my eyebrows. "I sure do love to remind you."

He nodded, spreading his knees farther. "Come on, Jimmy. I'm gonna die."

"You ain't gonna die. Nobody dies from not getting fucked quick enough."

He narrowed his eyes at me. "How do you know?"

"I know lots of things," I said, leaning forward and placing my dick where it needed to go. "You keep them hands on your thighs. Don't you dare touch yourself, Oscar."

"I won't. I won't. Only fuck me now. Plea—"

I breached him in one firm push, which cut off his begging and caused a sharp gasp that became a deep-throated groan as I slid all the way in in one smooth motion.

"Oh, fuck. Oh, Jimmy." He cried out. "Yes. Oh, yes. Oh, gawd."

I was as desperate as he was, and I found a quick and punishing rhythm, living for his soft cries and curses and yelps.

"You like this, Oscar? You like me just taking my own pleasure, no matter what?"

"Oh fuck. Just use me, Jimmy. Do whatever you gotta do to get off."

Well, since that was the case, I wasn't gonna drag it out, even though he felt so good I kind of wanted to. But I'd waited too long to get inside him, and I was so close to spending. For once I wanted to just let it rip and not be concerned about him — and he'd given me permission.

All of a sudden, the thought of it, of using him as a vessel for my lust and my pleasure, made me crazy.

"You take it, boy. Take this cock, and you'll take my seed when I give it you, won't you — and thank me after?"

Oscar made the most endearing whimper as he pulled his knees to his chest, blinking up at me like I was some stranger he'd created from his own imagination — which, maybe I was at this moment. Strands of sweat-damp hair fell o'er his cheek and forehead, his face red and glowing with his enjoyment at being used and debased in such a way.

"I'll take it. I'll take it all, whenever you need to give it."

I groaned and fucked him faster, harder, until I my breaths came in harsh gasps.

"I'm gonna fill you with my seed, boy. Fill up your little belly so full, you'll — "

Oscar threw his head back and cursed so loud that the sound tore through my body and gave me just what I needed. I plunged deep and stilled as I saw stars when the sensations took me o'er. I spent without a worry as to Oscar's pleasure, only concerned with my own and how using him made me feel — and with the realization that he'd let me do this, given me permission to be selfish and act like an animal what only wanted to breed and didn't care about anything else or understand that t'was impossible.

We could pretend t'was something that could happen if we tried hard enough. I'd give him all my babies if I could, though he'd make a questionable mother.

A strange sound bubbled up from me as I lay spent between Oscar's thighs, as Oscar squirmed and grunted. T'was exhausted amusement at the turn my thoughts had taken.

"Oh gawd. Oh gawd, Jimmy. I need to come. I almost came just then, knowing you'd spent in me. That was so dirty and good."

I opened one eye and glanced at him, feeling lazy and sated and in no rush to return the favor.

"You'll come when I'm good and ready to get you off."

He inhaled a breath and stilled, his ass clamping down on me as he gave a frantic cry, and I felt his spend, hot and gushing between us. I held him through his spasms then watched as he collapsed like a rag doll into the bedsheets.

"Oh, Oscar," I said.

"I'm sorry. I'm sorry."

I lifted myself up on one elbow and traced Oscar's lips with the tip of my finger. "I reckon you're gonna be."

His eyes widened. "What?"

"You know I gotta spank you now."

He shuddered. "You do?"

"I do," I said. "You were supposed to wait until I had my mouth on you."

"I know it. I tried!"

"Maybe I gotta give you proper motivation," I said, sitting up and pulling him with me, ignoring the mess on both of us. I arranged him o'er my lap and smoothed my palm o'er his sweet, pale buttocks.

He gazed back at me from the mattress, his head sideways on the sheet. "Can you hold my wrists?" He reached his arms back and crossed his arms.

"Sure. That's a good idea. It'll keep you from escapin'."

I grinned and took his slim wrists in one hand, feeling all the urges I'd tamped down while we'd been at Clarence and Irene's break free in a wild temptation to do everything that tempted me before we went back. I didn't know what time t'was, and I didn't care. Hopefully we'd make it back for supper, with Oscar's ass pink and sore from the spanking—and maybe another fucking.

* * * *

Turned out we did make it back, a bit later than we'd planned. From the look Irene gave me, I expect she knew what had kept us—or at least had a general idea.

She didn't know that Oscar's buttocks were pink and tender, or that I'd left another load inside him that had dribbled out in bits o'er the course of the hour we'd waited before starting back, so's he wouldn't stain his union suit. I figured if there was any miraculous chance Oscar *could* get with child, it'd be from today.

Oscar walked with a distinct swagger, as if he'd pulled *me* o'er his knee and given *me* the hiding of a lifetime and not been the recipient of my hand, which, to be honest, was a bit sore. Not as sore as Oscar's ass, though. T'was hard to believe that Oscar could walk, to be fair, after the pounding his behind had taken from my hand and my cock, let alone prance about like he owned the fucking world.

I saw Irene watching him with her hand on her hip and a certain knowing in her eyes. I swear, nothing could get past that woman.

"Oscar, you're dancing about like the Queen of Sheba. I take it you had a nice afternoon?"

At least he had the courtesy to blush. "I did. How was yours?"

Irene glanced at Clarence. "T'was fine. Only probably not as fun as yours."

"I got a bum leg, woman. Jesus," Clarence grumbled.

"Uh-huh," Irene said. "I don't see anything wrong with your hands."

I almost choked on my own spit. Clarence turned bright red and gave Irene a look. Then he turned to me.

"I'm not so sure I can recommend marriage, Jimmy. Not at this moment."

Irene laughed, hearty and full, and it filled me with warmth and gaiety.

"I expect the wind was high on your way over. Your hair looks awfully unkempt," she said to Oscar, then put a finger to her chin in contemplation and narrowed her eyes. "Though you would have worn a hat—"

Oscar ran his fingers through his hair. Perhaps we should have tidied up more before we came back, but we were worried we'd be late.

"Naw, my hair's just gettin' too long. Needs a trim, I s'pose."

Oscar's hair was awfully long. T'was starting to get in the way and easily tangled, though it still looked all right.

"I've got a pair of shears. If you like, I can give your hair a trim after supper. Jimmy's, too."

We looked at each other and shrugged.

"Sure," Oscar said. "I s'pose it wouldn't hurt."

After a delicious meal of bear steaks, mashed potatoes and turnips, Irene set up the straight chair in the kitchen, sat Oscar down with a cloth o'er his shoulders and got to work.

I was sitting in the living room with Clarence, talking about the horses and how we needed to get Dixie re-shoed in the spring, and when he'd start working at the blacksmith's again. T'was so warm and cozy in that room I plumb forgot what Irene and Oscar were up to until a strange looking young man came in the room and grinned at me.

"What the—" I said, standing up. "What the *hell?*"

Oscar's smile wavered. He lifted a hand to his head. "Don't you like it?"

I barely recognized him.

Irene had shorn most of his long hair off. T'was cut so close on the side and around his ears that he seemed a different person. I was speechless. I gaped at him, trying to decide what I thought of it, until Irene came forward and spoke to Clarence.

"What do you think?"

"Looks good. I think it's just a shock to poor Jimmy, that's all."

Now that I was becoming accustomed to it, I did like it. The cut made him look older and younger at the same time. His mouth looked too big for his face in the most charming way. His wide brown eyes popped now that they weren't competing with his hair. I'd forgotten that his eyelashes were so long. Even with the shorn hair he looked pretty, with those plump lips and his pale complexion that reddened so easy. He seemed vulnerable and more delicate now his slim neck was exposed.

"You look—" My mouth had gone dry. He looked so good but so damn different. "You look good. You look—younger, I think?"

"Really?" he said, fluttering his eyelashes. "How much younger?"

Good God. I really didn't want to think about that. He'd looked young enough before, and now he looked even more like a kid. T'was distracting in a way I didn't want to think about.

I shrugged, not answering.

Clarence laughed. "You do look a bit like a fresh-faced youth, Oscar. I s'pose when you're forty and you look thirty, that'll be a good thing."

Oscar snorted. "Forty? You think I'll live that long?"

"Jesus, Oscar," I said, not wanting to think about any other possibility, "I sure hope so."

"Yeah, me, too, I guess. There were times I didn't think I'd make it to twenty, honest to God. But I've got you, now, and we seem to be doin' all right. Maybe there's hope for me."

"Sure there is," Irene said, reaching up to tousle what was left of his hair. "Anyway, it's your turn, Jimmy. Come and sit in this chair, please."

"Fine." I supposed I could use a bit of a trim. "I only need a little taken off."

"So, not as short as Oscar's? He did ask for that, you know."

"Oh, I see. No, you can go that short if you want. I'm used to having it like that. I just wasn't prepared to see Oscar with his hair so short."

"He's a very handsome young man."

"Yes, he is. More 'n I deserve, really."

Irene came around in front of me, frowning. "Well, now, Jimmy Downing, you're not exactly hard on the eyes, either."

I laughed and said, "Sure," although I didn't truly believe her. I still thought t'was a miracle that Oscar found me fetching.

Irene grabbed the looking glass from the counter and held it in front of me. I started in shock, seeing my face in it so close.

"You think that isn't a handsome face? *Psht*. You two are gonna have all the girls in Port Essington in a tizzy."

I didn't want to look at myself because I saw my brother Robert in that reflection, too — which only made me think about all of the mistakes of my past again.

"Well, I hope not," I said, as Irene put the looking glass down and went back to her trimming. "Won't it seem strange that we're not on the prowl for wives?"

"I suppose. You'll have to come up with some reason why you're not interested in that," she said. "Could be as simple as liking the bachelor life and not wanting to be tied down. Say you want to keep your options open for future travel, and you have no interest in having children."

"Yeah, which is true enough unless Oscar was able." I grinned. "I swear, if I could get him with child, I would."

"Not for lack of trying, I'll bet. But I know what you mean. Sometimes I think t'would be nice if I could bear Clarence's child. But, then again, we like our life here, and we have time to be with each other with no distractions."

"True enough."

"I reckon there are enough children in the world. Maybe too many. Cities are getting awfully crowded now, and the world's changing so much. Why, I heard that some people in Vancouver have automobiles! Imagine that. And I thought the railroad was strange."

"Land sakes. I heard about them things. Seems awful dangerous."

"Yes, they do. I'll stick to horses. They're nicer, anyhow."

When Irene had finished my hair cut, she took the towel off and wiped my neck, then shooed me out to the living room so she could sweep up the floor.

Oscar glanced up from his seat beside Clarence. He had his slate and slate pencil in hand. We'd brought it to show Clarence and Irene how much he'd learned.

"Oh, Jimmy, you look so good! Not that you looked bad before, but you look so professional now."

"Professional? What the hell do you mean by that?"

"Why, like a fine gentleman, that's all," he said. "Anyhow, look what I wrote!"

He passed me the slate. On the blacking, in capital letters, was written JIMMY.

I blinked down at the neat letters. "That's very good, Oscar."

"Clarence helped me to know what letters to put down," he said.

"Here... Give me the pencil," I said, holding out my hand.

"Why? It's spelled right, ain't it?"

He passed me the slate pencil. In my careful hand I wrote OSCAR underneath JIMMY and gave it back to him.

"That's *my* name, ain't it?" he said in hushed tones.

"Yes, it is. That's us, together...always."

* * * *

Irene and Clarence held our wedding ceremony the following weekend. T'was a bit of folly, but I reckoned Irene and Oscar enjoyed it.

Irene wore a pretty blue dress, and Clarence wore his suit. Oscar and I didn't have anything fancy, but I borrowed a hat from Clarence and Oscar borrowed a tie.

Clarence conducted the basic ceremony. He had us take each other's hands and promise to love and honor each other for the rest of our lives. That's when it all became real to me, and I couldn't believe this young, handsome man was willing to stay with me forever. I stumbled o'er some words of emotion and I needed to sit down. Oscar sent a worried glance Irene's way then joined me on the couch.

"You okay, Jimmy?"

"Yeah. I'm —" I gazed into Oscar's sweet brown eyes, my hand going behind his neck as my fingers wove through hair that wasn't there anymore. "I'm just so grateful to have you, Oscar."

His eyes went wide. "*You're* grateful?"

He covered my hand with his own, as Irene and Clarence stood watching.

"Do you remember when you came across me in Dawson City?"

I nodded, my hand cupping his shorn head, that seemed smaller and more delicate than ever.

"Of course, I do. I thought you were a kid because you were so skinny and dirty."

Oscar blinked, and I could see the memories of that day in his eyes. "I'm the lucky one, Jimmy. If we hadn't found each other—" He inhaled a shaky breath. "I don't wanna think about it."

"Neither do I," I said. "But we did, and we'll always have each other," I said, leaning in to kiss him softly. "And now we've got Clarence and Irene, too. Our lives are richer than I ever expected."

Chapter Sixteen

Wolves

Clarence was able to start doing his own chores after about three weeks of recovery, though I'd told him to pace himself and get Irene's help if he needed it — or send her for one of us. But his leg was healing fine, and his limp had become less noticeable. I reckoned the muscle would take longer to heal, but regular movement would help.

We returned to our little kitchen-house after spending most of January at Clarence and Irene's. T'was strange at first but appealing to have some privacy. We went back to their place often o'er the next few weeks, whenever the weather was decent, to check in and make sure Clarence was managing.

Oscar had asked Irene to sew us some thick curtains for the windows in the small house. He'd claimed t'was so the sun wouldn't wake him up so early, but he and I knew t'was so we could close them when we got up to our games in the off chance that someone stopped by for an unexpected visit.

They proved useful about a week or so after we put them up. We were only getting started, kissing and touching each other, when we heard boots outside and a knock at the door. We jerked apart like we'd been burned and gazed at each other, thinking the same thing about them good, thick curtains and being glad we'd drawn them.

"Who's there?" I asked, getting up from the bed and glancing at my rifle, which was in its place against the wall by the door.

"It's Carson Moore."

"Oh!" I said, checking that Oscar had all his buttons done up before I pulled the door open and smiled at Carson. "Howdy! Great to see you!"

T'was good to see him. Carson smiled and took off his hat.

"I figured I'd come along and check on the two of you, make sure you weren't freezing to death out here."

"Good idea," I said.

Carson had told us how he and Tim Jensen hadn't thought to check on Oscar's uncle after his young wife had died and he was out here all alone. In the spring, when he didn't come to town, they had found him out here, dead in his own home. His horse was in the barn and had starved to death.

"Come in. You know it ain't much, but it's warm. Can I get you some tea or coffee?"

"Some coffee would be nice," Carson said, hanging up his coat and taking off his boots.

I found the coffee pot and filled it with water, then added the coffee grounds and put it on the stove to boil.

"So, how are you two?" Carson said, turning a chair around and sitting down.

"Good," Oscar said, sitting on the edge of the bed and acting like we had not been cuddling and kissing on it together when Carson arrived. "We're gettin' to know our neighbors."

"You are?" Carson said. "That's wonderful."

"Yeah, Irene cut my hair. See?" Oscar ran his fingers through his hair — what was left of it.

"Looks very dapper."

"Why, thank you."

"I suppose it's real good to have neighbors out here."

"Especially when they have a proper house with different rooms and even a piano," I said, smiling at Oscar.

"I'm glad they've been so welcomin' to you two. I don't know them all that well. They generally keep to themselves."

"Well, we're good friends with 'em now. We spent Christmas Eve at their place," Oscar said. "T'was nice to be so welcome, wasn't it, Jimmy?"

"Sure."

Carson looked from one to the other of us. "Well," he said, "I'm glad that I don't have to worry about you."

When the coffee had boiled, I poured it into cups and served it out.

"Ah, that's nice," Carson murmured. "You like it strong like I do."

I shrugged. "No point in making weak coffee. A cup of coffee should make you perk up and take notice."

Carson laughed. He looked about at our little abode, and I followed his gaze. That's when I noticed the jar of saddle grease on the bedside table and just about died.

"It's real nice and cozy in here. I'm glad we were able to get your stove put in and the sink pump working," he said, meeting my gaze and not indicating any kind of unsavory suspicion.

Thank God. If he did mention it, I'd just say I was sitting on the bed cleaning some of the tack, which seemed plausible, considering the limited space we had. I tried not to think of it and hoped Oscar wouldn't see it, panic and do something even more suspicious, like get up and try to hide it. T'was only a jar of saddle grease. I expect a regular person wouldn't think anything of it.

"Yeah, so'm I. Thank you so much for all your help, Carson. We wouldn't have been able to get this far without you and Tim Jensen," I said.

"I'm happy to do it, Jimmy. Seems a way to make amends for what happened to Oscar's uncle."

"T'wasn't your fault," Oscar said firmly, sipping his coffee.

"Well, now, I suppose I know that. But I keep thinking that one or the other of us could have ridden out to check on things, like I did today."

"Everything looks clearer in retrospect," I said.

Oscar screwed his face up. "What's that mean?"

"It means, when you see everything laid out in the past, it's easier to see what might have been done differently. But when you're caught up in it, it ain't always so obvious."

"Oh."

Carson eyed the slate that Oscar had left on the table. It still had our names written out together, and I hastened to explain.

"I'm teachin' Oscar to read and to write," I said. "He ain't had any proper learning, and I mean to fix that."

Carson moved his gaze to Oscar. "That's very responsible, Oscar. There're a lot of people who can't read and write, but 'tis a good skill to have, especially now the world's getting more and more confusing."

"Yeah, I reckon. It ain't easy," Oscar bemoaned.

"Nothing of value ever is."

Oscar nodded, sipping his coffee, and glancing at me nervously. I reckoned he was wondering same as me if Carson could see anything suspicious around the place.

"Still, you're lucky to have a teacher as kind and patient as Jimmy," Carson said.

Oscar grinned. "I suppose. Although, we seem to get on each other's nerves more'n more."

Carson laughed, and I thought t'was wise for Oscar to pretend that. Well, maybe he wasn't pretending. We did get on each other's nerves a bit. But we always made up real nice after we bickered, so there was that.

"I don't doubt it. Well, it's not that long till spring, and we can start expanding the place and give you two some more space. I imagine that second bedroom will be welcome."

Oscar looked heavenward and put his hands together in a silent prayer. "Oh, t'will. I can't wait to be able to sleep all alone without someone snorin' and kickin'."

I sat up straighter. "At least I don't pass wind all the time."

Oscar shot me a look of real indignation. "Maybe not. But when you do pass wind, e'en if I don't hear it, it knocks me flat."

"Well, good thing you're lyin' down, then."

Carson laughed so hard that he almost spilled his coffee.

We spoke about how the weather had been, how Onyx was working out and if we needed anything from town. I said I thought Clarence and Irene were gonna take the sled to town next week, and we'd either go with them or get them to pick up what we needed. He didn't need to bother himself, but I appreciated him asking.

"Well, then, I suppose I'd better get back. When do you want to start working on the house again?"

I shrugged and glanced at Oscar. "I don't know. April? Or will it be too muddy?"

"I reckon we can at least start planning by then. And we'll start as soon as we're able."

"Sounds good."

"Bye, then."

After he'd left, Oscar and I stared at each other until we were sure he'd gone, then let out equally relieved sighs.

I nodded toward the jar of saddle grease. "I hope to God he didn't see what that was."

Oscar followed my gaze and blanched. "Oh shit."

"Or that he figured I didn't have anywhere comfortable to sit to clean the leather gear. I don't know."

"I got worried when he looked at the slate. I'm glad you explained," Oscar said.

"Yeah, I figured t'would make sense. And it does. You need to spell both those words and more."

"Yeah." Oscar made a face. "'Tis a goddamn shame we have to lie. 'Tis even harder after bein' ourselves with Clarence and Irene."

I walked o'er and lifted the edge of the curtain, making sure Carson had gone. Then I took Oscar in my arms and held him close, nuzzling his neck and kissing him in that soft place where there wasn't much stubble.

"I know it. But 'tis the only way we can do this. And 'tis worth it, ain't it?" I said, pulling back and looking him in the eyes.

He nodded. "'Course it is. I'll lie to the Pope for you and our life together, Jimmy, e'en if he was standing right in front of me."

I arched a brow. "Well, hopefully it won't ever come to that."

* * * *

Irene had been thoughtful enough to let us bathe at their place once every week. She'd said t'would be a kindness to them as well as to each other, and I had to agree.

They had a full-sized tin tub, and we could fill it with big pots of hot water from the stove. T'was a luxury we'd got used to while we'd been spending most of our time there, and t'was a nice way to check in with them each week. She and Clarence handled our clothing, too, since they had a small room for washing and we didn't. T'was very nice of them, and it took a load off of what I had to do around the stables and the cooking and cleaning at our place.

Every Friday we'd saddle up Onyx and Dixie and ride out with a bag full of laundry, since Irene had offered to take care of that, too. She didn't mind. We'd ride home with our cleaned things the next day, after staying up late playing games and listening to Irene and Oscar at the piano then staying the night so we didn't have to worry about riding home. Oscar and I were blessed, and that was a fact.

The last Friday in February, we set out for their place. The sun had gone down, but the full moon shone so bright that we'd dispensed with a lantern. We hadn't been riding more than a few minutes when a chill went down my spine as a wolf's howl broke the quiet of the night.

"Jimmy!" Oscar said, his body stiffening as he pulled Onyx up sharp.

"I know. I heard it," I said as I stopped Dixie beside them.

Oscar's eyes flew wide with fear, and Onyx didn't look too happy, either. Her ears lay flat and she stepped forward and back, as if she couldn't decide which way to go.

"Should we go back?" Oscar asked.

"Shh-h."

The forest was peaceful and quiet again. Maybe t'was nothing. We waited a bit longer but didn't hear anything else.

"I think it's gone," I said. "Let's keep going. It's only a little farther to their place."

And, to be honest, I was looking forward to a good meal, a bath and being neighborly with Clarence and Irene.

"Okay," Oscar said, but he didn't sound so sure.

We quickened our pace, and we thought we'd be okay. In fact, I started to relax when we got within sight of the Trelawneys' picturesque home. I turned in my saddle to say as much to Oscar when I caught sight of a slinking form about ten meters away.

"Oh shit. Oscar, go. Get to the barn!"

There was no way I was risking him and Onyx with the wolves. If those bastards had to get someone, they could have me...not him.

"But—" he said, his head turning so his gaze could follow mine.

"Do as I say!"

My tone brooked no argument and, as Oscar was used to responding to my orders, he turned around and kicked that horse toward Clarence and Irene's place.

I reached behind me and grabbed my rifle, bringing it o'er my head as Dixie recognized whatever was loping in the distance and whinnied. She shied to the left as I squinted into the silvery moonlight.

"C'mere, you bastard," I whispered as I lifted the rifle to my shoulder, then spoke in a calmer tone to Dixie. "Easy, girl. Steady now."

I saw movement out of the corner of my eye, and Dixie moved to the right this time. I turned my body and took a shot that rang out in the quiet of the night.

I didn't hear a whimper or a thump, so I supposed I'd missed. With any luck, the beast had been scared off, but there might be others lurking close by. So, I placed my rifle in front of me and kicked Dixie toward the barn.

As I rode, I saw Oscar reach the barn and slide off his horse, undo the latch and open the big wood door. He slapped Onyx on the rear, and she hoofed it inside.

"What're you doin? Get in there!" I shouted.

But Oscar only stared at me, and I could see now he had his revolver in his hand. *Of all the stupid*—

"You get in that barn!"

I heard another shot and, for a second, I thought t'was Oscar, but he was staring at the house and had lowered his shooting arm. Clarence stood in the light from the open door, with his rifle to his shoulder. There was another crack of the gun, and I heard a sharp whimper as the bullet found its target.

"Get in the barn, both of you," Clarence said. "Take care of them horses, and I'll make sure you're covered when you come to the house."

I slid off Dixie and gave Oscar a glare, pointing at the revolver in his hand. "Put that thing away. And get in the barn like I told you."

He looked as if he wanted to argue, but he said, "Yes, sir," instead. He turned, pulled open the barn door and went in, leaving it ajar so I could ride Dixie in. I slid off her, shut that door and latched it tight.

"Holy fuck, Oscar. Come here."

"What?" he said, his eyes wide.

I took two strides and grabbed him, spinning him around and landing a volley of hard smacks on his behind.

"Ow! Jesus!" he yelped, and I forced myself to stop, even though I wanted to keep going, I was so mad.

I held him still, my fist wrapped tight in the neck of his coat while I tried to steady my breathing and at the same time listen for any sounds outside that would mean the wolf was still there…or wolves.

"I'm sor—" Oscar started.

"Shh-h. Quiet."

He shut up and stayed still in my grasp. I'm sure he sensed my anger, and I'm certain t'was burning on the skin of his ass, even now that I'd stopped. I didn't hear anything except silence outside, so I expected we were safe. But it had been a close one.

I turned to glare at Oscar.

"What the fuck did you think you were gonna do?" I said, my voice shaking.

"I—I know how to shoot, Jimmy. I was trying to protect you," he said, in a husky, frightened voice that made me regret my hasty punishment.

I blinked. "I know. I know you thought you were — "

He stood up straighter and shook me off, lifting his chin. "I ain't a child."

We stared at each other for a long moment.

"I know," I said.

"I have practiced, and I can shoot well," he said, dusting himself off.

"I know."

"So why can't I make up my own mind?"

My heart was breaking.

"Because I got a lot more experience than you about guns and wolves and — and risky situations. You need to listen to me and do what I say."

We stared at each other, and I could see he wanted to fight me on it.

"Oscar..." My voice was calmer now. "You're so good at obeying me when it ain't even a life or death situation. Why can't you listen to me when it matters?"

He looked down at the ground, then back up. "I just thought I could help."

I stepped forward and put my arms around him, pulling him into an embrace. He stiffened and resisted for one brief moment, then he let himself be coddled and petted.

"I know you did. But the best way for you to help in that situation was by doing what you're told. I know you ain't a child. You're a smart man, and you are a good shot. But, like I said, I been in close call situations most of my adult life, and I know what to do. You need to remember that." I pressed him tight to my heart. "Because you are the best thing in my life, Oscar Yates, and I don't plan to lose you to some stupid, hungry wolves." I choked up on that last part.

Oscar wrapped his arms around me then and pressed his head to my shoulder. "I'm sorry."

"I know. And I'm sorry for whackin' your poor behind." I pulled away and frowned at him. "You okay?"

He nodded then grunted. "I can take that and more. You know it."

I rolled my eyes. "Come on now. Let's get these horses put up so we can go inside."

We made sure all the animals were fed, watered and settled before we went to the house. True to his word, Clarence stood right outside the door, on the porch, with his rifle at the ready as we crossed the yard while Irene watched out of the window.

"I ain't seen any more of 'em," Clarence said. "I think I got the one that was after you."

I couldn't remember hearing another howl while we were in the barn, but t'was a relief to get inside the house.

Irene grabbed Oscar and hugged him, then did the same to me.

"Oh my goodness. Sometimes I think living out here in the bush is a fool's idea. But mostly it's all right. And nothing beats having your own stretch of land."

"We're okay," I said, though Oscar and I exchanged a glance. "I reckon if we hadn't had that business on our previous journey, I wouldn't have panicked so much. T'was only one wolf."

"Maybe," Clarence said, moving the drape so he could see out of the window. "Maybe not."

His eyes moved back and forth as he scanned the yard, but he didn't say anything more.

Chapter Seventeen

Besieged

Irene served up some rabbit stew and biscuits, then we had our baths. She got the water heating on the stove, and we filled the tub when t'was warm enough. I reckoned when they did their baths, the tub was in the kitchen, but when we had ours, we put it in Clarence and Irene's bedroom so's we could get some privacy. We were good friends, true enough, but I didn't reckon they needed to see my bits or Oscars, unless t'was absolutely necessary, like in the case of Clarence's injury.

I stoked the fire in the fireplace, so the flames rose and the wood crackled as sparks flew up into the chimney.

I let Oscar go first, while I lay on the made-up bed and watched. It reminded me of that first night in the hotel in Dawson, when I'd paid for him to have a badly needed soak and a wash, when we'd barely known each other and I was still trying to pretend my only interest was in helping him. The truth of t'was that I'd been drawn to him in other ways from the beginning, but I hadn't understood it.

Well, I understood it now. Watching him relax and enjoy that steaming hot water, his hair wet as he soaped his lanky body, made me all kinds of crazy. I wished we could have baths like this at our place, because it always made me want him. He caught me looking and gave me a leer.

"Why, hello, Mr. Downing. Fancy meeting you in this fine establishment."

I rolled my eyes. "Very funny."

"Why don't you come on o'er here?"

I blinked. "What?"

"I said, why don't you come on o'er here?" He spoke low and breathy, so the others wouldn't hear. I glanced at the door.

"To do what?"

"Well..." Oscar drawled, looking at the door and back at me, then quirking the corner of his mouth. "You oughta check to see if I did a good enough job."

I narrowed my eyes, but my dick had taken notice the moment Oscar had shucked his clothes and stepped into the tub.

"Oscar Yates," I said, sliding off the bed as quietly as I could, "are you asking me to come and bathe you?"

Oscar's lips parted as the heat flashed up between us like it always did. Sometimes, t'was a calm, steady ember, and other times, like now, t'was a conflagration.

"Maybe."

"We're gonna have to be quiet," I said. "If Irene and Clarence are wise to what we're doin' in here, we'll never hear the end of it."

"They won't care." He shrugged. "And you're only gonna help me get clean, Jimmy."

"Oh, I see."

I strode to the tub, where I stood looking down at him in the water, all wet and slippery and warm. I wanted to get in there with him, but I reckoned the others would have heard all the splashing. So, I went to my knees instead and picked up the washcloth.

I swallowed thickly while Oscar gazed at the cloth in my hand. "Where do you – need help?"

The tub was long enough for a fella to sit with his legs bent, and the back of it extended upward in a gentle slope for comfort and ease. Oscar leaned his head back and turned to gaze at me, as he spread his legs so that his knees rested against the sides. His cock, in a state of semi-arousal, was visible under the water.

I shuddered.

"Please clean my little nubby, Mr. Downing. I been dipping it into all sorts of mischief, and it's very, *very* dirty."

"*Oscar Yates.*"

He blinked sedately at my astonishment, like a cat that has dropped a mouse at your feet and doesn't understand why you're not pleased.

"Goddammit," I cursed, because now I was here I *had* to touch him, and I didn't know how we were gonna keep quiet. "You are a naughty, dirty boy, Oscar, and I reckon I'd better help or you'll be in that tub all night."

Oscar inhaled a tremulous breath, and his cock went to full stand while I watched. Then he made the most lovely, soft moan, that could have simply been from the pleasure of the warm water if anyone had been listening.

I leaned forward so that my mouth was right at his ear.

"You put your hands on the edge of this tub and don't move 'em," I said, as soft as I could.

Water dripped from his hands and wrists as he obeyed me, the movement making tiny splashes and swirls.

"Now, don't make a sound."

I rested the cloth o'er the edge of the tub and rolled up my sleeve, taking my time. When I'd rolled up my other sleeve, I leaned forward and placed a soft kiss on his lips. Then I reached into the water and traced my fingers up the inside of his leg, from his ankle to the place where his thigh met his groin.

"Oh, fu—."

"Shh-h."

I did the same on the other side. Oscar clutched the tub as he tried not to move. His breaths came quicker. His eyes flashed wide when I circled his cock.

"Oh, God," he moaned.

"Quiet, or I'm gonna go back onto that bed and let you finish this yourself."

Oscar's whispers came quick and desperate. "You could do that, Jimmy. You could watch me pleasure myself in this tub. I'd enjoy doin' that for you."

The thought of t'was tempting, for sure. "Not yet."

He nodded, the frown of displeasure on his face amusing to see.

I stroked his cock with lazy fingers until his forehead relaxed and he gave a pleasing sigh. His thigh muscles quivered as his cock moved under my hand. He gazed at me as I stroked and teased him, his knuckles white and wrinkled on the metal edge of the tub. His absolute trust and willingness to let me take control always laid me flat. How could a person give themselves up to someone like he did? Even when he'd barely known me and I'd told him I was a thief and a murderer, he'd given me his trust and his loyalty in an instant.

I pushed those thoughts to the back of my mind, and continued with my gentle torment, until I worried he'd spend in the water. Normally, once one of us had bathed, we topped up what was in the tub already with a pot or two of hot water. I didn't want to explain to Irene and Clarence that we needed to fill the whole tub again and why.

So, I released him and braced my hands wide on the edge of the tub. I had a good idea how we could both stay clean.

"Stand up."

He stared at me for a moment. "But I'll get cold."

"Wrap that towel around yourself then. But don't get out."

He did what I said, the water sluicing off him as he rose up like a slick sea creature, beautiful and smooth, his cock sticking right up like a divining rod. He grabbed the towel off the chair and quick-dried his hair in a couple of rough swipes, then wrapped it around his shoulders, gazing down at me as I tried to calm my breathing.

"You need to stay quiet," I reminded him.

Oscar nodded. "I will."

"I hope so. Otherwise, you can explain to Clarence and Irene."

He gave me a brief reflex smile that disappeared instantly with the anticipation of what was coming. I gave him a stern look, that made him stutter a deep breath, then I leaned forward and swallowed his nubby to the root.

Perhaps I should have started slower, because Oscar expelled a loud grunt and jerked, causing water to splash out of the tub. I pulled off in a flash as his eyes went wide and he turned his head toward the door.

Sure enough, footsteps sounded outside and a knock followed.

"Everything okay in there?" Irene said.

"Yes," I said, too quick to allay suspicions. "Fine. Oscar just stubbed his toe."

"Oh dear. I wish that room was bigger."

"He's just finishing up. We'll be coming out for more hot water soon so's I can have a soak."

"There's two more pots on the stove, ready whenever you are."

"Thank you kindly."

We heard Irene walk away. Oscar's dick was still at attention, mostly because I'd been stroking it softly through that whole conversation while he tried not to choke on the sounds he wanted to make.

Our gazes met, and I narrowed my eyes.

I mouthed the word 'quiet', and he nodded.

I leaned forward, and this time took him into my mouth slowly as he clutched the edges of the towel and watched. He smelled of soap and water and man, and I breathed him in. I circled his thighs with my hands to hold him steady while I went to work, feasting on his cock as quietly as I could until he gasped and flooded my mouth with his spend.

His look of gratitude and the untidiness of his damp-dry hair gave me everything I needed as I reached into my trousers and pulled my dick out of my union suit. I shoved the cloth from the tub into my mouth to stifle my noises as I brought myself off in a few harsh yanks, shuddering and spending o'er my fingers.

Then Oscar stepped out of the tub, steadying himself on my shaking shoulder, and knelt on the mat in front of me, licking all of it up while I looked on in amazement.

When he was done, he smirked from under his lashes, and whispered, "I reckon you don't even need a bath now, Jimmy, I cleaned you up so good."

I rolled my eyes and wiped my mouth. "Hmm, it might seem suspicious if I didn't."

"I suppose."

I grabbed another towel and dried Oscar's lightly haired legs while he watched.

"I feel like the Queen now. You're a lovely houseboy," he said, resting his hand on the top of my head. "I reckon I could get used to this."

"Better not," I said, pushing off the floor. "Now get dressed so you can help me refresh the tub. It's time for my soak."

"Well, it's a good thing we both got off because I'd probably wanna get in there with you."

"In this tub, that would be a pretty tight fit."

"I don't think I'd mind."

* * * *

Once we were bathed, dry and dressed in clean clothes, we made our way out of the cozy bedroom and into the kitchen where Irene and Clarence had cleared the table and set out a checkerboard.

Clarence went in and banked the fire in the bedroom, and he and I emptied the tub, then dragged it out to the mud-room in back where t'was stored. While we were doing that, a wolf howled close by — then another and another after that, until a whole chorus of wolves were howling in the night, sounding so near to us that I started to worry about the horses in the barn.

Clarence and I exchanged a sober glance, then we went back into the house. Irene and Oscar were sitting at the table. They glanced at us, their faces grim and pale.

"You hear that?" I said.

"Yep," Oscar muttered. "They're close."

"Too close," I agreed. "I don't like it."

"Neither do I," Clarence agreed.

He walked to the front window and moved the curtain aside, peering out into the darkness. He was quiet for a moment. Then he cursed.

"What is it?" Irene said.

"Wolves. A whole pack of 'em. Maybe nine? Could be more."

A chill slid up my spine.

We were safe, there in the house, and the animals were secure in the barn. The wolves couldn't get at any of us. But the idea of being surrounded and unable to go outside without risking life and limb was not something I enjoyed, it turned out.

"I guess it's a good thing we'd planned on staying the night," Oscar said in a quiet, frightened voice.

The wolves started howling again, as if they were telling each other how clever they were to have trapped us here. Hopefully, they weren't trying to figure out how long they'd have to pen us in before we got desperate. I reckoned they weren't *that* smart. But they were intelligent animals—pack hunters that used strategy and cunning to get their prey. I knew that much.

"It's all right. They can't get at us or the horses."

Clarence looked at me. "That's true. But those horses are gonna need feeding and watering come morning."

I gave a little nod. "Hopefully they'll be gone by then."

"Hopefully."

"Well, there isn't much we can do right now," Irene muttered. "We might as well carry on with our evening. Those wolves can prowl around all they want, but they're not going to ruin our fun."

"Sure," I said. "Let's try and forget about 'em."

We did try—and partly succeeded. T'would have been easier if they didn't start howling every twenty minutes. There was a tension in the air, because we could sense them, and they could sense us. I only wondered when they'd give up hope that they could have us.

Oscar asked if Poke was safe in the stables at our place, in case the wolves gave up on us and went there.

"The stables are sturdy, and the door is latched. He'll be just fine."

I didn't mention to Oscar that Poke would shudder in fear if a pack of wolves surrounded the stables and started howling, as they were doing here. I tried not to worry about that. Of course, even if this pack of wolves wasn't right outside of the place in the morning, they might be nearby still. We'd have to be real careful doing the chores and riding out.

Anyway, there was nothing we could do about that now.

Clarence got out the whiskey and the gin and that settled some of our uneasiness. We played checkers and ate popcorn that Irene made and slathered with salt and butter. T'was just as pleasant as usual, only with this thing hanging o'er us that we knew we'd have to deal with tomorrow.

Around about midnight, I realized I hadn't heard their howls in a while. I glanced at Clarence.

"You think they're gone?"

"Maybe. Anyway, at least we'll be able to sleep."

Turned out that was a wildly optimistic statement. Clarence and Irene said goodnight and went into their bedroom and shut the door. Oscar and I laid out our bedrolls on the floor in the sitting room and doused the lamps. Before we went to bed, we peeked out of the curtains.

"I don't see any," Oscar said.

"Me, neither."

The night seemed peaceful and quiet, though the moonlight showed us dozens of tracks in the snow outside.

Oscar and I huddled together in our union suits under the blankets, the fire banked but still providing heat, and the wood stove burning hot and bright between the hinges in the iron door. It took me a long time to fall asleep, although Oscar started snoring softly, wrapped safe in my arms.

I finally dozed off. When I woke, sunlight streamed in between the curtains and Oscar stirred in my arms.

"What time is it?" he whispered, covering my hand with his and playing idly with my fingers.

"I don't know. I can't see the clock. From the slant of the sun, though, it must be around eight, maybe?"

Oscar hummed contentedly and wriggled against me. I circled my arms tighter around him and buried my nose in his clean hair. He made a soft noise and clasped my hand, pushing it down his body and o'er his cock that was poking up under his union suit.

"You know, Clarence could come outta that room at any moment...or Irene."

"Sure," he breathed. He worked two of his buttons loose, shoved my hand inside the cloth and pressed it against the burning flesh of his nubby.

"We'll need to tend to the animals soon," I breathed, circling it with my fingers. I kissed the lobe of his ear and licked along his throat to indicate that I was, in fact, interested in pleasing him, but I was unsure of how much time and privacy we could count on.

Oscar turned his head and pressed his nubby into my hand. He blinked up at me with a heartfelt need burning in his eyes.

"I reckon you need to attend to *this* animal first," Oscar said in a sensuous, sleep-soft tone, pushing into my hand again.

I chuckled deep in my chest. This man was irrepressible — or, at least, his cock was.

"Don't you think we took enough chances last night?"

"No, Jimmy, I don't. I need you to take another chance right now. Won't take long, I promise."

The bedroom door opened with a creak, and I froze, as did Oscar. My eyes locked on Clarence as he stepped out of the bedroom and shut the door with care behind him. He took a step forward, then saw us.

"Sorry. Did I wake you?"

"No," I hastened. I slid my hand out of Oscar's long underwear, kissing him on the cheek in apology as Clarence raised a hand and turned away.

"I gotta make coffee. If you wanna continue, I can pretend not to notice."

The heat rushed into my face, but Oscar outright laughed and pulled my hand back to his cock.

"Okay," he said. "G'on, Jimmy," loud enough that Clarence heard.

"I can't. Oscar, I can't," I said, my wide eyes on Clarence, whose shoulders were shaking as he got the pot and pumped some water into it.

Oscar sighed and pushed my hand away, then the blankets.

"You ain't no fun."

He stood, all rumpled in his red long underwear that he fastened up as he gazed down at me in disgust, shaking his tousled head.

Now Clarence did laugh. "My Lord, you two sure are entertainin'. I'll say that much."

"Hmph," Oscar pouted. "*I* ain't feeling very entertained right now. Anyway, I need to use the privy."

"I reckon all of us do. I want to go with you," I said, standing up and finding my trousers and socks.

"Now you're talkin'."

"Not for that. I wanna make sure them wolves are gone. I'm taking my rifle and escorting you. Then you can stand outside the privy with it and guard me while I go."

"How about we all go," Clarence said. "I can take Irene when she wakes up."

"All right."

The expedition was a success, and we didn't see or hear any wolves nearby, even though the tracks in the snow made me anxious.

"How many do you reckon were out here?" I asked Clarence.

"Too many."

The sun shone warm on the snow and made it sparkle. T'was hard to imagine any danger on a day like this, but I was still wary. I walked Oscar back inside then Clarence and I went to tend to the animals.

When we'd finished and left the barn, the front door to the house opened and Oscar peered out with a frown. "Irene needs the privy bad. I was thinkin' about takin' her myself, but I knew you wouldn't like it," he said, "even though I've got the revolver."

"No, you did the right thing, Oscar," I said.

Clarence moved toward the porch. "She can come now. I'll take her."

"Okay." Oscar disappeared and, in a moment, Irene hastened out. She must have been wearing her coat and boots already, poor thing.

She tried to laugh it off but was in some distress.

"Goddamn wolves," Clarence said. "I hope to fuck they stay away."

He stuck close to Irene while I went inside.

"I'm proud of you, Oscar," I said. "You did the right thing by waiting for us."

He shrugged. "I ain't never seen a woman needed to piss so bad. I told her to use the chamber pot, but she said she expected you'd be done soon."

"Yeah, we need to empty those. Let's do that, then they won't have to."

We dumped the two china pots out back—we were lucky they had more than one, although I suppose we could have used a regular pot—and cleaned them before setting them back in their places.

By the time we'd finished, Clarence and Irene had come back.

Now Irene really was laughing. "My goodness. I thought I was gonna explode—or let go and flood the house if you didn't get back in time."

Oscar laughed. "Yeah, you looked a fair bit uncomfortable."

"I went twice in the pot since yesterday. Not sure why I was so desperate." She flipped her loose hair off her face and grinned, looking like a schoolgirl with her dimple. "Anyhow, I feel much better! I'll start making breakfast."

We ate flapjacks, eggs, ham and an orange each. Oscar peeled his orange like t'was a treasure—and it sort of was. I felt the same when the tender flesh exploded between my teeth.

"This tastes like summer," Oscar moaned. "*So* good."

Irene and Clarence exchanged a look and a smile. They were charmed by Oscar, almost as much as I was.

"Yes, it does. Makes me feel better after a restless night," I said.

"Well, it looks like those wolves have found some other place to go. But you boys can wait a bit before you head home if it makes you feel better," Clarence said.

"I ain't in no rush," I said, helping myself to another flapjack.

Oscar gave me a look to say that he was eager to get me alone, but he'd just have to wait. I wasn't risking those wolves coming back just so we could get up to some of his sexy mischief.

Chapter Eighteen

Domestic Quarrels

A few hours passed with no sign or sound of the wolves. I didn't want to wait too long, in case they did come back and we were trapped there again. We had to get home to feed and water the poor mule.

The sun was high in the sky when we saddled up the horses. Clarence had accompanied us to the barn, his rifle at the ready. He'd promised to cover us as we rode away, but I kept my rifle on the saddle in front of me, nevertheless.

The sun was high and bright in the blue sky, and the beauty of our surroundings didn't go unnoticed. But I couldn't enjoy it as much as I wanted to. My gaze switched between Oscar and Onyx in front of me and scanning the trees on either side of us, while I listened for any sign of the wolves. But for most of the short journey, all I heard was the crunch of hooves in snow and the call of forest birds mixed with the chatter of angry squirrels.

The abrupt caw of a crow to my left startled me so badly that I reached for my gun then cursed when I realized t'was nothing to worry about. Those goddamned wolves had ruined my peace of mind, and I was all kinds of annoyed. I needed to get Oscar home and tumbled good and proper, which would make the both of us feel better.

We made it to the stables without incident and found Poke to be happy and content, with Sprite keeping him company in the stable and lots of warm hay to eat and sleep in. We wouldn't have left him if the cold had been severe, since he'd miss the warmth from the two other horses in the small space. But the temperature was mild, and he was nice and warm. The cat could come and go through a small hole in one of the stalls that was too small for a wolf or any other predator. Both the mule and the cat seemed in good spirits — not acting spooked or as if they'd feared for their lives, and we hadn't seen any wolf tracks beyond the immediate surroundings of Clarence and Irene's homestead.

We took Onyx and Dixie into the barn and unsaddled them, gave them a brushing and put them up with some grain and fresh hay, then gave the same to Poke. Oscar brought some fresh, unfrozen water in from the pump for them to drink. Even though we hadn't seen any wolf tracks, we'd decided to keep the animals in the barn today. They'd gotten plenty of exercise o'er the last few weeks, and one day at rest wouldn't hurt. If we didn't see any wolves around for twenty-four hours, we'd put them in the paddock tomorrow. The cat followed us out of the barn and o'er the snow toward the house. I reckoned she was eager to get back to the comfortable, pillowy perches that she favored.

I was just about to turn to say something lewd and enticing to Oscar when I felt a hard thump in the middle of my back. It took me a second to realize t'was a balled bit of snow and not a wolf attacking, what with the way my nerves were still in a heightened state. Once I'd figured it out, I dropped the laundry bag in the snow and placed my rifle against the door, then turned to face the little bastard.

He was already rolling up another one and threw it right at my face. I opened my mouth to utter a curse as I jerked away, but he must have planned for that and the damn thing hit me square on the chin, with half of it ending up inside my mouth.

His laughter, which t'would have been music to my ears on any other occasion, only pissed me off more.

"Oscar, you little shit," I growled, tired and fed up with everything. He thought he was being fun and flirty, but all I wanted to do was get inside, shut the door and fall into bed with him. Since he was preventing that, I decided to subdue him out here.

I took three strides and grabbed his elbow, tripping him up so he fell into the snow. Then I dropped down, covered him with my body and pinned his mischievous hands down.

"My nerves are a fucking wreck. Stop instigatin'. Get in that house, and get on your knees for me — or maybe o'er my lap so's I can give you what for."

There was enough genuine anger and impatience in my voice to turn Oscar's fancy, and sure enough, he made a meek sound of surrender. Then he licked his lips and sighed in such a languorous, seductive way that I could barely contain myself.

"Good boy," I said, letting go of his wrists and sitting back on his calves as a wolf howl broke the silence.

We scrambled up off the ground and made for the house. I grabbed my gun as Oscar fumbled with the latch string and pulled the door open. We got inside and I bolted the door behind us as my heart pounded in my ears. I'd never gone from excitement to dread so fast in my life, and I didn't want to again.

I stared at Oscar, and he stared at me.

"Fuck," I said.

"But we're safe now," Oscar said.

"Yeah. And the stable's shut up tight, so the animals are safe, too."

Then Oscar's eyes blew wide. "Where's Sprite?"

I tried to remember. She'd been following us to the house, but then we'd got distracted. I didn't know where she was.

Another howl came then another, too close for comfort.

"I don't know," I said, realizing what that meant.

Oscar lunged for the door but I blocked him. "No! You ain't goin' out there."

"But Sprite!"

"She can take care of herself, and you know it."

"Against *wolves*?"

"She'll take off or go in the stable."

"We can go out and get her. You can bring your rifle," Oscar said, desperate and scared.

I narrowed my eyes at him. "I ain't risking my life and yours for a goddamn cat!"

He glared at me, and the emotions that skittered o'er his face finished with a bleak betrayal that flayed me to the bone.

"She's *my* cat."

"I know."

"She's more'n a cat, Jimmy. She's my *friend*."

"Well, I know that, Oscar, but—"

Just then, we heard her familiar mewl right outside the door and a frantic scratching.

"Jimmy!"

"I know. I know."

I hadn't *seen* any wolves yet, be we could hear 'em, and they sounded pretty fucking close.

"Take this." I handed Oscar the rifle. Then I grabbed the door latch and pulled it, shifting the door just enough for Sprite to shoot inside in a bundle of fur and snow. I slammed it shut and latched it good. Then I tried to forget the look on Oscar's face when he thought I was gonna leave her outside for the wolves.

By the time we'd taken off our things, we could see them. Six of them—big gray wolves, and they looked thin and hungry, sniffin', huffin' and prowling all around the little house. They must have been the same pack that were at the other place, but there didn't seem to be as many of them, which was less of a relief than one might think.

Six big wolves were still too many for one man to fight on his own. And even if both of us went out there with our guns, we'd be risking injury or worse. T'wasn't worth it. We'd just have to stay inside where we were safe and hope they'd leave before we had to go to the outhouse or the stables.

This felt different than it had at Clarence and Irene's. Our place was so small and had so little furniture, and there were only the two of us. Luckily, we had enough wood in the bin to start a fire in the stove and get some heat going, but we'd need more from outside by morning. With any luck, they'd be gone by then. And luck was all we had.

"Goddammit," I said.

"What?"

"I left our clean laundry out there."

Oscar went to the window and peered out. "Oh, yeah. It's there. Uh, Jimmy? One of the wolves is pissin' on it."

"Goddammit."

Oscar was silent for a bit. Then he said, "Now they're all pissin' on it."

"For fuck's sake," I said. "I've had just about enough of these bastards. Don't they got another place to be?"

I sat on the edge of the bed and put my head in my hands.

"I doubt it," Oscar murmured. "Anyway, they're just animals, lookin' for some food."

"I s'pose."

Oscar came around and peeled my hands from my face, gazing down at me with a look of determination.

"Maybe if we make lots of noise, it'll scare 'em away."

"What, like bangin' pots and pans?"

"Hmm, well, we could try that. But I was thinkin' more like spanking naughty boys who like to cry and scream and make a big fuss." He swayed back and forth, holding my hands, with a look on his face I knew pretty well. "Of course, it's up to you."

And maybe I was a fool for love because, even with a pack of bloodthirsty wolves prowling around outside, I couldn't think of a better thing to do just then. If nothing else, it'd take my mind off our situation and onto something much more agreeable. We were safe and sound and finally had some privacy. We might as well get up to mischief. And maybe if Oscar made enough noise, which wasn't generally a problem, the wolves would get spooked and leave us be.

I circled a hand around his slim wrist and pulled him on top of me, right where I was sitting. "All right. You wanna sacrifice yourself to *this* mean old wolf, that's your business. But I ain't bein' merciful."

"I don't want you to be merciful. I want you to be fierce."

I chuckled. "You are one naughty, naughty boy, Oscar Yates. And I'm glad to have the privilege of punishing you."

"You oughta be. 'Cause I don't let just anyone spank my sorry ass."

"I'm awful glad to hear it. Now pull them pants down and get o'er my lap."

"Yes, sir, I will. I aim to make so much noise those wolves run off with their tails between their legs."

Turned out the wolves didn't scare off that easy. But by the time I was done giving Oscar the hiding of his life then fucking him into the mattress, with the occasional wolf howl adding an urgent counterpoint to our coupling, I couldn't find it in me to care.

We lay there together in bed, listening to the sounds of the wolves and the crackle of the fire in the stove, and Oscar said, "Well, at least we ain't camping out on in the open and bein' chased by outlaws. I reckon we been in sorrier circumstances than this—and everything turned out all right."

I turned my head and gazed at him.

"That's true enough," I said, in a spent, soft voice.

'All right' was a subjective term, since I believed that Oscar was still traumatized by what had happened with Spook and Whitlaw. But we'd survived and made it all the way to Port Essington. And we were making a home here, together. No sorry pack of wolves was gonna take that away from us.

I pulled him in and kissed his forehead. "I love you, Oscar Yates. You know that, don't you?"

He grinned. "I do. And I'm thankful for it every day."

* * * *

The wolves were still there in the morning. They'd howled off and on all through the night, but we'd been able to sleep in bits. Still, when I peeked out of the curtains at dawn and saw them slinking around, some of them lying in the snow like they had nowhere better to be, my heart sank.

"They're still there, ain't they?" Oscar said, peering o'er my shoulder.

"Yep."

"Git! G'on, you bastards," he said, his voice at a conversational level. "We ain't got nothing for you."

"We're gonna need to feed the stock and give 'em water. I don't know what we're gonna do."

Oscar must have seen the concern on my face. He put a hand to my shoulder. "Maybe they'll be gone by lunch time."

"I hope so."

We had a chamber pot to piss in, and I supposed we could use a bowl or something for the other if we couldn't hold it, but neither of us really wanted to do that. We were doing our best to subdue any urges of that sort until we could get to the privy.

We had some cheese and bread for breakfast, and I made coffee, which tasted very civilized and welcome, with the wolves hanging about outdoors. When we were done, I looked around the little place and sighed.

"Well, we might as well do some cleaning and get this shack polished up while we're stuck inside."

I held the broom out to Oscar and picked up a rag. Oscar stared at the broom in my hand.

"I think I'd rather take my chances with them wolves."

"Very funny. Here. Take it."

He took it, with a look of displeasure on his face like he was touching something distasteful.

"It's a goddamn broom. It ain't gonna hurt you."

"I ain't so sure about that."

I stared, perplexed, at him. I'd never met anyone so against doing domestic chores. He was fine in the stables. He'd muck out stalls and shovel shit. He'd done all right when we were traveling. But now that we actually had a small house to live in, he didn't seem to want any part in keeping it up. I don't know if t'was because he thought those were women's jobs or if he simply couldn't be bothered because he'd never had to take care of his own place before. But t'was getting to be a sore point, and I guess the stress of those wolves had got to me.

"Oscar, for fuck's sake. I can't keep this place up by myself. Sure, it's small and all, but it takes a lot of work to keep a house clean and presentable."

Oscar wrinkled his nose. "Presentable? Who we gonna present it to?"

I raised my arms like t'was obvious. "Why, anyone who comes o'er. I don't want people comin' in here and thinkin' we live like animals."

"Well, I don't think—"

"Oscar, shut your trap and sweep the floor."

He glared at me. Then he stuck out his tongue.

I held his gaze and tried to convey how annoyed I was starting to feel. His tongue went back in his mouth, and he stood there, fidgeting with the end of the broom.

"Oscar."

"What?"

"How sore is your ass from that spanking?"

"It's...it's a little sore."

"Well, if you don't start sweeping this floor in a minute, it's gonna be even sorer."

He laughed. "That ain't the threat that you think it is."

"Oh, I see. But what if I said I'd spank you up against the wall until you cried and didn't let you spend. What then?"

He stared at me like he couldn't believe what I'd said. Then he laughed, loud and genuine.

I put my hands on my hips. "What's so goddamn funny?"

"You are. You should know by now that anythin' involving spankin' and cryin' and keeping me from spendin' is right up my alley. That ain't *no* threat, Jimmy." He enunciated each of those last words distinctly.

I crossed my arms o'er my chest. "Is that a fact?"

"Yep."

"Well then, I'll just ignore you. Give me that." I reached for the broom, and he hesitated before passing it to me. But then he did, watching me warily.

I took the broom and moved past him, nudging him out of the way as I got to work. I didn't pay any attention to Oscar, just went about sweeping the floors. He was nice enough to get out of the way, at least, but I didn't even care. I would have swept around him. I figured for a man that liked attention so much, this would be an effective way to punish him for being lazy and unhelpful.

This situation with the wolves had turned me into an old grump, 'tis true. But t'was about time Oscar helped out around here. We all had to do things we didn't like once in a while. And I'd be damned if I was gonna do it all.

For a little while he sat on the bed and watched. Then he looked out of the window, pretending to ignore me. Then he tried to distract me by lolling about and trying to look fetching. He took off his shirt and rolled the sleeves of this union suit up, then unbuttoned the top few buttons. He fluffed up his hair and lounged about like a lady of leisure, stretching this way and that, trying to look provocative. And if I'd been in any other mood, I'd have surely attacked him. But I was determined to teach him a lesson.

So, I focused on my work. I swept the floors and loaded the stove with wood, then noticed the dirty dishes that we'd left, despite my best intentions. I went to the hand pump and filled the sink with water, then grabbed a rag and started washing. I whistled a bit to keep up my spirits as I worked, the well-water cold from the ground but still getting the dishes clean.

I had just about calmed myself down doing this repetitive, banal work, when I felt something brush my elbow. I looked up and Oscar was standing beside me with a dish towel.

"I guess I'll dry," he said in a chastened tone of voice. His cheeks were a little pink, as if he'd realized what a child he was being and was shamed by it.

Instead of thanking him, like he was doin' me a favor and not his duty, I said, "Okay."

He was quiet for another moment. Then he cleared his throat.

"I'm sorry."

I nodded. "Okay."

"I reckon these wolves have gotten to me, too. When do you suppose they'll go?"

I looked out of the window and saw three of them lying there, all relaxed and lazy, as if they had all the time in the world.

"I don't know. Soon, I hope."

"I'm worried about Onyx."

"The horses and Poke will be fine for a little longer, I reckon," I said. "But we'll need to tend to them by nightfall."

While I was watching the wolves, all three stood and at the same time looked toward the barn, their ears perked up and their bodies on alert.

What in tarnation?

I heard them before I saw them — the jangle of harnesses and the whoosh of a sleigh, and Clarence's voice yelling out, "Haw, haw! Go on! Git!" as he rode his team hard and fast toward the pack of wolves in our yard.

The wolves scattered, but not before Irene had aimed and shot at one of them. Oscar and I watched as the wolf jerked back and fell, blood oozing from a fatal shot to the side. T'was so quick it didn't even cry out.

The sight of Irene Trelawney, standing up in the sleigh, wearing a buffalo coat like Clarence and aiming her rifle at those goddamned wolves, would be seared into my memory for the rest of my sorry life.

She aimed at another wolf and shot again, hitting her target, while Clarence kept up his yelling and yipping.

"Stay here," I said to Oscar. "Don't you dare leave this house!"

"I won't," he said, and I believed him. He was glued to the window, watching our rescuers disperse the wolves that had kept us pinned all night and most of the day.

I jammed on my boots and grabbed my rifle. Making sure there weren't any wolves right out front, I unlatched the door, stepped out into the snow and shut it behind me. I heard the latch click as I raised my rifle, scanning the snow for the retreating pack.

Chapter Nineteen

A Wagon Ride

"They're gone," Clarence said. "My wife scared them away."

He slapped his thigh and laughed, the sound ringing in the air.

"I reckon they won't be back," I said, grinning.

Irene, still upright in the sleigh like a warrior priestess, her hair gathered in an untidy bun, face flushed and a huge smile spanning her pretty face, lowered her rifle and nodded. "I got three of those bastards. Did you see me, Clarence?"

"I saw you. I did."

"Jimmy? Did you see?"

"Mrs. Trelawney, you may be as good a shot as I am."

"Is that good?"

She delivered that line so serious that for a moment I took it to heart and felt a bit…insulted. But then I saw the glint in her eye, and all the stress from the last twenty-four hours came out in huge breathless guffaws. I was laughing so loud I almost didn't hear Oscar's voice.

"Can I open the door? I feel like I'm missing a party."

"Sure. No wolf is gonna go near that woman—or any place she's ever been, I figure."

The latch scraped, the door swung open and Oscar grinned, squinting into the sunlight.

"That was the most amazing thing I've ever seen!" he said. Then he frowned, as if the words he'd said had jogged an unwelcome thought.

He glanced at me, and I saw the memories of an outlaw being blown to bits all o'er him by a perfectly aimed bullet.

I shook my head. We didn't have to revisit that right now.

Oscar's smile returned, though t'was somewhat shaky. "Well, Jimmy's a good shot, too. I feel so protected with the two of you watching my back…and Clarence."

Clarence hitched the horses and got out of the sleigh. He walked around and helped Irene down. Irene leaned her rifle in the front of the sleigh and gave her hand to Clarence.

"My lady," Clarence said, leading her down like an empress.

"Good sir."

Clarence wrapped his arms around her and hugged her tight, kissing her on the lips with obvious passion. Irene giggled like a girl and let herself be manhandled.

Oscar and I shared a glance.

When they were finished and walking toward us, I asked, "What are we gonna do with them?" I pointed at the three dead wolves in the blood red snow. "I reckon we should get the pelts, at least."

Clarence wrinkled his nose. "We've eaten wolf at times. I don't recommend it. Irene's a decent cook, but she can't even make it taste good."

"I've eaten it when I had to," I said. "Not partial to it. There's enough other game around here that I don't feel desperate."

"You think those wolves that ran off will come back?" Oscar said.

Clarence, Irene and I exchanged glances.

"I doubt it," I said. "The rest of that big pack had already gone somewhere else, and I reckon the ones that got away from Irene will be long gone."

Oscar grinned at Irene. "You were incredible. I reckon those wolves are gonna tell everyone they meet about the wild man with long hair and wearin' skirts that killed their brothers in about five seconds with fire from a stick. You'll be a legend!"

Irene rolled her eyes. "I'm glad we decided to come by. I got to thinking and said to Clarence, we'd better go check on Oscar and Jimmy. T'would be the neighborly thing to do, knowing there are wolves around."

I stepped forward and held out my hand to Irene.

"We thank you, kindly. You're as brave as a lion, Irene—and Clarence, too. You took a risk for us, and we're mighty thankful." I looked down at the snow, then back up at them. "If that huge pack had surrounded you, the sleigh wouldn't have been much protection."

Irene grabbed my hand and pulled me into a hug. "It all turned out fine, so what's the point of fretting?"

I held her close, truly grateful and impressed. I pulled back and gave her a look. "I don't ever wanna be on the bad side of you, Irene Trelawney. Jesus."

She gave me a sober look that was tempered with a bright glint in one eye. "No, you don't."

"Me neither," Oscar added. "We're mighty thankful. We should feed and water the horses and Poke now, Jimmy. They must be hungry, poor things."

"We'll put up your team as well," I said.

But Clarence shook his head. "You let Irene and me take care of the horses. You and Oscar best get to skinnin' and disposin' of those wolves. You don't wanna leave them out here bleeding all o'er the place, or you'll have every other predator around. I'm surprised the buzzards aren't already circling."

T'was a good plan. We got our coats and, after we'd each taken a turn in the outhouse, we gloved up and I showed Oscar how to skin a wolf and clean the hide. Then we made a bonfire in the snow and burned all the other bits so they wouldn't attract attention. The scraped pelts would hang outside and, with no blood on them, they wouldn't be a draw to other animals.

By then, Clarence and Irene had finished in the barn and gone inside. Oscar and I washed off at the pump and went in, glad to be where t'was warm and bright and there were no wolves circling.

"What's all that?" I said, seeing food laid out on the counter.

"We brought sandwiches," Irene said with a smile. "Help yourselves. I had some of that bear meat left, and there's cheese and some of the fine English mustard I bought."

"That'll hit the spot," I said. "Thank you."

"You're welcome, Jimmy," Irene said. She gazed around her at the little house. "My, this place is so clean!"

I smiled. "Well, we didn't have much to occupy us this morning, since we couldn't go outside." I glanced at Oscar, and he had the decency to look a mite ashamed about his earlier behavior. "Oscar was a big help. It didn't take long once we set to't."

He sent me a grateful glance and sat in the chair.

"Your place is always so tidy and fine," Oscar said. "I reckon we got used to that."

"Nonsense. I am *not* the best housekeeper. Clarence does his share."

Clarence smiled benignly as he chewed his bear sandwich. "I don't see why Irene should have to do it all. If she can shoot bears and wolves, I suppose I can pick up a cleaning rag once in a while."

T'was a nice afternoon then, with no wolves bothering us and good neighbors to chat with. Clarence and Irene left in their sleigh before too long, so they could get home before darkness fell. And Oscar and I went to bed early, since our sleep hadn't been ideal the night before.

* * * *

We were right about the wolves. They were gone, and they didn't come back.

We continued to be cautious, because there were other predators about, but we didn't have any problems after that. February ended and March went by, and before we knew it, t'was early April and the snow was almost all melted. T'was boggy in places, but we figured we could get started on building up the rest of the house soon. Irene and Clarence offered to take us to town in their wagon so's we could get our supplies back home, and we accepted.

T'was nice to go all together in the wagon. Clarence and I chatted about the weather and how plentiful the hunting was, and Oscar and Irene sat in the wagon box, giggling and conspiring.

They let the two of us off at Jensen's so we could see Carson and Tim and discuss our plans for the homestead. Clarence and Irene continued on to do some errands and promised to meet us at the general store in an hour or so.

T'was early afternoon, so the saloon was almost empty. Carson saw us as soon as we walked inside.

"Hello! I wondered when you two would make an appearance." His smile was warm and genuine, and I felt grateful again for the hospitality we'd found in this place.

"Carson, how are you?" I asked.

Oscar tipped his hat in greeting.

"I'm just fine," he said. "Glad the snow's gone. It's a lot prettier out where you folks live. Here in town, it just mostly makes a mess."

I laughed.

"What can I get you?"

"I'll have a beer. Oscar?"

"Sure, that sounds good."

"Is Tim around? We wanted to see when you'd both be available to get started on building up again."

Carson nodded. "I'll get him."

"Thank you."

Tim came back with Carson in a moment, and Carson went to pull our pints.

"Oscar, Jimmy, good to see you. How did you weather your first winter in Port Essington?"

"Well, except for dealing with some wolves and a bear, we did all right."

"Good God," Tim exclaimed.

We told him about Clarence's encounter with the bear and about the wolf pack.

"I'm glad to live in town, and that's a fact. Glad everyone's safe and sound," he said.

"I reckon I'd like to spend the next winter in a bigger place, though," I said wryly, and he laughed.

"I reckon so. When did you want to get started?"

I glanced at Oscar who shrugged, but I said, "I guess, as soon as 'tis convenient for you two?"

Tim nodded. "I'm busy this week, but next week I'll have time to sit down with you to plan out what we're gonna do, and we can get started the following week. How does that sound?"

"That sounds perfect. Thank you."

By the time we'd finished our beers, t'was time to meet Clarence and Irene at the general store, so we took our leave.

The wagon was hitched up outside the store, and Clarence and Irene were inside putting things on the counter and getting their purchases put together. We waited for them to finish then put our own orders in. Oscar and Irene argued about which candy was the best, and Oscar bought a bag full. But he asked for another paper bag and divided his candy up, giving half of it to Irene.

"Oh, Oscar, I can't accept this!"

"'Tis only a bit of candy. 'Course you can."

She looked at Clarence for guidance.

"For God's sake, Irene, you saved him from a pack of hungry wolves. You can take his candy." He rolled his eyes and went back to looking at a stand of rakes in the corner.

"See?" Oscar said to Irene. "I *owe* you some licorice and gum balls. Here… Take it."

"All right. Thank you, Oscar." She gave him a kiss on the cheek that made him blush and smile. "I quite enjoyed the candy you gave us at Christmas," Irene said. "Seems like when you become an adult, you don't think of buying candy, unless you have wee ones, I suppose. But I don't honestly know why." She opened the bag and peered inside it, her eyes going wide. "Oh my. Look at this, Clarence. There's even a bit of fudge!"

Clarence smiled and shook his head.

"If you're nice to me, I may share some of it," Irene said with a lilt to her voice.

Clarence snorted. "I'm always nice to you."

Irene sighed. "I suppose that's true. I'm a lucky woman."

"Yeah, you are."

She shrugged and winked at Oscar, her face a picture of good humor.

I felt envious of the easy way they had together, even in public, because Clarence looked like a man and was supposed to be a man, and unless he exposed himself, nobody would ever know he didn't have a dick the size of a truncheon in his pants. It almost made me wish that Oscar could get away with passing as a woman in public, but t'would be a lot to take on, and he probably couldn't pass anyhow. He wasn't like Cal, who truly believed herself to be a woman, surely seemed one and preferred to be called she/her and wear dresses and pretty things all the time — or when t'was safe to do so, at least. I couldn't imagine Clarence as anything other than a gruff fellow after knowing him so long, and I figured what was in his trousers didn't matter. There was more to being a man than a cock and balls, and there was more to being a woman than being able to bear children.

I figured people could make up their own minds about who they wanted to be, and they were the only ones who could know for sure.

* * * *

That night, lying in bed together after a busy day and a quick tumble between the sheets, I asked Oscar if he ever thought about his parents.

He gave me a strange look.

"Not really. They're long gone and a part of a past I don't wanna recall, mostly."

"Mostly?"

"Well, I remember bits of my life before we ever went to Dawson City. Seems I was happy then. Not sure why my folks decided to up and go all the way north like that. But I reckon t'was the promise of gold. They figured they'd be so much better off, when t'was the opposite that happened."

"I'm sure they weren't the only ones."

"No, they weren't. Why do people always wanna get rich, Jimmy? Why can't they be happy with what they've got? I'm sure we didn't have much where we were, but I do remember bein' happy when I was real young — playin' in the grass, feedin' the chickens, ridin' in the wagon. I remember a quiet, plain life, but t'was a good one." He gazed at me out of fathomless brown eyes. "Will you be happy with a plain life, Jimmy?"

I blinked at Oscar for a second, then gathered him against me, nuzzling his neck and kissing his ear. "A plain life with you is better than a life of riches with anyone else," I said, and I meant it. "I reckon we got enough money to finish this here house with a little bit left, but then we're gonna need to get jobs and figure out a way forward. But I know we can do it, and I can't think of anyone better to do it with."

* * * *

The following week, we rode into town to meet with Carson and Tim again.

"You know, we could build a two-story house, instead of trying to fit everything on one level. They're all the rage, now, and they do look nice."

"Won't that be more complicated?" I asked, while Oscar looked at Tim's sketch with a growing excitement.

"Not really. I helped my cousin build a place for him and his wife, the other side of Spokshute Mountain. Turned out awful nice. Wasn't anythin' fancy, and I expect we can build one for two bachelors just the same."

Oscar was nodding. "Why, that sounds fine! Then I can put a whole floor between me and Jimmy's snoring."

"Well, we can put two sizeable bedrooms upstairs, so you'll have a wall between you, anyways. And downstairs, you'll have your kitchen and a sitting room and a back storage room, if you like, or a parlor."

"What's a parlor?" Oscar asked.

"'Tis a more formal place to sit with your guests for short visits, rather than bringing them into the sitting room, which is more relaxed," Carson explained, glancing at me. I think he had some idea that Oscar's upbringing hadn't been ideal, but he didn't know quite how lacking it had been.

"I reckon we ain't got no need of that. A larger sitting room and a small back room for storage will be fine," I said.

"Sure enough," Oscar agreed. He beamed. "My goodness, I'm getting excited. I ain't never had a proper house before."

Tim nodded. "Well, this house will have enough room for four people to live comfortably, since one or both of you might want to bring a bride in eventually."

"Sure," I said, pretending that was a real possibility.

"I reckon," Oscar agreed, doing his best not to glance my way.

We wanted to get started as soon as possible. Tim introduced us to the operator of the sawmill, and he said he could get us what we needed to begin as early as the following week. We'd use spruce timber for the framing and oak for the floors. Tim and Carson said they'd use their wagon to bring it out to the homestead when the order was ready.

The amount of work we had ahead of us was intimidating, but t'was thrilling to think of building on to the space we already had. The kitchen had been cozy during the cold weather but had begun to feel claustrophobic and tight, especially whenever we'd had other people come by. The new house would have space for a suitable dining table, so we could have a few folks o'er for a meal on occasion.

Clarence and Irene had told us to invite Tim and Carson for supper at their place on Sunday evening, since that was the only day of the week the saloon was closed. They had accepted, and Oscar and I had to remember to be friends while in company—a tricky prospect since we were used to being ourselves at the Trelawneys'. But the idea of having a relaxed meal with Tim and Carson and giving them something in the way of a thank you for helping us out so much, was very appealing.

* * * *

Clarence and I went hunting and returned with two large geese, which Irene roasted up and served with mashed potatoes and turnip from the cellar. There was fresh butter, thick gravy and wine to drink, which Tim had brought. And for dessert there was a lemon meringue pie, the likes of which I'd never seen in my life. The top of it sloped out of the pie dish in lightly browned peaks of white sugary goodness, and the main part was a tangy yellow lemon curd that set my tongue to dancing.

"Irene, this is the most delicious pie I've ever had," I said. "Where'd you learn to make it?"

Irene smiled, pleased as punch at the praise. "My mother used to make it, and I learned it from her. She was a wonderful baker." Her smile wavered, as if she were fielding fond memories.

"Well, it's truly delicious," Carson said, cleaning the last bit off his plate.

"Would you like another piece, Mr. Moore?" Irene asked.

"Call me Carson, please. And yes, as a matter of fact, I would."

"Anyone else?" Irene asked, her gaze sliding around the table.

We all raised our hands and Irene laughed. "Well, then. We might as well finish it."

She sliced up the rest of the pie and served out the pieces. We ate our second helpings with as much gusto as the first ones.

"I can't finish mine," Oscar said, setting his fork on the side of his plate. "I'm sorry."

Tim eyed it. "Do you mind if I have it?"

"Not at all. Glad it won't go to waste."

"So'm I," Tim said. "My goodness, Irene, if I'd known you were such a good cook, I'd have befriended you long ago."

Irene smiled. "We've been a mite too standoffish, I suppose. T'was Jimmy and Oscar who showed us that. And we're just so glad you and Carson are helping them build their homestead."

Clarence nodded. "Yes. T'will be nice to have two homes to go back and forth between next winter. And Jimmy can practice his cooking."

I blushed. "That sounds mighty nice. I've never cooked for more'n a couple of people."

Tim gazed at us with the shiny eyes of someone who'd had a good meal and just enough wine.

"Well, I reckon you two oughta start showing yourselves around town a bit more, now that you're getting settled. P'raps it's time to think about bringing a woman home to do all of that for you." He focused in on Oscar. "You might not be ready, but a man of Jimmy's age should be thinking about getting married."

Oscar and I exchanged a glance.

I cleared my throat. "You don't think I'm too old? I'll be thirty-seven next month."

"Well, you're a little past your prime, I suppose, but you don't look it. And lots of young women these days prefer to have older husbands."

"I suppose," I said, trying to seem like I was thinking about it. At least the blush that came to my cheeks would seem an appropriate reaction.

"In fact," Tim said, wiping at his mouth with his cloth napkin, "the annual spring social's coming up next Saturday at the church hall. I reckon you fellas should make an appearance. That'd get tongues wagging, and I'll bet the eligible girls will be settin' their hats for at least one of you, if not both."

I didn't know what to say, so I latched onto the only thing I could think of. "Well, if I were to get married, though, we'd need an even bigger place, wouldn't we?"

"Now, not necessarily. I've heard of two couples sharing a homestead. We could just build another house — or even just add on another bedroom."

Oscar's gaze was going back and forth between me and Tim Jensen. And Irene was watching, too.

"Now, hold on a minute. Who's to say Jimmy even wants to get married?" Oscar mumbled.

Carson and Tim laughed, as if not wanting to get married was the silliest thing they'd ever contemplated.

"Of course, he does," Carson said. "Don't you?"

"Well, I — Now, I don't know. There ain't nothing wrong with it. I just never really thought about it all that much."

"Never thought about it? At the age you are?"

I scrambled for something that would sound reasonable. "It always seemed it would be too much trouble. I don't know if I'd make a very good husband."

Oscar laughed, and everyone turned toward him.

"Sorry. I'm just trying to imagine Jimmy as a husband, and I'm not quite sure that I can."

I gave him what I hoped was an insulted look. "Well, now, that's uncalled for."

He snorted. "Sorry. It's only 'cause of all the smelly socks you leave everywhere and the habit you have of chewin' on your fingernails."

That was just—not even true. I did bother my nails sometimes, but Oscar was the one that left his stinky, dirty clothes everywhere, not me.

I arched a brow. "At least I don't chew my food like a goddamn animal."

Oscar narrowed his eyes and crossed his arms o'er his chest, and I realized we might be giving away more than we thought we were.

Tim looked back and forth between us with amusement on his face.

"Well, then, what about children? Most people want to carry on the family name…"

I made a face. "I ain't never been all that fond of 'em."

T'was the truth, although I'd really never been faced with dealing with any young'uns for any period of time. It certainly wasn't anything I felt I needed or wanted. I figured there were enough young'uns around on this here Earth that we didn't need any more. And there were a lot of children brought into this world who weren't cared for properly.

That was one other thing I loved about being with Oscar. Even though in my silly fantasies I might imagine having a child that looked like him, I was relieved that t'was something we'd never have to worry about. I expected there were too many children that had come along as the result of the love between a man and a woman that naturally produced them, when those people couldn't afford to care for them or maybe even didn't have the capacity to love them the way they should.

Chapter Twenty

A Birthday Party

It took the better part of a month to build our home, with Carson and Tim and Clarence and Irene helping when they could. Clarence was back working in town at the blacksmith's shop, but he had weekends and evenings off and helped us out then.

We were truly blessed to have such friends, and I did begin to believe that God might have actually forgiven me for the things I'd done, even though I'd always regret them. The heaviness in my chest had eased, and the dreams had stopped. For once in my sorry life, I felt like I might be on the right path, if there was a right path for anyone. Everything did seem to be falling into place.

T'was exciting to watch our house go from a one-room kitchen with a stove, to a two-story house with a staircase and two bedrooms upstairs, and so much space downstairs that it almost made me dizzy. T'was a lot of hard, physical labor, but Oscar and I hadn't ever shied away from that. Our muscles got thicker and stronger, and we felt good about helping to build our own home.

Carson and Tim had enough experience to know how to build a good house, and Oscar and I did as we were told — and learned much in the process. There were a few close calls, but nobody was severely injured or killed, so that was a blessing.

Oscar and I even had some leads on jobs that we might take, come summer. Tim said he'd gladly hire Oscar to serve behind the bar in his saloon, since he was young and not hard on the eye, and he thought I might find a place in the general store, to load and unload stock and maybe even help with the ordering. I had experience transporting goods and some knowledge of accounting.

There were more folks in Port Essington for the summer than there were in the winter, so the businesses often hired folks for seasonal work, like Clarence's spot with the blacksmith, but they would keep you on through the colder months if they could. T'was good to know and something to think about, once the work on the house was done.

Mentioning my upcoming birthday had been a mistake, and Oscar wouldn't let up until I gave him the date. When I did, he smiled with a secret in his eyes and nodded.

"All right, then."

On the anniversary of my birth, Irene had us for supper, and they made a big fuss o'er me, which was strange. I hadn't had a birthday party since I was a little 'un, but t'was nice. Although, when the meal was done and no dessert had been produced, I was somewhat disappointed.

"Ain't you got somethin' sweet for us, Irene?" Oscar asked, tapping his fingers on the tablecloth.

"Well now, I don't know. Is it anyone's birthday?"

I shook my head, amused beyond words by their unsubtle reference. But I kept my mouth shut.

"Why, I believe it's Jimmy's birthday, Irene," Clarence said.

"Why, I think you're right!"

She disappeared into the kitchen, and I turned to Oscar.

"What on earth is going on?"

"You'll see."

After a few moments, Irene came out of the kitchen carrying a large cake on a pretty platter, with candles in it that were aflame. She nodded to Oscar, and he started singing a simple song about a happy birthday with my own name in't, as they looked in my direction and joined in.

My face heated at the attention, but t'was sweet of them to sing to me. Irene placed the cake on the table at my place.

"Now, make a wish, Jimmy, then blow out the candles."

I looked at Oscar, who was glowing with happiness at the surprise.

"Well — what should I wish for?" I asked.

Oscar rolled his eyes.

"I can think of lots of things, but you ain't supposed to tell us. That way, there's a chance it'll come true."

"I see," I said, then closed my eyes, thinking about what I truly wanted.

I wanted this new house we were building to be the beginning of a wonderful life for me and Oscar, and I wanted Clarence and Irene to be our friends forever, and I wanted… I wanted to see Miss June and Cal and the girls again, sometime.

I took a deep breath and blew out the candles, getting every one of them.

"There! Now there's a real good chance your wish will come true, Jimmy."

I circled my arm around Oscar's waist and pulled him against me. "I truly hope so."

Oscar leaned in to whisper, "If you wished for some gamahouching tonight, I can pretty much guarantee that one's gonna happen."

I lowered my hand and swatted him sharply on the behind.

"Oscar, we're in company."

"Well, maybe you shouldn't spank me, then," he said in his regular voice, and Irene dissolved into laughter while Clarence put a hand to his chest in false modesty.

Irene got a hold of herself.

"All right, now. Who wants a piece of this delicious cake I made?"

She carved out thick slices and handed them to us on blue china plates. Oscar took one bite and closed his eyes, moaning as if he were in the throes of passion. I took a bite of my piece, and I couldn't blame him for it.

"Oh my God," I murmured as I chewed, covering my mouth so nothing would escape or be visible between my lips. I paused to enjoy the rich, fudgy taste of it before I swallowed. "Irene, this is — this is — like Heaven."

I licked my lips and cut another piece off with my fork, getting some of the icing this time.

"Irene, this is your best cake yet," Clarence declared. "Is this why you wanted to buy the imported chocolate?"

"Clarence, you knew when you married me that I had expensive tastes."

Clarence rolled his eyes, but he was glowing with pride. "Ain't that the truth."

Irene shrugged and ate some of her piece.

"Oh my. Yes, it is good. When's your birthday, Oscar? I'll make the same cake for you if you like."

Oscar stopped chewing and swallowed, then screwed up his face.

"I think 'tis in August."

We stared at him.

"What? Does a fella need to know the exact date?"

It did seem strange that he didn't know it.

"I suppose not," Clarence said, the first to get o'er the shock. "Why don't you pick a day, and we'll celebrate it then."

"Sure, okay. How about August tenth? That's easy to remember," Oscar said, side-eyeing me to see what I thought of that.

I smiled and inclined my chin. "August tenth it is, then. Good to know."

I reached o'er and placed my hand on top of his, squeezing softly. He turned his palm up and squeezed back.

* * * *

By the time the siding and shingles went up, t'was the end of May and the spring social was only two weeks off. The house was finished, and we had started arranging our furniture — what little we had — about the various rooms. We graciously accepted donations of a few items no longer needed by the Trelawneys and Carson and Tim.

Every time I climbed the narrow stairs to the second story bedrooms, I was amazed to have such luxury. Part of me regretted that the dirty, stolen money we'd taken from Spook and Whitlaw had paid for this place, but another part of me decided t'was fair to use it for something good. Those nasty fellas had wrecked most of my life—and Robert's, too. So, I felt t'was bringing some kind of balance to the universe when Oscar and me used it to make a comfortable life for ourselves. It gave me the chance to make restitution for all those things I'd done. I planned to be a decent man—a responsible citizen who helped his neighbors and loved his partner until the day he died. I could only hope that God would feel that t'was enough.

We'd put a single cot into the second bedroom, but the main bedroom had our big wooden bed frame in it, and a little desk at one end, where I could sit and go o'er the accounts. We'd extended the stove pipe from downstairs so it passed up through this room now, and next winter it would keep us almost as warm as it had when we'd slept downstairs. And there was a proper fireplace in the living and dining room with a sturdy brick chimney.

T'was a good, strong house, and we were lucky to have it. In our cozy bed upstairs one night, I asked Oscar why he didn't know his own birthday.

He shrugged and tried to distract me by sliding his hand under the covers and circling my cock. That technique tended to work, but not this night. We'd stopped wearing our union suits now that the weather was warmer, and t'was nice to be able to access each other's parts so easy.

But I took his slim wrist and gently lifted his hand away. He turned surprised brown eyes my way, blinking in confusion.

"Why don't you know your birthday, Oscar?"

He faltered, his face betraying a mix of embarrassment, frustration and a spark of anger that flared then disappeared.

"I don't know."

A cat's mewling interrupted us, and Sprite landed on the bed beside me, snuggling into my hip and wrapping her tail around herself as she started to purr. I gave her a stroke and turned back to Oscar.

"Didn't your folks make note of it? I mean, when things were better for you all?"

"I don't rightly remember. I think— I'm fairly sure t'was in August."

I stared at him, wondering at parents not making a fuss about their child's birthday. It seemed so strange that he wouldn't know the day, but perhaps I was being simple. Maybe birthdays weren't as important for some folks as they were to others.

I knew when my birthday was because my mama would always make something special for me on that day. But that didn't mean everyone was so lucky. And I'd goddamned near almost forgot it, since you can bet the gang didn't care one whit about them things.

"Well, how do you know… How do you know your age, then?"

Oscar looked scared now, as if I'd caught him out about something, and an icy shard of dread sliced through me.

"Oscar. You're twenty-one. You told me you were twenty-one, and I believed you."

"I *am* twenty-one," Oscar stated, licking his lips and nodding as if reassuring himself. "Or thereabouts," he added in the softest of voices, glancing at me from under his lashes, like a frightened child.

All of a sudden, I knew in my heart that Oscar was likely *not* twenty-one, and could have been as young as eighteen, but hopefully — *hopefully* — was at *least* twenty. Then, gazing into his eyes and seeing the fear there, I decided it didn't matter.

He was my sweetheart and my home, and I didn't care about the numbers. There was no question he was a grown man — his deep voice and the hair on his face and his parts made that obvious. Even though t'was on the sparser side, t'was there. His skin, though t'was softer and firmer than mine, was thick and rough enough to be a man's.

We'd keep on going with the age he hoped he was, and he'd turn twenty-two in August. Irene would bake him a chocolate cake, we'd sing him the birthday song and I'd take him to bed with all the gentleness and strictness that he wanted.

"All right," I said, sliding my hand up behind his head and bringing his mouth to mine.

He put his arms around me and held me tight, as if he was worried I was gonna blow away in the wind and leave him all alone to make his way. And I would never, ever do that.

* * * *

If we had to go to this spring social, we needed some new clothes. We'd made do with what we had, mostly, except for the union suits and some warmer things we'd purchased for the winter.

"Do we really want to spend money on fancy clothes, Jimmy? We're startin' to run out of cash, ain't we?" Oscar said, after we'd rode into town and stabled the horses at Jensen's.

"Not quite yet. But we're gettin' low enough that we have to be mindful."

"Well, then, why're we gonna go and buy these fancy outfits? Just for one party that we don't even wanna go to?"

I sighed and nodded.

"I know, but I've thought about it, and I think 'tis wise to go and to make a good impression. The easiest way to do that is to look the part of respectable gentlemen. And, you know, if we're livin' here, there's a chance we're gonna be invited to other things. Maybe we should put in an appearance at church now and then."

Oscar looked like he'd eaten something sour. "Aw, Jimmy. Don't say that…"

I laughed and shook my head. "My goodness, you sound like a child."

He side-eyed me. "I hate goin' to church. Why do I wanna listen to a bunch of men what think they know how to speak for God when I can talk to God all by myself from wherever I am and get a more honest answer?"

"I know, I know. I didn't say you had to believe what they were sayin'. But maybe we oughta go on occasion."

Oscar gave me a look. "You make me go to church, Jimmy, and I'm gonna make you pay."

"Oh, really?"

"Oh, yes, really."

I laughed. "How are you gonna make me pay for takin' you to church?"

He seemed to think about it for a moment. We were walking by the river now, with nobody else anywhere near us. The pungent scent of salmon and fish guts floated on top of the salty, ocean smell.

Oscar spoke in a stage whisper, his gaze furtive.

"Well, maybe I'll suddenly develop a modest streak, and I won't want to tumble very often. Hmm? You never know, Jimmy, surrounded by all that 'purity', maybe some'll rub off on me."

I grinned wide instead of laughing out loud because I couldn't even imagine it. I put my arm across his back like we were only friends sharing a good joke.

"That ain't never gonna happen."

Oscar's lip twitched, as if he were about to laugh, too, but wanted to be stern and serious.

"It might!"

"Well, I'll take my damn chances," I said, removing my arm and giving way to a small laugh. "Or maybe, we'll be so frustrated by everything the damn preacher says, we'll just go on home and show all the ways that we honor each other and celebrate the goodness of God in our own way."

He did smile then and shook his head.

"Fine. I suppose that's more likely."

"I suppose it is. Mayhap we'll have to celebrate God's goodness even more enthusiastically to make up for what some people are sayin' about Him…or Her."

Oscar's face screwed up. "You think God's a woman, Jimmy?"

"Maybe? Why couldn't God be a woman? Or maybe God's not a man or a woman, but just a force, like gravity, that holds us all together, e'en though when men twist words up like they do, it mostly tears us apart."

"Hmm-m. You got some strange ideas, Jimmy Downing."

"Me? As I recall, you're the one introduced *me* to all the strange ideas."

"Well, maybe that's true."

"Pretty sure it is."

"Now you just be quiet and buy me some nice clothes."

"Yes, sir."

We smiled, our eyes sparkling with good humor as we walked along beside the Skeena River to the haberdasher's.

Chapter Twenty-One

Being Sociable

"Jimmy, I can't tie this goddamned cravat!" Oscar growled as we got ready to head out with Clarence and Irene to the church social.

We'd spent a good bit of coin at the haberdashers, getting sorted out with some fine clothes and new, shiny, city boots to wear. I reckon Mr. Trilby who owned the place thought we were highly amusing fellas, the way we argued and harangued each other while we looked for some decent threads. We tried for some honest-to-goodness masculine goodwill disguised as crass jibes, the way regular men might act who were forced to spend all their time together. I supposed we were on our way to being known as eccentric at the very least, which was better than the truth, to be sure.

"Here... I'll help you," I said. I'd managed to get myself kitted out with only a bit of difficulty. The shop keeper had shown me how to tie the cravat, and I'd practiced some in the meantime.

Oscar turned his gaze on me and whistled. "Ho-ly. You look… You look so" — his gaze moved from the top of my head to the toes of my new boots, o'er everything in between. He swallowed — "temptin'."

I blushed and moved behind him, even though he seemed to want to keep looking at me.

"Here… 'Tis easier this way," I said, taking hold of the ends of his cravat from behind and tying it as I had my own. Irene had given us a small square mirror with a wood frame to hang in our bedroom above the wash basin. We stood before it now as I tucked the ends of the burgundy cravat into Oscar's fine embroidered waistcoat. T'was gray silk with gold thread in intricate designs, not unlike those on his new pocket watch.

"*I'm* temptin'? I don't rightly know how I'm gonna keep my hands off *you* tonight. Honest to God."

T'was truly gonna be an effort not to reach out and touch him, but t'was one I would have to make.

I finished with his cravat and slid my hands up o'er the embroidered front of the snug vest. "Hmm, this looks mighty fine on you, Mr. Yates. You'll drive the young women wild."

Oscar grinned at himself in the mirror as our gazes met in the reflection. "You reckon?"

"Oh, I know it."

He nodded sharply, satisfied. Then he turned in my grasp and gazed at me with eyes on fire. "If only they knew."

"We'd better hope they don't find out."

He reached out trembling fingers and touched them to my starched white collar, then ran them o'er my royal blue cravat, as if t'were made of gold and not silk, which was fine enough.

"Do we really gotta go through with this? Can't we just stay home and"—his gaze flew o'er my silver waistcoat and back to my face—"pretend we're at a dance where we can be together the way we like?"

I backed up a step and took Oscar's hand in mine, bringing it to my lips for a kiss. "We have to go, my love, but I reckon we've got time for a dance."

Oscar blinked, his cheeks flushing in a delightful way. "But…we ain't got any music."

I shrugged, my gaze taking him in in all his fine, tailored glory. He looked like a prince to me in them fancy clothes that almost looked tailored because they fit him so well. His hair had grown out some and the wave had come back as the strands fell atop his ears and swooped o'er his forehead. He'd looked good with it cut short, but I preferred it this way.

"Who needs music?" I whispered, pulling him against me and taking his other hand as I waltzed him around our brand-new bedroom.

He inhaled and smiled as I led him across the wood floor.

"I didn't know you could dance. Why didn't you say you could?"

He truly seemed surprised, and I didn't want to tell him that when you're an outlaw, the days and nights can be monotonous. I *really* didn't wanna tell him t'was Spook who taught me, because I figured t'would upset him. So, I simply shrugged as if t'were nothing and carried on, since now he seemed like a princess who'd only just discovered she was royalty.

"Well, I'm a bit shy about it," I said. I stopped, pinning him against the wall so I could press myself against him. "I ain't that good."

"Jimmy, you're—" He parted his lips on an indrawn breath as we gazed at each other, our faces inches apart. "You're the best thing I ever—"

He blinked rapidly, as though he was trying to keep his feelings in.

So I kissed him, slow and long and tender, and pretended not to notice the tears that tracked down his cheeks.

A faint jingling sound came from outside. I stepped to the window and moved the curtain to make sure t'was Clarence and Irene. We were all going in the wagon to keep our clothes from spoiling.

I kissed Oscar a final time, and we gazed at each other with sobering looks.

"You got your watch?"

"It's here," he said, reaching into the small pocket of his waistcoat and showing it to me. "By my heart."

"Sweet, sweet boy."

"I can be sweet when I wanna be." He grinned.

"And saucy the rest of the time."

"Because you like that."

I laughed. "I surely do. Now, you ready? We gotta put on a good show, and we might as well start as soon as we leave this house."

Oscar nodded. "I'm ready."

We'd already discussed how we'd handle it if any women paid undue attention or wanted more of us than we wanted to give them. Luckily, the manners of the time were based on modesty and politeness, so I figured we'd be able to avoid any direct overtures.

I may have underestimated the determination of the young ladies of Port Essington.

Ten minutes after we'd arrived to the church hall, Oscar was surrounded.

Tim and Carson had been sure t'would be me getting all the attention from the ladies, but it turned out to be Oscar. I couldn't help feeling somewhat amused by it, although Oscar seemed less so. He looked like a rabbit caught in a trap until I'd rescued him.

"Jimmy," he said, gazing about the hall at all the people, and watching the group of young women who had accosted him going to search out the refreshments. "I'm not sure this was a good idea."

"I know. But we only have to stay until Clarence and Irene want to go home."

"I don't think that's gonna be anytime soon."

I glanced o'er to see Clarence and Irene dancing together, seeming to be in a private world of their own making. Clarence was dressed similarly to me and Oscar, but Irene wore a beautiful peacock-blue dress in silk and satin with fine lace and small bows all up the back, her hair done up in a fancy style. I did feel envious of the fact that they could live so openly, with the secret of Clarence's sex hidden away like t'was. But if t'was ever discovered that he was different to other men, and that he and Irene were intimate like a regular married couple, I reckon it would be the end of all that. So, Oscar and I would guard that secret for them and hope it never became known, just like they would guard ours.

After a spell, the young ladies returned like bees to a flower and spoke to both Oscar and me. I started to wonder if it had been a mistake to buy such fine clothes, as it seemed we made quite a statement. The times I'd catch the eye of Tim or Carson, they seemed awfully amused at our predicament.

We attempted to make polite conversation, but I knew Oscar was hating every moment of it. The women seemed excited to be at a party and were in very good spirits, and most were all right to talk to, though some made their interest in us as marriageable prospects more obvious than others. I recognized the girl that had been at the counter in the general store a few times, peering at Oscar with something akin to hunger.

Oscar refused to dance with any of them, using the fact that he didn't know how as an excuse. I politely declined at first, in the interests of staying near him. But I realized fairly quick that it seemed queer for me and Oscar to be standing together for so long, and I decided to take up some of the offers I received.

I danced with several different ladies, some of whom seemed more interested in Oscar but simply wanted an opportunity to dance with a handsome stranger. I was a decent dancer, too, as Oscar had discovered earlier, and the women, though not ideal, were better to dance with than Spook, who would turn and spit into the dirt now and then and insult me when I messed up. So I took deep breaths, smiled and nodded, and made pleasant, benign conversation, being vague about my life and my interests.

I focused on the fact that my ma had been a schoolteacher, and that's why I knew how to write and read and figure well, which was a truth that I clung to like a lifeline. She was the only thing that made me fit for a respectable life, and I sent a prayer up to her. Even though she'd left me too soon, and the loss of both my parents had led Robert and me into a life of thieving, at least she'd given me some kind of legacy I could hold on to.

And now I was teaching Oscar to read and write, and to do more and more complex sums. He had a sharp mind and an excellent grasp of human behavior, and that was a fact. Add some book learning to that and no one would be able to stop him. He was young enough that he could learn some valuable skills, and he'd always have the means to keep himself fed, even if something happened to me.

I didn't want to think about that, but sometimes it occurred to me that I was probably gonna die before him, and what would he do then? At least we had Clarence and Irene, and Tim and Carson to rely on for help. I supposed either one of us could get sick or have an accident and perish at any time. There wasn't any way to control that, and t'was no use trying. I just had to put it out of my head.

"You look a bit gloomy, Mr. Downing," Miss Bess Taylor said as I led her about the dance floor and tried to avoid the press of bodies on each side.

"Oh, I'm sorry." I gave her a half-hearted smile. "Sometimes I think too much."

"What're you thinking about that makes you so sad?"

I shook my head. "Why, nothing important. You're a fine dancer, miss."

She smiled, and she truly was a pretty thing. Her hair was as black as Onyx's coat and her eyes were blue. She had freckles scattered across her cheeks and her pert little nose.

"Why, thank you so much, Jimmy. My brother taught me when I was real small. He loves to dance." She nodded at a young man a bit older than Oscar, dancing with another young woman. "He's here with his wife."

"I see. They do make a fine couple."

"Do you think you'll marry?" Her bright blue eyes peered into mine with undisguised intention.

I blushed. "Well, now, I don't know. I'm fairly…set in my ways, to be honest. I don't reckon I'd make a very good husband."

"Really? You're awful handsome," she said, giving me a look I knew well, though usually it came from Oscar, which I much preferred.

T'was so strange to think on't.

While I was living with them outlaws, I'd have traded my soul for an opportunity to dance with a pretty girl like Bess, make small talk and have a good time with regular people who weren't set on robbing and stealing and killing. But now my life had gone in a different direction — one I hadn't foreseen — and though t'was still enjoyable, my heart and my desire lay with the fella leaning up against the wall with a frown on his face, checking his pocket watch as he kept an eye on me and Miss Taylor.

When the dance was o'er, I thanked her and returned to my place beside him.

"What's the matter with you?" I asked, although I was pretty sure I knew.

"Nothin'."

"Well, you look pretty sour. You'd better turn that frown around or folks'll think you're a mean little bugger."

"I don't care."

"Yeah, you do." I leaned in to speak in his ear. "And if you don't start lookin' more congenial, I'll ignore you when we get home instead of givin' you the hidin' that'll make you happy."

He blinked, licked his lips and tried to relax his features so he wasn't giving off such a cantankerous air.

"That's better," I said. I leaned in again. "Good boy."

His gaze flashed to mine and his cheeks flushed. "I don't like to see you dancing with them girls."

"And why's that?"

He put his face as close to my ear as he could without ending up in my arms, so he wouldn't be overheard. "Because I want to dance with you, Jimmy. And we can't. Not here."

"You're right. But we can do it at home. And we can do it at Clarence and Irene's," I said, taking a glass of punch off a tray that one of the ladies was carrying around. She smiled and moved on.

"I don't reckon we'll be going to more than one of these things a year, and I figure we can show our faces every spring and set the town to talking about who we are and why we ain't keen on hooking up with anyone. They'll make up their own minds about why that is. Nobody's gonna jump to the one conclusion that's the simplest, because most folks don't think that way. They prefer to ignore the things they don't understand, or that make them uncomfortable. They'll decide we're simply committed bachelors or too ornery for marriage, or that we simply ain't got no interest in it. There are people who are like that, and I reckon that's easier for most folks to deal with than the truth. So, it's best for them that we keep our secret, as well as for us."

"I suppose," Oscar said, sighing. "You look mighty handsome is all, and I wish I could show you off as my husband."

"I know," I said. "We'd best stop talking about this, but I feel the same way. I want you to know that."

Irene came o'er and collapsed against the wall beside Oscar, lifting a hand to her forehead.

"Well, my goodness, I don't think I can go another round, Clarence! You've tuckered me right out."

Clarence had a very satisfied look on his face. "I reckon I have."

"You know everyone's staring at us? Because you're usually so grumpy and nobody ever knew you could have this much fun."

T'was true. The townsfolk did seem surprised by Clarence and Irene being here in the first place, and also because they'd spent the entire social dancing together.

Clarence shrugged. "Hmph. They can be surprised. I don't care a whit."

"Ah, there you go. Back to your old self, now," Irene said, grinning at him fondly. "Now everyone can relax."

Clarence narrowed his eyes at her. "You watch yourself, woman."

But Irene only laughed and turned to Oscar. "How are you and Jimmy doing? Are you ready to go home or do you want to stay a bit longer?"

"Home," Oscar said. "Please."

"Oh, Oscar," Irene murmured, giving him a kiss on the cheek. "I'm so sorry."

"It's fine. I just want to go home."

She looked back and forth between us. "Clarence, you'd better get the wagon."

Chapter Twenty-Two

Reparations

Irene, who'd spent the entire evening with Clarence, declined to sit with him in the wagon and insisted on getting into the box with Oscar and me. T'was covered with a wool blanket so our fancy clothes would stay clean. We arranged Oscar in between us and leaned against the sides of the wagon box, gazing at the trees beside the dirt road and the stars o'er our heads.

Irene produced a flask from inside her skirts and offered it to Oscar, who took it with a grin. He had a long swallow then passed it to me.

"Irene, you're all right," I said.

"That punch was fine but, goddamn it, I need a real drink," Irene said, throwing her arm around Oscar.

"How did you enjoy it, Oscar?"

"Truly?"

"Truly."

"I hated every minute of it. I hated that I couldn't walk in there, hand-in-hand with my husband, and show him off as mine."

I chuckled. "You know, you don't own me. I may be your secret husband, but I can dance with a girl if I want."

Oscar swiveled his head around and pinned me with a glare.

"I suppose you can." He gazed at me in silence for a few moments, while Irene took another swig of gin. "You know that girl couldn't handle a cock the size of yours, Jimmy, nor a hidin' like you enjoy givin' me. *Psht.*"

Irene's eyes went wide, and she put a hand to her mouth to stop her laughter. I reached o'er and took Oscar's hand. He didn't want to give it to me, he was so mad. But I dragged it to my knee and held it there.

"I reckon you're right. And I ain't got no interest in her. But it ain't gonna kill you to watch me dance with a girl or two once a year to keep up appearances."

"Hmph. I don't know about that."

Irene put her hand on Oscar's knee. "Oscar, you know you're a hell of a lot prettier than that girl, don't you?"

I could have kissed Irene that second. That was the exact right thing to say to Oscar just then.

He shrugged, because of course he wasn't gonna admit that that was exactly what he wanted to hear.

I squeezed his hand and leaned in close. "Irene's right. I bet most of those girls and women were lookin' at you and imaginin' how you'd look with no clothes on."

He pulled back and gave me a quizzical look. "Are you drunk, Jimmy Downing?"

I laughed. "On fruit punch? Fuck no."

"You truly think those women were hot for me?"

I gave him a leer.

"Why wouldn't they be? Don't tell me you don't think their fancy airs and polite manners don't hide needs and wants as powerful as ours. But they can't show it any more'n we can. The whole world's fucked up, and that's the truth."

"Amen," Irene said.

And Oscar laughed. He turned his hand up under mine and twined our fingers together.

"You know what, Jimmy?"

I gazed at him with fondness and a simmering desire to get him alone. "What, Oscar?"

"When we get home, you're gonna have to prove how much you care for me, to make up for dancing with other folks all night."

I grinned and leaned in to kiss his cheek. "I look forward to it."

Irene threw her head back and laughed, her voice drifting up to the stars that looked down on us and twinkled in complicity.

Irene and Clarence dropped us off, and Irene climbed up into the wagon seat with her husband.

"Good night, boys! Don't stay up too late lovin' on each other."

Clarence rolled his eyes and shook his head.

"Now don't think you're off the hook, Clarence Trelawney. I'm gonna expect some sweet talk and soft handling once we get home."

"Don't I know it," Clarence said in a long-suffering tone. But he winked at us and *chirrup*ed to the horses. He nodded toward the porch of our house. "You'd better let your poor cat in."

Sure enough, Sprite was walking back and forth in front of the door, winding her body this way and that, scowling at us and mewling as if she were scolding us for being gone so long.

We waved them off and walked up the steps of our new front porch. Oscar took hold of the door handle, but I stayed him with a hand to his shoulder.

"Oscar," I said.

I turned him around. Then I put my hands on either side of his face and gazed into his eyes. T'was dark but for the silver moonlight that shone onto us from above.

"I love you, and you are the only one for me. You know that."

He swallowed then nodded. "I know."

I smiled and traced my thumb along his chin and his lower lip. "And we're standing here, on the porch of the home we helped build. *Our* home...that we're livin' in together."

He gazed at me, waiting for me to continue as Sprite's mewls punctuated our conversation.

I swallowed thickly, full of the emotion I felt all of a sudden.

"And this home knows the truth. This home and this land know we're married, in our hearts and souls and" — I quirked my lip as I scanned him — "bodies."

Oscar smiled shyly.

"And t'will always know that — and so will we."

"I love you, Jimmy."

"I know," I said. "Now let's go inside, so's I can show you just how much."

The empty house greeted us with its silence, but for the ticking of the clock in the sitting room and the woosh of the cat as she took off up the stairs. We lit one of the oil lamps and followed her up, to where another clock in our bedroom made its heartbeat heard, keeping watch as we took off our fine clothes and hung them in the wardrobe. We were silent as we did it, stealing surreptitious glances at each other's slowly revealed nakedness in the lamplight.

Up here, we could leave the curtains open a bit, because no one was likely to come upon us, and the moonlight streamed in onto the coverlet of the bed, which was right below the big window.

Irene had given us a quilt that she'd sewn as a wedding gift, and it made our bed a precious thing. We made a point to fold it up and lay it aside when we got up to nonsense, because t'was so fine and so much delicate work had gone into it. I did that now, and turned down the blankets as Oscar finished taking off his things and climbed up onto the linen sheets. He sat back on his heels and watched me with an almost reverential air. T'was not something I was familiar with, since he was normally playful and crass during our coupling, but it seemed to match with the moonlight and the sober words we'd spoken on the porch. The cat jumped up onto the folded quilt, as if I'd placed it there for her, and curled up into a ball, blinking lazily and yawning, purring with contentment.

There was a sacred feel to the space tonight.

I got onto the bed in front of him and cupped his chin, guiding his mouth to mine and taking possession of it in a soft, sensual way that brought a sigh to his lips. He could never truly understand how precious he was to me, but I could show him with the way I treated him in these moments.

He wrapped his hand around my cock, dancing his fingers along it as it rose to a stand, eager for him after a long night of manners and necessary subterfuge. I gasped, and my kiss became more urgent as he opened beneath my hunger, wrapping his arms around me and tugging my body close.

I slid my hands down to cup his buttocks, squeezing and stroking that cherished part of him, pulling his cheeks apart and swiping a finger o'er his hole as he shuddered and pressed against me.

He moaned against my mouth, and I broke away to pepper kisses along his neck and throat, inhaling the scent of his sweat and the heady tang of our arousal.

"Lie down, on your back," I said, smoothing the hair from his brow as he nodded and did so, gazing up at me with the trust of an acolyte. My heart clenched at the faith he had in me, and I pushed the sentiment aside so I could focus on what I was doing.

"Spread your legs," I grunted, as I grabbed the jar of saddle grease from the side table and opened it. "And bend your knees."

His chest rose and fell as he did what I asked, without any wisecracks or rude comments. I figured he sensed the atmosphere between us and was humbled by it, just as I was. He watched me silently, except for small sounds of pleasure, as I got him ready for me. Then I put the jar aside and hovered o'er him, taking in his beauty and surrender with wide, grateful eyes.

I kissed him again, showing him just how much I cherished him and what we did together. Then I rubbed his soft entrance with the tip of my finger until he sighed and let me inside.

"Jimmy," he moaned, his arms out to either side in religious supplication to my sacred devotion, as I fingered him gently and thoroughly in preparation for me.

Finally, I pressed the head of my cock there, as Oscar's lips parted and I breached him, pressing into him like a baptism. Oscar's eyes closed and he gasped as I pushed in all the way, our bodies fitting together like they always did, and finding home here as well.

When I was fully seated, I slid my arms under him and held him tight, while his went around me and our mouths met again. I wasn't in no rush tonight. I needed to show him how much I loved him and how the things we had to do in town meant nothing to what we were to each other.

I made love to him for a long time, gently, carefully, to show him that. I gave him everything of myself and took comfort in his acceptance of my offering.

As I drove into him slowly and torturously, his nubby got harder and harder and leaked all o'er his belly, until with a soft cry, he spent with a gush of wet warmth, and I followed right after, emptying inside him with a gasp and a quiet groan as our bodies shuddered together.

T'was sweet and soft and perfect.

Afterward, we lay together for a long time, gazing into each other's eyes and listening to the breeze in the freshly leaved trees outside the open window, until we fell asleep, in our brand-new house, beside the Skeena River in a little town called Port Essington.

Want to see more from this author?
Here's a taster for you to enjoy!

Northern Horizons:
Return to Telegraph Creek
AE Lister

Coming June 2023

Excerpt

By the middle of June, summer weather had come to Port Essington.

We'd folded and put away our woolen union suits and winter jackets in a cedar trunk that we kept at the foot of our bed. Now we went about in shirtsleeves — rolled up — and lighter trousers. I wore cotton underthings, but Oscar couldn't be bothered, liking to feel as naked as possible, I supposed. I could barely get him to wear shoes half the time. He'd say shoes were for chumps and laugh in that way he had that put all my sensible arguments to rest.

Our friend, Irene Trelawney, had shown us a swimming hole on the other side of their property, and I could barely keep Oscar away from it now that the weather was warmer. The kid wanted to strip every chance he got, and I can't say that bothered me, except that we had to be careful out here of someone coming upon us in a clinch. Though it seemed unlikely that would happen, considering how isolated we were, it made me nervous. Still, we'd indulged ourselves with a quick gamahouche or a hasty fuck out by that swimming hole more than once, and nothing had ever come of it. I don't think the folks in town knew about the place, and t'was nothing to remark upon, although t'was a pretty spot, and Oscar loved it so. He'd spent most of his life in a city, so it didn't take much to impress him when it came down to it.

Evenings out here were something special. After a winter stuck inside of our small kitchen, we reveled in all the outdoor space, spending a lot of time on the porch, in the paddock with the horses or riding over the homestead and beyond.

Carson and I had walked the ten-acre property back when we'd first seen it, and now that we'd prettied up the space, it felt good to be landowners. The outlaws I'd run with had scoffed at folks owning land, being settled and staying in one spot all their lives. They'd glorified the nomadic lifestyle that was the only one they could possibly have and pretended to ignore its disadvantages. But I'd only ever wanted a spot to call my own, where I could make an honest life for myself and, if I were lucky, for someone else.

I'd not expected a twenty-one-year-old man-child to be the bride of my dreams, but there t'was. Oscar was my love, and I was his — and there weren't no turning back from that solid fact. And we didn't care a whit what other people might think, except we kept our deeper feelings to ourselves, since the laws in this beautiful land were harsh on things that weren't understood. I'd take our secret to the grave if it meant keeping Oscar with me.

I leaned back in one of the rocking chairs Clarence, Irene's husband, had made for the porch of our brand-new house. The creak of the wood and the swoop of the runners going back and forth comforted me as much as the regular motion, and the peaceful sounds of crickets and birds soothed my mind. I gazed out over the grass to the barn, where our horses, Onyx and Dixie, and our sturdy mule, Poke, were put away for the night with a bit of grain and fresh hay. Sprite, the gray and white cat, perched on the railing to my left, one foot over the other as she napped, keeping alert for the rustle of field mice in the grass.

T'was a fine thing to sit in a comfortable chair on your very own property after all the waiting and hard work of building then have all the time in the world to think. We'd survived our first winter in Port Essington in less-than-ideal circumstances, having had only one very small room to live in. We'd expected to be isolated from people, hunkered down together out here in the wilderness, and instead, we'd been fortunate to meet Irene and Clarence, who lived about a ten-minute ride from our place and had secrets of their own.

They'd guessed ours right away, but only because they were keeping a similar one.

Clarence and Irene were married, and that was a fact. But there were specifics about their relationship they wanted to keep from the general public, and I didn't blame them. And Oscar and I were the same. But t'was a godsend that the four of us could be ourselves when we were together, and I hadn't expected to find such kindness and acceptance here. Even the folks in town, who believed that Oscar and I were bachelors and friends instead of lovers and soul mates, had been welcoming and friendly.

Carson Moore and Tim Jensen had aided us to plan and build this fine home, and they'd promised to help us find work in town for the summer and fall so's we could start making a proper living. The money we'd taken from the outlaws I'd killed back in September was dwindling, although it had made it possible for us to indulge in all kinds of luxuries that would serve us well in the future. We were gonna need at least one regular income, preferably two, in order to maintain the lifestyle we wanted. Not that t'was fancy, but we'd gotten used to being able to buy the things we needed and not having to settle for second-best. We'd invested in the stove, the new pitcher pumps and in this beautiful two-story house that would stand for years and give us shelter and comfort.

Our future looked bright and, for the first time, comfortable.

The screen door creaked as Oscar came out to the porch in his bare feet with his trouser legs rolled up. He'd pushed his shirt sleeves up, too, since he'd been washing dishes and t'was a warm day.

"What're you doin' out here, Jimmy?" he asked, coming over and giving the surroundings a quick scan before he bent to kiss me. We had to be careful out in the open, and t'was a shame, but I'd take it. We had the inside of this big place now to do as we pleased without worry, and that was enough.

"Just thinkin'…and enjoying the evenin'."

"Hmm," he said, sitting in the other rocker. "What're you thinkin' about?"

I smiled at him. "Mainly, about how happy I am."

Our gazes held, and he gave me a slow, sultry smile then turned to gaze out at the barn and the paddock, peaceful now with the livestock put away.

"I'm glad."

I waited for him to say he was happy, too, and when he didn't, I cocked my head at him.

"Are you content, Oscar?" I asked, "now we got this place built and a few weeks of leisure before we need to get jobs?"

He frowned and turned to me. "'Course I am. You really gotta ask that?"

I nodded. "I reckon 'tis important to ask it once in a while for any two people makin' a life together."

He raised an eyebrow. "You don't suppose I'd tell you if I *wasn't* happy."

I laughed. "Oh, I'm pretty sure you would. That's true."

He leaned forward in his chair and put his hand to my knee. "You be sure to tell me if *you* ain't happy, won't you, Jimmy? And I promise to do anythin' I can to make things right."

"Oscar—"

"I will. I'll make sure you're happy every day, Jimmy Downing."

I covered his hand with mine and squeezed it.

"Oscar. I can't even imagine bein' unhappy with you by my side. You do make me feel wonderful every day, Oscar Yates. Every fucking day I wake up next to you and every day I go to sleep beside you, I'm content— more content than I have any right to be."

* * * *

"We goin' into town?" Oscar said a few days later. "We ain't got no more potatoes, and the sugar's gettin' awful low."

"You and your sweet tooth," I said, rolling my eyes.

"Don't you mean my sweet ass, Jimmy?"

"Sure."

I glanced over at the plain wood dining table we'd helped Tim make. Oscar was sitting in the chair with his bare heel up on the seat like a ten-year-old. I expected he was still stuck somewhere in his childhood in a lot of ways because his older years had been so rough. I didn't care, and, in some ways, I found it charming and sweet.

"How are those sentences coming along?"

"I'm almost done. I think I'm gettin' the hang of it."

He stood and brought the slate to me with a smile.

I looked over his work with some satisfaction. His penmanship was getting better. I'd buy him some paper and a proper lead pencil in town so he could practice on that instead of the slate.

"That's very good."

He nodded and gazed at me with a hopeful expression. "Can we get another book? Since we're finished t'other?"

"Sure. Or we can borrow one from Irene and Clarence. They've got lots."

He frowned. "Well, we *could* do that, but then how are we gonna build up our library here?"

"Our *library*? My goodness, I got you reading and now you want your very own *library*?"

He laughed. "Well, just a small one. I never knew books were so enjoyable, Jimmy. I'm glad you taught me to read, e'en though I was grumpy about it at first."

"Yeah, you were pretty grumpy…until I promised to reward you with a spankin' if you did good, rather than use it as a punishment."

Oscar winked. "What can I say? I like bein' over your knee."

"And I like havin' you there—and havin' you everywhere else in this house."

The house had been mostly complete for a month now, and we'd gotten up to mischief in almost every damn room. There still wasn't much furniture, but we made do, and we did have an old settee of Clarence and Irene's in the parlor and a chair that Carson had given us.

Seein' as we'd fucked over saddles and tree stumps on our journey, t'was a far sight more comfortable in our own home, even though it might not be the coziest of setups just yet.

"Now I *don't* wanna go to town. I wanna stay here and have a tumble," Oscar murmured.

I gave him a stern look. "I reckon that's what you wanna do most of the time, and most of the time I indulge you. But we need to go to town, so you best get ready and go saddle that fine horse of yours."

He grinned and sighed. "Yes, sir. I will. But...if I'm a good boy in town, will you fuck me later?"

"For certain."

"And maybe spank me?"

"I'll definitely spank you."

"In the sitting room?"

I gave him a look. "Sure. Why the sitting room specifically?"

He shrugged and went redder.

"I don't know. It feels dirtier and more wrong, somehow, and I like that. Because it feels like...it feels like we're thumbin' our noses at polite society. Fuckin' in the parlor, my goodness, let alone that we're two men doin' it. And it reminds me a bit of Miss June's, where we could say whatever we wanted in any room, and there was all kinds of mischief goin' on everywhere."

I walked over and took his chin, kissing him with softness before gazing into his brown eyes. "I like the way you think, Oscar Yates."

* * * *

The weather was warm and pleasant for our ride, and t'was nice to breathe the air that smelled of new growth and blooming wildflowers. Oscar was almost as good a horseman as me now, and Onyx and he had developed a close partnership.

He loved that horse so much, and she loved him. Together they made a good team—just as good as me and Dixie. Maybe better, because though Dixie and I cared for each other, she was a practical consideration, and I reckon she felt the same about me. I'd be sad when she died, but I reckon Oscar would be devastated when the time came for him to say goodbye to Onyx, even more than he'd grieved for his first horse, Sprite, after which he'd named his kitten.

Oscar went out riding every day, now that the weather was better. Irene would often join him, since they seemed to enjoy talking to each other and their characters were similar. I loved that Oscar had such a good friend in Irene and that Clarence and I got on well. I tried to join them when I could, so Dixie would get some exercise.

In town, we hitched the horses outside the general store and went inside, the jingling of the door making our presence known to the gentleman working there, I believe his name was Samuel, behind the counter. He glanced up at us and smiled, then seemed to start.

"Oh, Jimmy Downing! You're the man I need to speak to."

I was caught off guard for a moment. "I beg your pardon?"

Samuel grabbed a piece of paper from the counter behind him and came around, handing it to me.

"A fella came in here and gave me this here letter for you. Said it was real important and asked if I could make sure you got it. I figured you and Oscar would be in here this week, and if not, I'd have given it to Tim or Carson to bring out to you."

"A letter?" I glanced at Oscar, but he seemed as confused as I was.

"T'was a fella wearin' soft bear-skin trousers and embroidered boots—one of the Tsimshian people. He spoke English pretty well, and he said t'was a message from some folks you know in Telegraph Creek. They needed to get a word to you, and he said he'd take it. I reckon they probably paid him to do it...at least I hope they did. That's a long way to travel."

Oscar and I exchanged concerned glances. I opened the envelope, unfolded the letter and started to read it right there in the store, because I'd never expected anything like this and I needed to know why Miss June might reach out to us, when she didn't even know for sure we were here.

Dear Jimmy,

I'm hoping this note finds you and Oscar, because I don't know what else to do or who else to turn to. You and Oscar were always so kind to Cal, and she's in a bit of trouble right now.

"It's Cal," I said.

"What's wrong?" Oscar replied, reaching for the note.

"Shh, I'm still reading."

He let his hand drop and stayed quiet so I could finish.

At least I think she must be. She hasn't been back to see us since she left three months ago. And she promised she'd let us know how she was getting on, so we didn't worry. The man she left with, who said he was going to marry her, is someone I didn't entirely trust, although he claimed he was after the best for Cal, and she believed him. You know my girls don't have their pick of men except the ones who come to visit them here, and there's not often a man who really would do good by any of them.

But Cal was a little bit in love, and she was dreaming of a wonderful life and, well, I hope she got it. But, Jimmy, I don't think she did, and I'm scared to death of what might have happened.

If you get this letter, please think of us and consider coming back to The Angel if you can to help me find her. I don't know what to do.

Sincerely,
Your Good Friend,
Miss June Blaise of
The Angel,
Telegraph Creek, British Columbia, Canada.

I stared at the paper in a daze while Oscar tugged on my sleeve.

"What does she say, Jimmy. What about Cal?"

I looked up at him.

"She says Cal went off with a man to be married."

"Oh!"

"But…but she don't think things have worked out well, because Cal hasn't been back, and she promised she'd come to let Miss June know she was happy in her new life."

Oscar frowned. "If she said she'd come, she would. Cal would do what she promised, Jimmy."

"I know it…and so does Miss June." I licked my lips and scratched at my chin with the hand that wasn't holding the letter. "She wants us to come to Telegraph Creek."

Oscar stared at me. "She does?"

I nodded. "She doesn't know what to do, and she needs our help — to find Cal and do what we can."

Oscar was silent, which meant he was thinking about what I'd said and didn't know what to say. I couldn't blame him.

"'Tis a long way," he said.

"'Tis."

"And we're settled here, in our brand new, beautiful house."

I didn't reply. I'd already decided we had to go — or I had to. But I wanted to let Oscar come to that conclusion himself.

His forehead wrinkled. "Can I see it?"

I handed him the letter. "It's in cursive, but see if you can read it."

Oscar's gaze tracked Miss June's neat writing. It took him a while, and I could see his mouth moving as he made out the words. I doubt he read every one, but he'd be able to get the gist of it.

Finally, he looked up.

"Jimmy, I'm worried about Cal."

"Me, too."

"Do you…do you want to go?"

"I reckon I have to. But you can stay here if you want."

Oscar gazed at the door we'd come in only moments ago, when things had been much less complicated. Then he looked back at me.

"You ain't goin' anywhere without me, Jimmy Downing," Oscar said, in a firm tone that brooked no argument. "Don't even try."

I smiled, relieved. I felt a bit of guilt, as t'would be safer for Oscar to stay here with Clarence and Irene, but I wanted him near me. I couldn't bear the thought of leaving him, even for a month or two. Anything could happen in this wilderness, and if we met up with trouble, at least we'd be together. And as dangerous as it might be to travel again, we knew we had a safe place in Telegraph Creek with Miss June.

"I wouldn't think of it."

I took the letter from him and folded it up, placing it in my pocket for safe keeping.

"I suppose we should buy supplies for our journey since we're here, rather than things to stock our cellar."

I sighed as Oscar's gaze met mine with a look of regret. I supposed the days of relaxin' on the porch and fucking in the sitting room were over, at least for now.

About the Author

AE Lister/Elizabeth Lister is a Canadian non-binary author with a vivid imagination and a head full of unique and interesting characters. They have published 10 books, one of which received an Honorable Mention from the National Leather Association – International for excellence in SM/Leather/Fetish writing.

"Sensual and visceral BDSM." – Amazon.ca

AE Lister loves to hear from readers. You can find their contact information, website details and author profile page at https://www.pride-publishing.com

PUBLISHING

Sign up for our newsletter and find out about all our
romance book releases, eBook sales and promotions,
sneak peeks and FREE romance books!